THE HUNTING FIELDS

THOMAS FINCHAM

The Hunting Fields
Thomas Fincham

Copyright © 2025
All Rights Reserved.

AUTHOR'S NOTE
This book is a work of fiction. Names, characters, places and incidents are products of the author's imagination or are used fictitiously. Any resemblance to actual events or locales or persons, living or dead, is entirely coincidental.

The scanning, uploading and distribution of this book via the internet or any other means without the permission of the publisher is illegal and punishable by law. Please purchase only authorized electronic editions, and do not participate in or encourage electronic piracy of copyrighted materials. Your support of the author's rights is appreciated.

Visit the author's website:
www.finchambooks.com

Contact:
contact@finchambooks.com

Join my Facebook page:
https://www.facebook.com/finchambooks/

THOMAS FINCHAM

A RONAN CARVER NOVEL

PROLOGUE

The Magnolia Hotel of Omaha, Nebraska, was designed in the style of the roaring twenties. Morgan Unger liked the place very much, especially the cozy but luxuriant ballroom he stood in now.

His face hurt from smiling. His shoulder hurt from waving and shaking hands. But he kept on going. The crowds flooded in and out. His constituents, coming to show their undying support. Or to tell him what a wretched job he was doing.

Senator Unger took it all with the same warm greeting and vow that he'd do better in his next term. "Vote for me," he'd say, "and I'll devote the next six years to *you*."

It hurt. Every second of it. This schmoozing didn't come naturally. He'd rather be drinking in a backroom, or flirting with one of the cocktail waitresses.

"Excuse me, Senator?" a bespectacled man said. His name was something like Leonard or Bernard (Unger wasn't sure which), but he was a librarian at a middle school. "Could we talk for a moment about literature?"

"Of course," Unger replied with a gracious nod. The same nod he'd been doing all afternoon. Come to think of it, his neck was starting to hurt, too.

"The sorry state of the average school library is a sore spot," Leonard or Bernard went on. "The books are falling apart. So are the shelves. And don't even get me started on the computers."

"Computers," Unger sighed. "I don't know much about them."

"Then allow me to educate you. The ones at *my* school are still running Windows Vista, an operating system that was considered inferior even when it first came out. I know what you're thinking now."

How do I get out of this conversation? Unger thought.

"You're thinking why don't we just upgrade to a newer OS," said the librarian. "We tried that. The hardware isn't compatible. That's how old it is! The kids can barely play *Oregon Trail*. It's a travesty, but our schools would rather funnel money into sports than—"

Someone cleared their throat. Unger felt a tap on his shoulder. He turned his head. Saw a sharp-chinned man with narrow black eyes. It was Colonel Paul Bell. He held the highest office in the Nebraska State Patrol, and he had been an ally of Unger's for many years.

"Sir," Colonel Bell said, "there's something you need to hear."

Unger nodded. "I apologize, Bernard, but…"

"It's Leonard," the librarian said.

"Excuse me. I've had a long day and heard many names. But I'll remember what you said, don't you worry."

He clapped Leonard on the shoulder. Then he turned and followed Colonel Bell.

"Thanks for saving me," he said quietly as they entered a back hall. "It was getting tiresome out there."

Bell grunted. "Don't thank me yet. Sir…"

They stopped walking. Faced each other.

"We lost track of the target," Bell said.

Unger clenched both fists. But the friendly smile was still frozen on his face. "Where?"

"Just outside North Platte."

Unger exhaled. "This could be the end of everything, Paul. Get your people on this. I want every state cop in Nebraska on the hunt."

ONE

Annie Carrol.

It was a name he would never forget. No matter how many nights passed. No matter how many days he wandered through. No matter how far he went. To the ends of the Earth. To the stars. To a place beyond time.

She would be there. A ghost entwined with every piece of him.

Ronan Carver tried many ways to forget. One of them was beer.

It had been years since he'd known happiness.

But this would suffice, he thought. Sitting in small-town bars. Knocking back a cold brew. Not to get drunk, or even to get buzzed. He just liked the ritual. The taste. The history in every amber drop.

All the way back to Neolithic times in the Middle East, and then to Germany in the early medieval period, where the addition of hops made beer what it was today. It connected him to the past. Rooted him in time. Kept him from floating away.

"Bartender," Carver said. "I'll have another one."

The curly-haired bartender smiled at him. "Slow down there, chief. Two beers in an hour and a half? Might have to cut you off."

Carver chuckled and looked around. The bar was small and dark, with a low ceiling, and far more patrons than it could comfortably hold. He didn't know what the place was called, but he did know it was in a town called Lexington. In the great, flat, seemingly endless state of Nebraska.

As for how he'd ended up here…

He could hardly recall.

Seattle was the last place he'd spent more than a night in. Since then, he'd been running. Somewhat from the FBI—though he was unsure they were even looking for him.

For the past few years, he'd technically been a member of organized crime. A double agent working under a drug trafficking kingpin who called himself Everest.

Everest had sanctioned the murder of Annie Carrol, a journalist—and the love of Carver's life.

He'd had his revenge. Carver had helped out the Seattle FBI office in the process by clearing their head agent's reputation. A good deed, he thought. And an agent named Jo Pullinger seemed to agree. She was the one who'd let Carver go.

But the bureau at large had plenty of reasons to still be looking for him.

If they were, he'd be waiting. But he wasn't about to make their job easier. One more drink and he was out of here. No more stopping until he reached Iowa.

"Got something on your mind, friend?" the bartender asked. "Lady trouble?"

Carver smiled. "One last beer. Then I'll be closing my tab."

"You got it." The man shrugged and walked away.

Carver took another sip. He set the bottle down, suddenly aware that someone was behind him, standing way too close. He could smell their breath. It had alcohol on it, something stronger than beer.

"You're right," a slurred voice said. "One more beer. Then we're kicking you down the road. Don't you know this bar is only for locals?"

Carver took another drink. He moved slowly. Relaxed.

"Hey," the drunk said, more loudly. "Did you hear me? Get out of my bar. Or I'll throw you out."

The problem could no longer be ignored. The last thing Carver wanted was a beer bottle smashing into the back of his head. So he turned on the stool. Stood up. Towered over the tattooed punk standing before him.

The punk was backed up by several friends, all equally wobbly on their feet. Carver almost laughed.

"What do you want?" he asked.

The punk recovered from the shock of Carver's height and went back to sneering. "I want you to get out. Actually, I want to beat your ass. How about that?"

Carver nodded. "I know guys like you. I've fought them before."

"Izzat right?" slurred one of the other men.

"That's right. You probably struck out with every woman in here. Now you want to heal your bruised egos by finding the biggest guy in here and making him bleed."

"Shut up," the head punk snapped. He rolled up his sleeves. "Are we doing this or what?"

"You're too drunk to fight me," said Carver. "But I'll let you substitute in a sober friend. If you have any of those."

The punk grinned. He held up a hand and waved toward the door. The bouncer of the place, barrel-chested and thick-bearded, came over. Pushing people out of his way like they were made of paper.

"That's Kev," the punk said. "He's my cousin. And he hasn't had a drink since he got out of prison."

TWO

There was no getting out of this one. Carver knew it right away. He was going to have to fight. He motioned the bartender over. Handed him some cash.

"I won't be back," he told the man. "But your bouncer might be. Depends what the doctors say."

Mocking laughter from the punks broke out behind Carver. When he turned to face his aggressors, their mirth petered out. Everyone was watching, other than a small collection of smart people who were currently fleeing the bar.

Kev the bouncer was big and mean. A bull of a man with an ogre-like face to match. He had a teardrop tattoo under one eye, and another tattoo on his neck that read KILL EM ALL in red font. Blurry and blown out. Definitely done on the inside.

"So," Carver said. "Where do you want to do it?"

Kev smiled. "I like this job. I want to keep it. So let's go into the parking lot."

Carver shrugged. "Doesn't matter to me. But I'll give you guys another chance to end the night peacefully. Stand aside. Let me walk out of here. You'll never have to see me again."

The punk leader scoffed, putting a hand on his big cousin's shoulder. "Can you believe this guy? Just cuz he's big, he thinks he can talk like that?"

"Like what?" Carver said. "I don't want any trouble. You probably don't either. If we do this, you're going to regret it. If you wake up tomorrow, that is."

Kev took a step forward, jutting his bearded chin in Carver's direction. "Did you just threaten my life?"

"No. I just think there's a good chance you'll end up in a coma. You might not wake up for another week or two. A month, maybe."

The punks all burst out laughing again, deriding Carver as if he were some kind of boastful wimp. Kev took a big breath through his nose. He calmed down, a technique he'd probably learned to try and keep himself out of trouble.

For a second, Carver thought the technique would work. Kev seemed to be reining himself in. But it turned out he was just getting himself ready for the fight.

"Let's go," he said.

Carver nodded. "After you."

Kev made his way to the door again, parting the crowd. Carver followed. The punks were close behind him.

Outside, Carver tailed Kev into the middle of the lot. The punks formed a ring around them. The combatants faced each other.

"How do you want to start?" Carver asked.

Kev raised his meaty fists, taking on the stance of a trained fighter—but not quite. His feet were all wrong. He stood like he was waiting in line.

Carver wasn't concerned.

A second later, Kev charged.

The bouncer was six-three or six-four, a couple of inches shorter than Carver. But he was heavier, more thickly muscled. His beard was fierce and neatly sculpted. But Carver had a feeling a glass chin hid beneath.

The more aggressive fighters were usually aggressive for a reason: they wanted to end things quickly, so their weaknesses couldn't be discovered.

It didn't matter. Carver already had the whole thing figured out during the walk across the bar. So far, it was playing out just like he thought.

He stepped aside at the last second, like a matador. The bull named Kev charged clumsily past. He tried to turn, but his feet slipped in the gravel.

Carver gave him a light kick in the back of the knee.

It was enough to send Kev to the ground. He landed on his face. His back half rocked upward like he was doing the Worm. A few guys in the crowd hissed in embarrassment. Kev's cousin started yelling.

"Get up! Break this guy's neck, Kev!"

Kev stumbled his way back to his feet. His beard was full of dust. Carver looked around the parking lot. The fight was already over. He was thinking of his next move. His car was nearby. He could be in it in ten seconds. Out of the lot in another five. Down the road and away, into the night.

The bouncer came charging back. His face was beet red. Anger was getting the best of him. He swung with a right hook.

Carver caught him by the wrist, and then he head-butted Kev straight in the nose. He felt a crunch.

Kev screamed and fell down again. Blood poured down his chin.

"Sorry about that," Carver said. "It was a little harder than I meant. Can we be done now?"

Kev swiped at his chin. Saw the blood on his hand. He gave Carver a terrified look.

Then his eyes flicked to his left, and the fear went away.

Carver turned to see what he was looking at and saw the tattooed punk leader sneaking up on him with an open switchblade.

The punk took Carver's boot straight to the gut. He grunted and folded in half. But he held onto the knife.

Carver grabbed the man by the arm and twisted hard. He heard bones breaking. Another scream of pain filled the night.

Grabbing the punk by the front of the shirt with both hands, Carver launched him through the air. He sailed eight feet across the parking lot and smashed through the windshield of a parked truck. A nice ride. Not a scratch on it… until now.

Oops, Carver thought.

"My truck!" Kev shouted.

Carver no longer felt bad. He strode over to his car, got in, started the engine, and left the bar behind.

THREE

Less than two beers. That was all Carver had. If he had stayed, he would have finished the second one. Maybe even had a third. But there was a shattered windshield back there. A shattered nose. And a shattered arm.

Time to get away.

But not too hastily. He didn't want to get pulled over for speeding. He didn't want some small-town cop with an attitude catching a whiff of beer on his breath.

Maybe they were already looking for him. Someone at the bar must have called the cops by now. And he was driving a distinctive car.

The windshield was cracked in two places. The side panels were rusting. On the surface, the car looked like it belonged in a junkyard. But under the hood, it was brand new. Souped up.

Carver had done some of the work, but most of the credit went to Harvey Carrol, Annie's father. They had been close long before her death. And in the wake of it, they were somehow even closer, despite the fact they rarely saw each other.

Especially now, with Carver on the run.

He glanced in his rearview mirror, checking for flashing lights. He saw none. Just the ordinary headlights of a few other drivers. The town of Lexington, Nebraska, soon faded into the distance.

Carver relaxed. Highway hypnosis took over. It wasn't hard to make his thoughts fade into oblivion. After all, he wasn't going anywhere. All he had in mind was going east. Reaching the next state. Eventually.

He found himself traveling back in time. Back to Annie. She was always there waiting for him. Whenever he needed her. Whenever he had a quiet moment like this, when he could visit her.

In this private area of Carver's mind, it was always a bright summer day. A light breeze blew through the pine trees and rocky valley of Idaho. It was a spot not far from the house where she'd grown up. A nice area. They used to visit it every weekend.

Annie was there, sitting on a blanket. Always smiling. Carver could only look at her and smile back.

After killing Everest and ending his quest for revenge, he worried the picnic spot would be empty the next time he visited. Annie's ghost finally moving on. The unfinished business wrapped up. Nothing holding her now.

But she stayed. Carver didn't know whether to be happy or sad. Sometimes he wished he could let her go. Other times, the thought of doing so terrified him.

He never spoke to her anymore. He'd already apologized a thousand times. And she knew he loved her. Of course she did. There was nothing left to say.

Carver came back to the present. Shaken out of his reverie by a bright light. Someone on the other side of the road, coming at him with their high beams on. He winced, holding up a hand until they were gone.

Then it was just him all alone. Under the big sky. Amid the endless farmland. He glanced at the passenger seat, where Annie used to sit and read while he and Harvey first started working on the old thing.

Just a hobby, back then. A fun side project. But when Annie died, they switched gears. The car became something more. A vehicle of vengeance. They turned it into what it was now: a restless beast under a corroded disguise.

Carver looked in the rearview mirror again, checking once more for cops. But he wasn't worried.

Even if they did come, he could outrun them.

FOUR

Carver continued to wander. Somewhere between the towns of Overton and Elm Creek, he turned left. Heading deeper into the countryside. He was alone on a narrow dirt road, driving past never-ending fields.

Now and then he saw a sign for a bigger farm. Or for small businesses that people were running out of their homes. A car detailer. A quilt crocheter. A guy named Jeff who made his own beef jerky.

It was nice to break up the monotony. It was late fall, heading into early winter. And while it was unseasonably warm, the farms lay empty and dead. Waiting for the spring planting.

It was dark out here. Far beyond any city lights, the night was like a thick blanket.

Carver drove slowly. Partially for safety reasons. Mostly because he wasn't in a hurry. He didn't even know quite where he was going. He was happy to get lost in the middle of nowhere. There was some food in the car. Bottles of water. If he had to sleep in his car...

It wouldn't be the first time.

He came to a crossroads. Unlike the others he'd just gone through, this one had a stop sign. There was no sign of other cars anywhere, but Carver played along. Smiling as he drew to a halt.

He waited for an imaginary car to cross the road. Drumming his big hands on the wheel. He glanced toward the passenger seat again. Reaching out, he flipped down the sun visor. There was a picture of her on it.

Annie.

Carver's smile turned bittersweet. He flipped the visor back up. Hit the gas to cross the intersection.

The car didn't move.

The engine roared, but it sounded different. Coughing and sputtering. Carver backed off, lifting his foot off the gas pedal. He put the car into park, turned the engine off, and then back on. He shifted into drive and tried again.

This time the car moved, though with a few complaints. It chugged, lurching forward. Then, with a huge groan, it started moving normally.

Carver sighed. Maybe this wasn't going to be a peaceful night after all. He thought about turning around. Heading back to the main road. He started to look for a place to turn around… then saw a sign for a town called Pomos. It was only three miles ahead.

Much closer than the highway at this point. The only question was, did it have an auto shop?

Carver decided to risk it. He babied the car forward, going even slower than before. Not like he was holding up traffic. He hadn't seen a single other car since making that left turn.

***

The car held out. It even started to perform better after a mile or so. To test it, Carver came to a stop again. Waited. Then tried driving. Once again, the engine complained. And once again, it slowly improved as he moved.

Soon enough, he saw the wooden sign ahead, painted in vivid colors. *WELCOME TO POMOS— HOME OF THE WORLD'S LARGEST ROOSTER.*

Carver spotted the rooster in question right away. It stood outside a farmhouse just past the sign. A giant statue on stilts. The size of the average water tower.

Not bad, Carver thought. *World's largest, though? Dubious.*

He drove further. Past more farms. And finally reached the town itself. He saw the usual destinations. A tiny grocery store. A firehouse and an elementary school. A post office. Gas station. Motel. Diner.

And, finally, an auto mechanic. The lights were all on. And the OPEN sign was lit up. Carver blinked, unable to believe his eyes. A small-town garage, open at ten PM?

He didn't think twice. He also didn't bother with his turn signal as he pulled into the lot.

FIVE

The parking lot was almost empty. Carver found a good spot, right by the big garage doors. He got out and walked up to the front door, pausing to read the name of the place: Pomos Mechanics.

Not original. But at least it was to the point.

He opened the door. A bell rang. He stepped inside, glancing around. There were two other customers in the shop. They seemed to be here together. So, they only really made *one* customer.

Carver strode across the lobby. It was clean, but smelled like rubber. Innumerable black scuff marks on the floor. A coffee pot gurgled in the corner. Coffee sounded good. But this stuff smelled bad. Like burned popcorn.

"Welcome, welcome!" the guy behind the counter said. He wore coveralls streaked with grease. A hat that looked like it had been through a wood chipper. His name was on his chest: ZEKE.

"Hello, Zeke," Carver said. "I was just passing through, but I ran into some car trouble."

"Oh, yeah?" Zeke beamed, fiddling with his hat. "What seems to be the problem?"

"I think it's a bad fuel injector."

"Ooh, a customer who knows his stuff. That's cool. We can take a look at that. I promise, whatever the issue is, we can fix it."

Carver smiled. "I don't doubt it. Do you think the motel across the street has empty rooms?"

"In Pomos?" Zeke scoffed. "You can probably have your pick of the litter, mister. But depending on how late you usually stay up, you might not need a room at all. We can get to your car right away."

Carver looked around again. "I was wondering why you were open so late. It can't be that you're catching up on your backlog."

"Oh, we had plenty of work today." Zeke waved a hand. "You're just catching us at the right time. We stay open late one night a week. It's all about customer service. Let's just get some paperwork started…"

He grabbed a sheet and a pencil. Sketched in the date and time.

"What's your name, sir?" he asked.

"I'd rather not provide it," said Carver.

Zeke looked up. "Why's that?"

"Because I have a lot of cash on hand. And I'm willing to throw in a tip for guys who do good work and mind their business."

Zeke nodded. "Well, then… um… Make and model?"

"1992 Camaro."

"Wow. Real oldster there. Hopefully, we have the parts around."

"You won't need the originals. Everything under the hood has been redone."

"Glad to hear it," Zeke responded. He didn't add anything to the paperwork. "If you don't mind me asking, where are you headed? You said you were just passing through."

"I'm heading south," Carver lied. "Into Kansas and then Oklahoma."

"Cool. Can I at least get a phone number?"

The phone Carver was using had been bought with cash only a few days ago. The definition of a burner. And since the paperwork didn't even have his name on it, he decided it was fine. He gave Zeke the number.

"Cool," the grease monkey said again. "We'll call you as soon as she's ready. Keys?"

Carver handed them over. A bad feeling suddenly settled in his stomach. But he chalked it up to reluctance. He didn't like handing the keys to his baby over. Normally he'd do the work himself.

But he didn't have that luxury.

What he did have was time. And an appetite.

On his way in, he'd noticed the town diner was still open as well.

SIX

Carver headed for the door. He noticed the two other customers looking at him. But he kept the paranoia at bay. He was used to the glances. The stares. It was what happened when you were six and a half feet tall, especially when your time in the Navy SEALs had packed your body with muscle.

He left the shop. The bell rang again. A cheerful sound. It dissipated quickly into the night. It was getting cold. Carver pulled his corduroy jacket tighter as he crossed the parking lot.

Briefly, he considered his car. It had a name. Harvey had decided it when they first brought the poor thing back from the scrapyard.

Her name was Victoria. It was what Harvey had picked out for the second daughter he never had. One failed marriage later, and the name ended up being applied to a rusted old car.

Later on, Annie told them how serendipitous the name was. Victoria was the Roman version of the Greek goddess Nike, who was known for her speed and athleticism.

Yes, old Victoria was fast. No doubt about it. The question Carver had was, did she have anything in her that he didn't want Zeke to see?

He thought not. The only somewhat questionable thing in the car was Carver's duffel bag in the backseat. It held a random assortment of things. Things he didn't think he'd need, but better safe than sorry.

There was nothing too alarming in the bag. There weren't even any guns. Anyway, Zeke would mind his own business—if he wanted his tip, that is.

Carver reached the road. He looked both ways out of habit. All he saw was dark blacktop stretching infinitely in either direction. He walked across it. Then down the sidewalk a quarter mile. Back the way he'd come originally.

The diner was still open, he was happy to see. According to the hours on the door, this was the only day it was open so late. They must have a deal with the auto garage. While people were getting their cars worked on, they could pop over for a bite to eat.

Works for me, Carver thought.

He went inside. A charming young hostess greeted him and led him to a booth. He sat down. By the time his waitress appeared a minute later, he was ready to order.

"Coffee," he said. "Decaf. Black. Cheeseburger and fries. Thank you."

"Any ketchup?" the waitress asked.

"Mustard, please," he replied.

"You got it." She walked away, still holding the menu she'd never had a chance to give him.

While he waited for his food, he kept his eyes on the window. Watching the dark, silent world beyond. Every so often, a car went by. One of them pulled in at the garage. The rest went on by. Just passing through. Same as him.

Then he saw a police car. A Nebraska state trooper. He pulled into the diner.

Just then, Carver's food arrived. He put the cop out of his mind for now, and got down to eating. He got through the burger in ninety seconds. Moved onto the fries. He dunked them in mustard, his preferred dipping sauce.

By then, the cop was inside.

The hostess brought him to a spot two booths down from Carver. He sat down and started perusing the menu. Carver took the opportunity to look him over.

The state cop was narrow-shouldered. A long, sunburnt neck. Matted down hair and a long, salt-and-pepper goatee. That was all Carver managed to get. The cop looked up, forcing Carver's eyes elsewhere.

Carver went back to eating. Sipping his coffee.

A minute later, he looked at the cop again.

He was still staring at Carver. With a purposeful glint in his eyes.

When the waitress returned, Carver asked for the check. He paid in cash, leaving a healthy tip. Then he got out fast.

SEVEN

Carver stepped outside the diner. He lingered on the front walk for a second, morbidly curious if the cop would come after him.

He didn't.

Carver walked away. He hurried back up the main road, along the sidewalk, into the quiet darkness of Pomos. It was peaceful.

Nothing much going on. All he saw were closed-up businesses. Houses in the distance, some with lights on. A dog barked somewhere.

This was the kind of place he liked. A place where nothing seemed to change. The rest of the world was in constant flux. Horrible things happened. People died. Entire towns, states, and countries were in upheaval.

But not here. Not in Pomos.

For a moment, he let himself imagine it. Living here. Maybe with Annie. They would raise kids. Walk them to school. Do corn mazes in fall. Hay rides out to the pumpkin patch. Come back to town just in time for a cup of hot apple cider.

Then he came back to reality.

His phone rang. He answered it with a stilted, "Hello."

"Is this the guy with the '92 Camaro?" Zeke asked.

"Yes."

"Your car's all fixed up. You can come grab it whenever you want, unless you're already settled in… We can hold it for you."

"No," said Carver, glancing back at the diner. "I'll be there in a minute."

He ended the call. Jogged across the road. Slowing to a fast walk, he made his way to the garage.

There was one less car in the lot. When he got inside, he saw the couple that had been here earlier was gone.

"I'm impressed," Carver said. "You guys really keep things moving."

Zeke gave him a grin. "We try. It helps when the jobs are easy. You were right about the fuel injectors."

Carver reached for his wallet. "How much do I owe you?"

"You were right about everything being new under the hood, too," Zeke went on. "Getting at the injectors was a walk in the park. In fact, I'm not even going to charge you."

"Not even for parts?" Carver asked.

"Nah. We're just happy to help you get on your way."

Carver nodded. He knew what had happened. Or at least he thought he did. Earlier, when he'd refused to give his name, Zeke had clocked him as some kind of fugitive. Which he was, in a way.

The mechanic was just trying to avoid any kind of connection. And yet he had agreed to fix the car. Nice guy. Or dumb. Sometimes the two were hard to separate.

"Thank you," said Carver. "I won't look a gift horse in the mouth."

Zeke held out a hand. The keys were dangling from his index finger.

Carver grabbed them. "Sure I can't give you a twenty, at least?"

"Nope," Zeke said resolutely. "We're just happy to help."

Carver shrugged. He was already putting the whole situation out of his mind. It was time to move on. He didn't like the way that cop was looking at him in the diner.

He was starting to dislike a lot of things that were happening tonight. It all felt surreal. And Carver knew what that meant.

It meant something strange was happening. He just wasn't aware of it.

EIGHT

Pomos faded like a dream.

Carver drove for another hour. Victoria performed perfectly. No more issues. She purred, carrying him at a steady fifty miles an hour. He headed east, finding his way to a random paved road. He didn't even know what it was called. What designation it went by.

The radio was on. A forlorn country song played. The windows were cracked, letting the night air flow in. It was chilly, but it smelled good, like fall leaves and corn husks.

For a little while, all was right in the world.

Then he saw the lights, flashing red and blue. He couldn't see their source just yet. It was somewhere over a small hill. But he saw the glow of the lights themselves, shining in a misty halo.

Unmistakable.

Carver kept going. Waiting for a speed limit sign. One soon appeared. The limit was fifty-five. He put on a little extra speed, getting close to sixty.

Maybe the cop was going somewhere else. He'd turn and disappear, leaving Carver alone yet again.

But the cop kept coming. He came over the hill. Carver saw the car now. The strobing light bar on top. But the cop wasn't going too fast. Sixty-five, maybe seventy. Gaining on Carver slowly.

Carver pushed his speed to sixty. Five over was forgivable in most states. He wasn't sure about Nebraska. But if the cop really was on his way somewhere else, he wouldn't care. He had bigger fish to fry than a minor speed violation.

The cop stayed where he was, gradually catching up.

Carver thought about pulling off to the side, to see if the cop would pass him. But then he'd be a sitting duck. Not a good idea.

He looked for other options. Side roads he could go down to disappear. But all he saw were long, straight driveways leading back to farmhouses. Everything out in the open. Visibility for miles in every direction.

That was also a no-go.

He glanced at the speedometer. Even at stock, the '92 Camaro could hit a hundred and thirty without too much trouble. In its current state, with a beefed-up frame and souped-up engine, it could break one-sixty without sweating.

Speeding away was always an option.

But far from a good one. The cop must already know what car he was in. Maybe even the license plate. If he ran now, he'd be putting himself on a great big radar.

There was really only one option that made sense, though it didn't feel good.

He looked in the rearview mirror. The cop had suddenly sped up. Going at least eighty, he surged up the road.

It was settled. Carver's hand was forced.

NINE

Carver slowed down, dropping below the speed limit. Then he put his blinker on, showing the cop he intended to pull over.

Right away, the cop hit the brakes. Dropping speed. Carver sighed. This was it, then. The cop was after him. It was unequivocal. Not that there was much room for any other possibility.

Carver let his right tires roll over onto the gravel. He pressed the brake pedal. Coming to a stop. The police cruiser settled in behind him. Parking about twenty feet back.

Nothing to do now but wait.

He left the engine running. From the glove box, he grabbed the vehicle registration, and then he slid his license out of his wallet, getting them ready.

Maybe this was just a routine traffic stop. Maybe he had been going faster than he thought. In that case, it would be over soon. Best-case scenario, he'd get off with a warning. Worst case, he'd have to come back to Nebraska for a court date.

Finally, the cop got out. He made a show of it. Slowly rising to a standing position. Stretching his arms and twisting his back. Then he slammed his door shut. Walked toward Carver.

When the cop crossed in front of his headlights, Carver saw his face. It was the goateed guy from the diner. The very same man who'd been giving him funny looks.

Any chance of an easy getaway seemed to fade in that moment, dropping away like a stone down a bottomless pit.

Carver pulled his eyes away from the side mirror. He gripped the steering wheel hard. Stared at the dark road ahead of him. He could get away. Victoria wouldn't fail him.

But running from the cops didn't sit well. He was no criminal.

He was a survivor.

And to survive, sometimes you had to do unpleasant things.

Why was the cop here? Had the FBI put out an APB on him? Was he wanted in connection with Everest's gang... or perhaps for killing several men at a shipping yard in Seattle?

Suddenly, the trooper was outside the window. The man lifted a flashlight, tapped the butt of it on the glass. *Click, click.*

"Sir," his muffled voice said, "please roll your window down."

Carver obliged.

For all the work that had been done on her guts, Victoria had never been given power windows. Carver had to grab a crank arm. Manually turn it. The window came down ever so slowly.

"Good evening, officer," Carver said. "Can I help you?"

The guy grinned. Showing big, sharp teeth. "Trooper Gibbs, at your service. What's your name?"

"Carver."

His next request would likely be to see ID. No sense in lying. But Carver didn't have to speak at all, so he didn't.

Gibbs nodded. "Fine. Maybe you'll answer this, at least: do you have any idea why I pulled you over?"

"I was going the speed limit," Carver said.

"A tad bit over," Gibbs grunted. "But that's not why. Would you mind opening your trunk for me?"

The trunk had nothing in it. Carver's duffel was in the backseat. If Gibbs looked in there, he might be in for a shock. But the trunk... other than a couple of extra jugs of water, it was empty.

"Sure," Carver said. He reached down, grabbed the lever for the trunk, and pulled until he heard a *thunk*. "There you go."

Gibbs smiled. "Thank you. I'll be right back with you. Just hang tight."

TEN

Gibbs slapped a hand on the roof of the car, and spat onto the ground. Clicking his flashlight on, he headed toward the back of the car, going very slowly. He even whistled, swaying side to side in a little dance.

"What is this guy on?" Carver grumbled to himself.

In his experience, there were two kinds of cop. First were the kids who saw bad things growing up. An abusive stepdad beating on their mom. A bully at school picking on anyone small and weak. Or maybe they were picked on themselves.

They joined the force to provide what they never had: protection.

Then there was the other kind of cop. The kind who did the bullying. Who now did the beating. Who saw the badge as armor against the very law they were meant to uphold.

Carver was trying to figure out which camp Gibbs belonged to. He already had a pretty good feeling it was the latter.

Gibbs reached the trunk. Carver felt the lurch as he opened it violently, slamming it upward. Clutching the wheel tighter, Carver held in his anger.

Nothing happened for a moment.

Carver turned around, trying to spot Gibbs. He couldn't. The open trunk lid covered everything. He didn't hear anything, either. It seemed like Gibbs was just standing there, staring at all the-nothing in Carver's trunk.

"Whatever you're after, Gibbs," Carver muttered, "I'm happy to disappoint."

Another moment passed.

Then everything changed.

First came the scuffle of boots on the gravel-strewn asphalt. The flash of motion as Gibbs sprinted away from the car. The snap of polished leather as he ripped his sidearm from its holster.

At the same time, Carver was moving too.

He faced forward. Unbuckled his seatbelt. Then stuck his hands out of the window, holding them up.

Gibbs ran across the road. Reaching a safe distance. Then he turned, aiming his gun at Carver.

"Sir, get out of the car!" he roared.

Carver hesitated. With his hands still through the window, he looked around, trying to figure out if he'd left anything in the trunk. But he couldn't think of a single possession. There was nothing that would cause this reaction.

He had done bad things. But he hadn't held onto them. At least not physically. Besides the mental baggage, he was pretty much clean.

As he glanced into the backseat, he saw something. The water jugs. He'd thought they were in the trunk, but they weren't, which meant the trunk was one hundred percent empty.

Or had been, until Gibbs opened it.

The trooper must have planted something. He must have seen Carver at the diner. Picked out a target for some nefarious purpose. To hit a quota of some kind. To get a commendation. A bonus. A raise.

There was only one possibility.

Carver was being set up.

"*Get out of the car!*" Gibbs screamed again.

"I'll need to take back one of my hands," Carver said. "Don't shoot."

"Just get out," Gibbs said.

Carver nodded. He pulled his left hand in, used it to open the door. He shoved it wide with his knee as he stepped out, rising to his full height.

Gibbs looked him up and down. Eyes going wide for half a second.

"Face the car," he commanded. "And put your hands behind your back."

Carver did exactly as he was told. He turned, looking over the top of the car. He crossed his wrists in the small of his back and waited.

Things had hit a new level.

He now had no intention of playing along.

ELEVEN

Everything was silent again. Carver stayed where he was, ready to be arrested… or so it appeared.

Gibbs also stayed put, as though he didn't quite know what to do. Or maybe he had a bad feeling.

You should, Gibbs. You should have the worst feeling you've ever had.

Finally, Carver heard it. Boots coming across the road, approaching from behind.

"Mr. Carver," Gibbs said, "you are under arrest."

Carver said nothing. There were a lot of things he *wanted* to say, most of them rude, some of them profane, but he kept his mouth shut.

He wanted to hear everything.

There was a metallic rustle. A ratcheting click. Handcuffs. Gibbs was pulling them off his belt, getting ready to slap them onto the wrists of his latest victim.

Carver had no idea why he'd been singled out.

But he was going to find the answer.

As soon as he felt the first touch of the trooper's hand, he turned around in a flash.

Gibbs had holstered his gun in order to work the cuffs. His mistake. Grabbing Gibbs by the right arm, he yanked up and twisted. Gibbs had to spin to keep his arm from ripping out of its socket.

From there, it was easy.

Carver used his foot, sweeping Gibbs's feet out from under him. The trooper went down on his back with a cry of surprise. Then a pained grunt as Carver's weight settled on him, a knee grinding into his chest.

Carver pulled the gun from the holster. He quickly dismantled it, tossing the parts in random directions. Gibbs watched, his face going red. From pain. From anger. From embarrassment.

He tried to fight, punching at Carver's side. But he couldn't move enough to generate any power. Nor could he reach Carver's head.

"I would say I'm sorry," Carver said. "But I don't know if it's true or not. Why did you try to arrest me?"

Gibbs let out a guttural roar in response.

Carver smiled. "Good. You're able to shout, which means you can breathe. Which means you can answer my question. But you're not going to, are you?"

Gibbs didn't say anything. Which, ironically, said everything Carver needed to hear.

No answers were forthcoming. He was pretty sure his assumption was right. Gibbs wanted to plant something in his car. Drugs. A piece of evidence. Whatever it may be.

The trunk was still open. All he had to do was look.

He turned his head to the left. Saw more lights speeding up the road. Backup was well on its way. By the look of it, they'd be here in less than a minute.

Time to go.

Carver ripped the cuffs from Gibbs. He lifted his knee long enough to throw the man over onto his belly.

"Hands," he ordered.

Gibbs complied. He laughed as the cuffs closed on his wrists.

"You're done, whoever you are," he said. "You aren't getting away."

"I disagree," Carver replied. "You're pretty close to my car, Gibbs. You might want to start squirming away. I don't want to run you over when I take off."

TWELVE

Carver got back in his car. He slammed the door and snapped his seatbelt on.

It was time to get gone.

His window was still open. It would have to stay that way. Cranking it up would waste time. He glanced through it, making sure Gibbs was moving.

He was. The trooper was worming his way toward the other side of the road.

Carver gunned it. Just in case he was still too close, he swerved right slightly, and then corrected straight. He put his wheels on the pavement. And drove.

Victoria roared with monumental power. The acceleration was crushing. The trunk slammed itself shut. Carver was shoved back in his seat. In the mirror, the flashing lights quickly began to fade.

But that only lasted a few seconds.

As soon as they saw he was running, they sped up. Straining against Victoria's force, Carver reached up. Adjusting the mirror. Making sure he could see what was going on. It was all about quick glances. If he had to pull his eyes off the road for longer than an instant, he was done.

He may have been driving a beast of a car, but the Nebraska State Patrol weren't exactly riding bicycles. They were catching up. Soon he saw them in his side mirror as well.

They were close enough that he could count them. Three cars. All being driven with great skill and grace. These guys knew what they were doing.

But so did Carver.

He knew the playbook they were working from. They had their set of moves. If it was just one car on his tail, it would have to try a pit maneuver. Nudge the back of his car. Make him spin out.

With three cars, they had another option. A better one, much harder to escape from.

A second later, they put the plan into action.

One of the cars sped up further, closing in on Carver's rear. Getting within a few feet. Carver let it come. It was only a matter of time before it happened anyway.

A second car surged forward, coming up on his left. If he looked over, he'd be able to see the driver. Look into his eyes. But he stared forward instead.

The third car hung back, waiting until it was needed. There was no room for it right now. No need for it. Carver was boxed in. He couldn't back off, or the car behind would hit him. He couldn't go left and make any kind of U-turn or breakaway.

All they had to do now was slowly chip away at him. Closing in. Forcing him to slow down. Then they could push him wherever they wanted. Get him to stop somehow.

They were doing their job well, Carver had to admit. But there was always a way out.

He started looking for one. And saw it. A dirt track leading into the countryside. But it was on the left side of the road. No way he'd make it with that cop car blocking him.

He let the dirt track go by.

Carver still planned on using it, as long as the next part of his plan worked.

A peek to his right told him it just might. The shoulder that way was wide. The culvert behind it was shallow, no steep drop-off. Just a gentle, grassy slope.

The cops were already killing his speed. He was going less than eighty now. Not ideal. Slower would be better. But he'd make it work.

He gave the wheel a tiny nudge to the right, slicing onto the shoulder and into the grass.

The cop behind him reacted. Also turning right, trying to stick with him.

Meanwhile, the cop to the left had no idea what to do. He kept on going, flying past. He slammed the brakes a second later, fishtailing in his attempt at a quick turnaround.

Carver went left, turning into the spot the second car had just left behind and heading back the way he had come.

As soon as he made the turn, he saw the third car charging toward him.

THIRTEEN

He thought he knew what kind of cop Gibbs was, but he had no idea about the driver of the third car. Was he sensible? Logical?

Or was he the kind of guy to take a head-on collision at seventy miles an hour?

Carver would soon find out. He pressed the gas pedal down. The tires screeched. Caught pavement. Sent him flying forward.

The headlights shone directly on his eyes. The flashing red and blue lights. Car Number Three was fast approaching, less than fifty yards away now. Forty. Thirty.

Carver saw the dirt track. He had found it again, even in the dark. But he'd be past it in an instant.

He made a quick turn. He felt the right tires just start to lift off the pavement. Victoria was getting ready to tumble. But with all the extra hardware Carver and Harvey had bolted into her, there was too much inertia.

She settled back down. And off Carver went, sending up a cloud of dust. Racing past a field of corn and deeper into the heart of Nebraska.

He wouldn't get to find out what kind of cop Number Three was after all.

The rearview mirror told him the cops were recovering. One was already on the track. It was soon joined by the others. The chase was back on.

This time, it would be slower going. Carver experimented with his speed. Each time he got to about fifty, he'd start bouncing all over the place, potentially doing damage to the undercarriage.

This track was rough. Full of potholes and old ruts. It was at least straight. For now.

Carver settled in at forty-five. He stared into the distance, looking for anything. Trying to figure out where the track went. If it dead-ended against a bunch of trees…

No time to think about that. The cops were gaining ground, catching him fast. Maybe their tires were better suited to the terrain. They didn't seem to be having the same trouble as him.

He sped up. Predictably, the car started bouncing again. But it also kicked up a lot more dirt, forming a dense cloud behind him. Maybe the cops would get lost in it. Swerve off the track. Crash into something.

It didn't happen. Instead, their flashing lights bored through the dust, coming up to meet him. They sandwiched him again, this time from three sides, owing to the flat landscape.

Left. Right. And back.

He was stuck.

The only way out was forward. But he'd have to speed up. That was a no-go. Too high a likelihood of losing control.

There was one other option. The last resort. Carver hated to do it.

He took one hand off the wheel, patted the dash.

"Sorry, old girl," he said. "It's either this or jail."

"*Pull over!*" a distorted voice crackled. One of the cops speaking through his PA.

But Carver couldn't pull over, not with cars on all sides.

The cop seemed to realize this. He added, "*Slow down. Come to a gradual stop. Do it now!*"

Not happening, Carver thought.

The car to his left suddenly swerved closer. He saw why a second later. A fence had appeared on that side, giving the cop less space to drive.

The fence looked heavy-duty. Thick wire. Maybe electrified. Thick wooden posts every ten feet. No way of knowing how far it went. It could end any second, putting them back on open ground.

The time was now.

Carver turned left. Sending himself careening toward the cop car.

FOURTEEN

The driver of the patrol car saw him coming. He yelled through his PA. No words, just a surprised scream.

Metal crunched on metal. The bumper and left fender of Carver's car ground against the trooper's car door. Carver did not relent. He dug in. Pushing the gas. Turning harder. Shoving the cop toward the side of the track.

And into the fence.

The cruiser slammed straight into one of the wooden posts. It was apparently set deep in the ground. It snapped off at the bottom, but not before caving the front of the car in. And popping the hood open.

The hood swung up fast. The hydraulic arm on one side broke. The whole thing flapped into the windshield, cracking it inward.

If that wasn't enough, the wire of the fence ripped free. It was sucked under and around the tires, making one of them pop. Sending bits of rubber through the air.

The police car came to a stop, spewing smoke and a series of angry cries. There were some bad words. Some nasty names. Carver ignored them.

He had bigger problems.

Swinging away from the fence, he fell back into the ruts of the dirt road. The other cars had gotten a little ways ahead. But they were braking now, trying to let him catch up so they could block him in.

But the fence soon ran out, giving Carver a wide berth to the left. He took it, rolling across dried corn stumps.

The other cars saw him make the move. In their haste to intercept, they got in each other's way. Both were forced to come to a complete stop.

Things were looking good. It seemed Carver would make a clean getaway. But he had learned a long time ago not to celebrate too early.

In the car closest to him, the driver's side window rolled down. A hand holding a pistol came out.

A second later, the shooting started.

Victoria's back right window shattered. Glass flew everywhere. More bullets hit the door, landing with hefty thuds. Carver cringed.

Then the shots stopped coming. He was ahead of the cops now. Were they afraid of shooting their windshields? Or something else?

Carver would take it either way. But he knew the bullets could start flying again any second. And Victoria was already damaged. He had no choice but to push the old girl further.

He pushed on the gas. Steeling himself for some nasty bumps. But they didn't come. The road was smoothing out. That was his cue to go even faster.

The troopers were moving again. The two remaining cars were back on the pursuit, racing toward him. They had learned their lesson and now moved in single file.

It didn't matter. Carver was gone. Or he would be in another minute. They couldn't catch up now. He was too far ahead.

Maybe it was time to celebrate. Carver almost did, a little fist pump and a smile. But he held back. Keeping his hands on the wheel.

He came over a shallow rise and saw the road ahead. Or rather, the lack of road. It ended less than a quarter mile away, right in the front yard of a giant farmhouse.

FIFTEEN

Carver cursed. He slowed down. There wasn't much road left. He started looking around, searching for other ways. Side paths. Driveways to neighboring properties.

No dice. The land sloped up in both directions now, ending in thin tree lines.

Once again, the only way out was forward. But even that was in doubt. The house was big, surrounded by different pens and fenced-off areas, along with a barn and a few silos.

Carver could only keep driving. And hoping.

As he drew close to the house, he saw that the track didn't end. Not where he thought it did, at least. It simply took a jog to the left, leading between the house and one of the pens. Beyond the pen fence, he saw big shapes. Cows, he thought.

The track was suddenly much skinnier. He slowed further, snaking his way into the front yard of the farmhouse. He was stuck now. If this was a dead end, his ride truly was at an end.

He took the jog to the left. Turned onto the next straight segment of the track. Now he could see that it did end. Fifty feet ahead. But there was no fence. No wall blocking his way.

Just a whole lot of open grassland beyond. The wilds of Nebraska. It was mostly flat, devoid of any real features. Not exactly the best place to get lost in. Even if he got miles ahead, he'd still be visible.

He had to find a way of slowing his pursuers down.

He checked the rearview mirror. The cops were coming, but they were a good forty seconds behind. Maybe enough time.

Carver stopped the car.

Jumping out, he ran toward the metal fence that held the cows in. He followed it back, looking for a gate. He found it quickly. It was latched, but not locked or chained.

He opened the gate and pulled it to a ninety-degree angle until it was jutting out straight across the road. It was eight feet long, barring the way completely. Nearly hitting the house itself.

Right away, the curious cows began to move. Two of them stepped through, approaching Carver fearlessly.

"Sorry, I don't have any food." He pointed toward the approaching cops. "Maybe they do."

A third cow came out, shuffling in between the others. A highly effective barricade.

Carver glanced at the house. Saw an angry bearded man watching him through a window. Carver pressed his hands together. Bowed his head. His best attempt at a non-verbal apology.

The man disappeared. Probably on his way to a gun cabinet. By the time he came outside, Carver would be gone.

But the two troopers would have some questions to answer.

Carver ran back to his car. He got in and drove, allowing himself to laugh now.

Somewhere behind him, the farmer started to yell. Flashing police car lights lit up the night, but soon faded as Carver entered the plains.

A few miles later, he looked back again. And saw nothing.

He was all alone, with nothing but the unknown ahead of him.

He had disarmed and cuffed one state cop. Sent another into a fence with great damage. Trapped another two with an angry, armed man.

After this, the entire Nebraska State Patrol would be looking for him.

And he still didn't know what kicked it all off.
What had Gibbs put in his trunk?

SIXTEEN

Speed was relative.

On the highway, or any paved road, thirty would feel dreadfully slow.

Out here, it was a different story. There was no illumination to see by. Carver only had his headlights. He wasn't afraid to use them. His taillights would still be visible for miles either way.

The headlights weren't enough, but he pretended they were. When he saw larger obstacles, he slowed down. Things like old stone foundations. Fenceposts. Even a few wrecked cars. He worked his way around them meticulously, vigilant for barbed wire or anything else that could pop a tire.

The land was flat. Devoid of trees. But there was still a surprising amount to contend with. Thick grass that tried to grab onto his tires. Prairie dog holes. Strange ruts that could be from anything. Maybe even an old wagon trail.

He continued for a couple more miles. Waiting. Watching for a good place to stop. Finally, the nervous energy caught up to him. And his bladder. He glanced in the rearview mirror. Saw only darkness behind him.

He stopped and got out. Left the car running. He stood alone in vast emptiness. The wind blew, rustling the dry grass. Turning slowly in a circle, he finally spotted where he'd come from.

The glow from the farmhouse was visible in the distance. So were the strobing red and blue police lights. Carver knew he'd gone at least five miles. But it looked like he'd barely gone too far.

Distances were deceptive out here in the plains.

Carver took a few steps away from the car. He took care of his business, careful which way the blind was blowing. Finished, he glanced at the trunk. Wondering if he should open it now.

Another look at the farmhouse told him it was a bad idea.

He saw the police cars now. Headlights coming his way. Two sets of them. They had only just left the farm, by the looks of it. It had taken them all of ten minutes to break free. To get the cows corralled. The farmer assuaged. The gate shut.

Now they were coming.

With all this open ground, they would have a harder time finding him. In the daytime, at least. At night, his taillights were a beacon.

If he could see them, they could see him.

Time to get moving again.

Carver got back in the car. He continued at twenty miles an hour, keeping a close eye on his six. The cruisers didn't seem to be closing the gap. Over the next few miles, they remained at the same distance.

Carver was impressed. Most cops would have called it a night by now. But these guys were persistent. The Nebraska State Patrol didn't mess around. But Carver had made them mad. He had outsmarted and out-driven them multiple times.

Now they knew his plate number. The make and model of his car. They knew what he looked like, thanks to Gibbs.

They would hunt him until one of two things happened: until he was caught, or until he managed to disappear.

It didn't look like he'd be caught, not tonight, so Carver turned his mind to other problems. Mostly, the problem of what was in his trunk. He figured it was something ordinary. Drugs, maybe. Or a weapon.

But maybe it was something wild.

Maybe it was a bomb.

That thought almost made him stop again. But he told himself he was being paranoid. A bomb made absolutely no sense.

Then again, none of this did.

SEVENTEEN

He could no longer see the police lights behind him.

It had been a few minutes since he last checked. The land had been declining for the past mile, sloping down into a shallow bowl. He didn't know whether he'd simply lost sight of his pursuers over the lip of that bowl, or if they had given up.

Either way, he saw his chance.

There were trees up ahead, a sparse thicket. Stunted by the constant assault of the wind. But it was broad enough. If he drove further toward the middle of it, he'd be hidden.

He made his way in. Going slowly now. He mostly let Victoria coast, not giving her much gas. Only little bursts here and there to overcome thicker clumps of grass.

Snaking his way between the gnarled trees, he traveled onward.

The underbrush grew denser. Bushes grew up here and there, making it harder to find his way. But he plowed ahead, crushing some of the foliage under his tires. The car was up to the challenge.

Finally, he hit the brakes. Put the car in park. He sat for another moment. Breathing. Waiting to see if anything would happen. Maybe a whole brigade of police cars would fly into this little forest, shattering his sanctuary with sirens and lights.

Nothing came.

He opened the door and felt the full force of the wind. He held on tight, keeping the door from being violently ripped away. Hauling himself out, he hit the button to pop the trunk. Then he forced the door shut again.

Carver shivered in the cold. The temperature was dropping. His body reacted to it, but his mind didn't. He didn't give the weather a second thought. Instead, he turned to his left. Walked slowly to the back of the car.

Gusts of wind buffeted the trunk lid, making it wobble up and down. Carver watched it. If there really was a bomb inside, it would be nice if he didn't get too close. Maybe the wind would eventually open it for him.

After twenty seconds, he gave up on that hope.

Putting one hand out, he wrapped his fingers around the edge of the lid and lifted it up.

He wanted to squint. To close his eyes. To hold his breath. He forced himself to look without fear. And saw the last thing he ever would have expected.

There were no drugs in the trunk. No contraband of any kind. Gibbs hadn't planted anything after all.

But there was still something inside.

Some*one* inside.

A woman. She was curled up. Her legs bent and turned to one side. Her back was flat against the trunk bottom. She stared up at Carver with a sheepish smile, holding her hands out in a placating gesture.

That was how he figured out her wrists weren't bound. There was nothing tied around her ankles, either.

"You're not supposed to be in there," Carver said.

The woman winced. "Sorry. This isn't how it was supposed to go."

EIGHTEEN

Carver reached in, grabbing hold of the woman's right wrist. He moved with lightning speed. Before she could begin to fight. First, he pulled her up so she was on her knees. Then he hooked his hands under her arms, lifting her up and out.

She started to slam her hands on his chest, pounding his pectoral muscles like they were a door she wanted someone to open. Her feet touched the ground. Carver quickly patted her down, taking her abuse with no reaction.

She had nothing on her. Nothing that he could feel, anyway. Which meant no gun. No knife. Nothing that seemed able to hurt him. He grabbed her right wrist again, then her left, catching her next attempt at punching him.

He stared her in the face. "Who are you?"

"Let me *go*," she demanded.

Realizing her legs were still free, she thrust a knee at him. Carver walked his feet backward, dodging the blow. Then he dragged her around the car. Shoving her against one of the rear doors.

"Don't try to hit me again," Carver warned her. "We're all alone out here. I'm a lot bigger than you. And I guarantee I'm better at hurting people."

Her eyes burned. "Is that a threat?"

"Take it however you want," he said. "Whatever stops you from fighting. The truth is, I don't want to hurt you."

Her features softened. "I don't want to hurt you either. Or anybody. Would you please let me go?"

Carver smiled. Shook his head. "Not until you answer some questions. Who are you?"

She groaned. "Fine. My name is Naomi Downes."

She'd rattled off the name quickly. Smoothly. Either it was a practiced lie, or it was the truth. Carver didn't care which. At the moment, her name didn't matter. There were more pressing matters.

"Where are you from?" he asked.

"Originally? Pomos," she replied.

Carver nodded. "That's the town where I got my car fixed earlier tonight. Is that where you squirreled yourself away in the trunk?"

"Yes," she admitted.

He kept staring at her, waiting for more. But she closed her mouth. Gazed back at him without fear.

"Naomi," Carver said. "Take a look around. What do you see?"

She didn't move her head. Her eyeballs flicked left and right, taking things in.

"Nothing," she answered. "We're in the middle of nowhere."

"That's right. There isn't anywhere for you to go. Not in a timely manner. And we've already established that fighting me won't get you anywhere."

Naomi frowned. "No. I guess that's true. You must have eaten your veggies when you were a kid, because you're the human equivalent of a brick smokestack. And these…" She turned her hands into fists, wriggling them in Carver's grip. "I wouldn't call them wrecking balls."

He smiled. Sizing her up. She was on the tall side for a woman. Five-eight or five-nine. Beautiful, with wavy black hair and sharp features.

A man of lesser discipline would be softened by her physical appearance. He would be taken in by whatever lies she was about to spew. Whatever requests she was about to make.

Carver was not that man.

But he did not fear her. With a final warning squeeze to her wrists, he stepped back and released her.

NINETEEN

To Naomi's credit, she did not immediately launch another attack. She also didn't run. She stayed where she was. Leaning against the car. Rubbing her wrists where his fingers had dug in.

"That kind of hurt," she said. With a smirk, she added, "You're a liar."

He was taken aback by the remark. But she quickly elaborated on it.

"You said you didn't want to hurt me. But I feel like I just had too-tight handcuffs on."

"I have real cuffs in my bag," Carver grunted. "I could remind you of what they feel like. I promise they aren't nearly as soft as my hands."

"You call your hands soft? With *those* calluses?" Naomi scoffed.

"Forget about my hands," Carver snapped. "Turn around. Face the car."

Her mouth fell open. "You sound like that cop. I think he said his name was… Gibbs?"

"That's right," Carver said. "Now turn around. I didn't pat you down very thoroughly before. I need to do it again."

She rolled her eyes. "Of course you do. Just be professional, okay?"

She faced the car. Putting her hands behind her head for good measure. Carver came up behind her. He used the back of his hand, running it up and down her back, and then her legs. He felt something in the back pocket of her jeans, pulled it out.

It was small. Rectangular. It had a cap on one end. He pulled it off, saw a USB plug.

"Flash drive?" he asked.

"Yup," she replied, in an annoyed tone. "And that's all I have on me. So you can keep your hands to yourself now."

He capped the flash drive again and considered keeping it. But he intended on getting this woman out of his life as soon as possible. He slid it back into her pocket.

"You're clear," he said.

"Told you," Naomi grumbled. Smoothing out her shirt.

"So, you're from Pomos."

She turned to face him, crossing her arms. At first, he thought it was a gesture of indignancy. But then he saw the goosebumps on her arms. The way she trembled. She was cold.

He didn't feel bad for her. Not at all.

"That's what I said," she shot back.

"I'm going to guess you didn't ninja your way into my trunk," Carver said. "First of all, the mechanics would have no reason to open it. Not for the work they were doing. You would have had to open the door. Popped it with the lever. Someone would have seen you."

She just shrugged.

"The car was fixed too quickly," Carver went on. "Which means there must have been people with it the entire time. It wasn't left alone. Not long enough for you to get in. Besides, Victoria's trunk lid is lightweight. You probably wouldn't be able to close it from the inside."

"Are you done?" she asked. "Wait, who's Victoria? Your car?"

"Someone at the garage helped you," Carver said, ignoring her question. "Was it Zeke? Must have been. He asked me about where I was going. I thought it was small talk. Now I'm not so sure."

Naomi shrugged again.

"Answer me," Carver demanded.

"Why?" she barked. "You're better off not knowing. Trust me."

"Not knowing the means of your stowing away in my trunk?" he asked. "Or am I better off not knowing *why* you did it?"

"The second one."

"Then you can tell me how you got in."

"Fine! Yes, Zeke helped me. I've known him my whole life. Not very well, but it's a tight-knit community."

Carver nodded. "So, I was marked. Probably no one else stopping by who was heading out of state. I'm sure all the other customers were locals. It had to be me."

Naomi grinned. "Wow. You're big *and* smart. That's quite the deadly combination."

"A lot of people have found that out the hard way," Carver told her. "Which makes you a lucky woman."

TWENTY

"Lucky?" Naomi sighed. "If you had told me that a few years ago, I would have believed you. But not now."

"I really don't care," Carver said calmly. "I want you to answer one more question."

"I'll try. No guarantees."

"Are the cops after you? Or are they only after me because they think I kidnapped someone?"

Naomi hugged herself tighter. "Like I said, you're smart. You can figure that one out on your own. For now… look, I'm really sorry you had to get tangled up in this. For what it's worth, I didn't pick you. Zeke did. I was hiding in the back of the garage, waiting for his signal. That's all."

"That doesn't help. Not at all. But I appreciate your attempt at an apology."

"Well, you should," she replied. Teeth chattering now. "Because I meant it. Can I get back in the car now? It's freezing."

Carver took a step forward. He put his hands on the roof of the car, blocking her on both sides with his huge arms. "Why should I let you do that?"

"Because I have nowhere else to go," she pleaded. "Please don't leave me out here."

"I'm still considering it."

"Please! I promise you *don't* want to know why I'm out here. Just… take me to the next town. Drop me off somewhere. I don't care. Just don't strand me in the middle of nowhere."

He stared into her eyes. She stared back. He tried to read something in her, a page from the book of her soul.

He didn't believe he could trust her.

But little did she know, he had quite a soft spot.

He pulled his arms back. "Fine. Next town. No further."

She let out a breath. "Thanks. I guess I am kind of lucky."

"You are," he agreed.

Naomi walked past him to the rear of the car. She stood waiting.

"You should put me back in the trunk," she said. "Probably safest that way. For both of us."

Carver smiled. "I don't know what's going on. But I know they're looking for both of us. Someone at the garage must have ratted your plan out to the cops. It's the only way Gibbs could have known to pull me over."

"Yes, that was my conclusion, too," she said quietly. "It wasn't Zeke, I know that. He likes me too much."

"You're on the run from someone. Now I am too, because of you. The cat's out of the bag. They know what car I'm driving. What I look like. They know you're with me. The only thing they don't know yet is my name. But they'll find out."

"I get what you're saying," she replied.

"You might as well ride up front," Carver added. "The trunk isn't even heated."

"It was fairly toasty."

"I doubt that."

"Well, I did say you were smart. Do you want to get out of here now?"

He answered by slamming the trunk shut. He went to the driver's side door. Got in. Naomi slid in next to him. She glanced at him warily as he turned the engine on.

Victoria rolled onward.

"I don't know your name either," Naomi pointed out. "I know I haven't been very... helpful. But I told you my name, at least."

"Your real name, right?" he chuckled.

"Yes, actually. Which I shouldn't have done. But I was panicking. I'm not used to this. You know, being a fugitive."

I am, Carver thought. *Getting there, at least.*

"So, how about it?" Naomi asked.

"It's Carver," he said.

"Is that your first name?"

He glared at her.

"Never mind," she said. "I'm shutting up now."

TWENTY-ONE

Trooper Gibbs gazed out into the darkness. He let the cold wind wash over him. Not much else he could do. He was caught. Sitting in the back of the ambulance, being fussed over by a duo of medics.

"Hold still," one of them said, dabbing a cotton wad with rubbing alcohol against a scrape on his cheek.

Gibbs hissed, jerking away. The medic glared at him. He glared back.

"I'm fine," he said. "Now get away from me. I don't need anything else."

The medic shrugged and let him go. Gibbs put his jacket back on. Striding into the road, a lonely country lane. Less than ten feet away was the spot where he'd been tackled.

It had hurt, having the big buy crushing him into the ground. He was bruised all over. But what really pained him was his pride. If he had been a bit faster... a bit smarter...

Getting locked up with his own handcuffs was the icing on the cake. The cake of humiliation. Gibbs was angry. He wanted revenge. He *needed* it.

There was another cruiser parked behind his, lights flashing. Gibbs approached the window. It rolled down. The driver smirked at him.

"Yeah, yeah, wipe that off your face," Gibbs snapped. "I'm all good to go here. What's the situation?"

"We tried following your boy," the other cop said. "But we didn't make it far. It was quite a merry chase. I just got word. A field office is being set up. It's going to be a whole manhunt."

"Good. Are we rolling?"

The cop nodded. Gibbs jogged to his patrol car, giving the ambulance a wave. He got in, waiting for his escort to get in front of him. He followed his fellow state patrolman into the night.

They soon turned off onto a dirt road. It was rough going. Along the way, they passed an empty police car. Hood up, windshield smashed. It sat amidst the wreckage of a fence.

That made Gibbs even angrier. But also a little less embarrassed. He wasn't the only one who'd been outplayed by the mystery man. Mr. Big, Gibbs wanted to call him. The name fit. Made him sound a bit like a mobster in a corny movie. But good enough.

He was led to a large farmhouse. A hay field had already been transformed into the field office. Two huge tents stood in it, along with a couple of trailers. One of them seemed to be giving out coffee.

Gibbs started to get excited. And confused. This was some real-deal stuff. Very official. And very fast. The state patrol always took things seriously, especially a case like this.

But this response was far from typical. What did they need a field office for?

He followed his escort into a makeshift parking area, which turned out to be another field. Gibbs doubted the farmer cared much. He'd probably been handed a check with a nice number on it. And it was just about winter. Nothing growing at the moment.

There were already a good dozen police cars here. Some other unmarked vehicles. A van. A truck. Gibbs found a spot and parked. He got out, wandering toward the coffee trailer.

Along the way, he spotted a familiar car. It had a scuff mark on its left rear fender, the result of a run-in with a traffic bollard a few months back. Gibbs smiled, increasing his pace.

He spotted her in line for coffee. Trooper Sanders, a good friend of his. She looked like a Midwest stereotype. Pretty in a plain sort of way. Blonde hair. Wrinkles on her face from way too much smiling.

"Sanders!" Gibbs called.

She turned back. Laughed and waved, flapping her fingers. She was at the back of the line. Gibbs joined her with no fear of cutting in front of anyone.

"Saw your car," he said. "Still has that ding in it."

"Oof," she hissed. "My fault. Distracted driver. Don't try and pull out of a parking garage while eating potato salad."

"It's certainly not on my agenda," Gibbs replied. "Any idea what's going on here?"

She grinned. "Free coffee and donuts."

He shrugged. "I was talking about the tents. I guess we're taking this thing seriously."

"Sure are. I dunno who this guy is you pulled over, but someone wants him bad."

Gibbs just nodded. The truth was, he knew a little more than he was letting on.

But he had been told not to talk about that.

TWENTY-TWO

Sanders and Gibbs got their stuff, a cup of black coffee and a cinnamon sugar donut for both. They joined the thin flow of foot traffic that was heading toward the tent. As they crossed the field, two more patrol cars pulled in from the main road.

"This is turning into some big thing," Gibbs grunted.

Sanders nodded. "All troopers within a forty-mile radius were instructed to come here."

Gibbs looked over his shoulder, at the parking area. "There were this many in forty miles?"

"Probably not," Sanders chuckled. "Like these latecomers, for instance. Everyone wants a slice of the glory, even if they don't know what the glory even is."

Gibbs pointed at the tent. "We'll find out in there, I guess."

Sanders dunked her donut in her coffee. Swirled it around a bit. Took a sloppy bite.

Gibbs knew more than she did. But he didn't have the full story. The *why* of it all. He hoped he was about to learn something, too.

All he knew was that he'd been given a task. From someone high up. He was in the right place at the right time. The right place happened to be the outskirts of Pomos. That was all, more or less.

He entered the tent behind Sanders. The thing looked like a pain to set up. It was bigger than the house Gibbs had grown up in. A canvas roof that probably weighed three hundred pounds on its own. Two dozen metal trusses held it up, supported by at least as many legs.

Most of the tent was filled with chairs. Half of them were filled. Gibbs and Sanders took two of the empty ones. They faced a makeshift stage, fashioned out of cinderblocks and plywood. Probably sourced from the farm itself.

On that stage, in an immaculately crisp uniform, was the man who had given Gibbs his special assignment.

Colonel Paul Bell.

Bell was the highest-ranking person in the Nebraska State Patrol. The top dog.

"Whatever this is, it's huge," Sanders muttered.

Bell stood with his hands behind his back. Confident. He waited, letting his eyes wander over the crowd, not minding the awkward silence.

A minute later, two more troopers hurried inside, sweaty and out of breath. They had sprinted from their cars. They fell into two seats.

"Is everyone here?" Bell said loudly. "Good. We can start. Ladies and gentlemen, this is a matter that concerns all staff of the Nebraska State Patrol. I'd love to address the entire agency, but time is of the essence."

He gestured to his left. An officer hurried away from the corner of the stage, passing things out from a file folder. A stack of headshots, showing the same woman.

"This is who we're looking for," Bell went on. "Her name is Naomi Downes. You'll find a dossier on the back of your photo. She's in possession of stolen material of a sensitive nature. She cannot be allowed to escape."

He sliced a hand toward the audience, indicating Gibbs.

"Trooper Gibbs has brought to our attention a second target, a man who is aiding Ms. Downes in her escape. His identity is currently unknown. But he's described as very tall and muscularly built, with light brown hair. If you see anyone matching that in the vicinity of Ms. Downes, chances are it's our guy."

Bell stopped speaking for about two seconds. Long enough for a trooper near the front to raise his hand.

"Yes?" Bell asked.

The guy put his hand down. "Colonel, what protocol are we looking at here? We want them alive?"

"It doesn't matter," said Bell, "as long as what Naomi Downes is carrying doesn't end up in the wrong hands."

TWENTY-THREE

Bell answered a few questions. Waffled on a bit longer about the importance of the mission. Then it was over. Everyone headed out of the tent, ready to begin the hunt.

Sanders got up. "Coming?"

"I'll catch up," Gibbs told her. "I want to ask him something."

She smirked. "Why didn't you just do that during the Q and A?"

Gibbs shrugged. "That's what everyone was doing. I don't want to be everyone."

Sanders frowned. She had no idea what he was talking about. But she left. Soon, it was just Gibbs and Bell in the tent.

The Colonel crooked a finger, summoning his minion. Gibbs got up, walked to the stage.

"Are you injured, Trooper?" Bell asked.

Gibbs shook his head. "No, sir. I'm good to go."

"I'm glad to hear it," Bell said, "but the Senator and I have our doubts about you."

Gibbs swallowed hard. His heart thumped in his ears. Suddenly, his mouth was dry.

He'd thought this was his ticket to greener pastures. A job in Unger's private security, maybe. Perhaps it would take him all the way to the Secret Service one day.

But he now had the feeling the rug was being pulled. He didn't know what to say. He knew he should say *something*. Defend himself. Save face. But he couldn't make his mouth work.

Bell lowered himself down. Sat on the edge of the stage. "You have an exemplary record, Gibbs. But maybe a state cop is what you were born for. Nothing more. That's nothing to be ashamed of."

"Sir, I can—"

"We thought you were the best man for the job," Bell added. "For chasing that tip we received from the garage in Pomos. But so far, your performance doesn't inspire confidence. You were incapable of subduing an unarmed man who had no idea what was even happening."

Gibbs shook his head. "I'm pretty sure he figured it out, sir. And he wasn't some regular guy. He must have some kind of training. I mean, he was *fast*."

"We'll find out who he is," Bell said. "Even if you're right, the point still stands. You're not suited for this assignment."

"And they are?" Gibb jerked a thumb toward the tent entrance. "They're all staties, just like me."

Bell sighed. "You're right. Obviously, I don't want to stop you from conducting your normal work. But I'm considering cutting you off from access to any privileged information."

"Don't do it," Gibbs said forcefully. "I failed this time. It was a learning experience. I'm not going to make the same mistake again. I'll find Naomi Downes, sir. She won't get away a second time."

Bell smiled weakly. "You have the fire, Gibbs. But do you have the talent to back it up?"

"One way to find out. Give me another shot."

"Okay, then. I'm willing to extend you that courtesy. I'll tell you what we know so far. The car you pulled over is registered to a man named Harvey Carrol. He lives outside Boise, Idaho."

"Okay, then," Gibbs said with a nervous laugh. "There's got to be a connection there. Some way of identifying Mr. Big."

"Most likely. We're working on that." Bell glanced at the entrance. Lowered his voice. "You've got one more chance, Trooper Gibbs. Don't blow it."

"I won't," Gibbs promised. "But I might need some help. Do you mind if I recruit a friend?"

Bell gave him a knowing smile. "Not at all. As long as she only knows what she needs to."

TWENTY-FOUR

"It's getting a little hilly now, huh?" Naomi observed.

Carver just grunted in reply. The stereotype of Nebraska being flat was mostly true. *Mostly*. Out here, the land rolled gently up and down. There were scattered thickets of trees. Some on hilltops, others in valleys.

It was difficult to drive through. Especially at night, with not even a walking trail in sight.

"At least it's a unique way to see the countryside," Naomi added, giving Carver a meek smile.

"Good way to damage your suspension, too," Carver pointed out.

"Come on. I know this thing's a beast. I could tell even from the trunk. It'll be fine."

It was his turn to glance at her, with a look of disbelief. "I had to stop at a mechanic earlier. Remember?"

"It was just a bad fuel injector," she replied. "Zeke told me. Easy fix. Could happen to any car."

Carver shrugged. She was right. Victoria *was* a beast. An unstoppable huntress. She could get through whatever Nebraska had to throw at her.

But the car was his last link to his old life. Nothing else he had with him was from those days. It was a connection to Annie. And he'd put plenty of sweat into the rebuild. He couldn't help but baby the thing.

Soon, the trees thinned out. In the distance, moonlight glinted off something. A long, thin line snaking across the flatter ground. If it was water, it was as still as ice.

"Hey, a road!" Naomi said.

Carver didn't say anything. He kept driving. He was already going slow. He went even slower as he approached the supposed road, and it was a good thing he did. The "road" turned out to be a deep canal. Stagnant water lined the bottom.

"No road," Naomi said, disappointed.

"No road," Carver agreed. "But it's a sign of civilization."

He turned left, following the edge of the canal. After a quarter mile, he spotted a bridge across it. But it was blocked by a hefty security gate.

"Private property," said Naomi.

Undeterred, Carver drove on. A canal was just a manmade river. And if you followed any river far enough, you'd find habitation. It was a guarantee.

As long as you didn't run out of gas.

A check of the gauge told him he had a quarter tank left. Victoria wasn't known for her stellar gas mileage. A tradeoff for her power.

Carver started to worry. Not about himself, about the car. If it ran out of gas, he'd have to leave it behind. Proceed on foot. Now that he had the State Patrol after him, there was no telling when he'd get back. If ever.

None of the worry showed on his face, or in his body language. He remained stoic, steering through the tall, dry grass.

He spotted something. A dirt track that ran alongside the canal. Just two lines running through brush. He steered onto it, increasing speed a bit.

Off to his left were houses. Clusters of farm buildings. A good sign.

Not long after, he found what he needed. An actual public road, cutting north. He turned onto it, crossing the canal on a bridge.

"Now we're talking," Naomi said.

"No, we aren't," Carver replied.

"I wasn't speaking literally."

"I was."

"You're a weird guy," Naomi remarked.

Carver said nothing. They came to a crossroads. He stopped, looking in all three directions. Left. Forward. Right.

To the right, he saw more signs of human existence. In the other directions, he saw nothing.

He turned right.

A little over a mile later, they reached pavement. A main road. There were no signs to point the way. Carver turned right again. This time, it was an arbitrary choice. But he committed fully.

Getting up to the speed limit, he sped toward whatever was waiting.

TWENTY-FIVE

It wasn't long before Carver saw lights up ahead. Enough of them to constitute a small town. He relaxed.

A minute later, Naomi pointed to a sign. "Kind of a nice name. Hopefully, it has a gas station, huh? Looks pretty small."

"It's the best we've got," he said.

She shrugged. "I wonder if it would be safe to turn your GPS on. Just for a minute."

"It could be. I've got a burner phone. Paid cash."

"Good!" Naomi held out a hand. "Give it here. Maybe I can find someplace better."

Carver pulled his phone out, handed it to her. "Knock yourself out."

She frowned. "This is a flip phone."

"It is."

"It doesn't have GPS."

Carver smiled. "It barely has text messaging."

She groaned, giving the phone back. "Oh well. Let's just see what Elyria has."

It didn't have much. They drove through the entire town in no time. Saw nothing but a bar. A post office. A church. Then they were back in the cornfields. Carver checked for traffic, and then did a U-turn to head back.

He pulled to a stop in the driveway of the church. It was dark and desolate. No one around. Not a single car in the parking lot. A parking lot which was made of dirt rather than asphalt.

"We can't stop here," Naomi said. "I need to get somewhere bigger. You know, with *stuff*."

"Stuff?" he asked.

"Yeah. Like, people who can help me, since you're not willing to."

He turned to her. "Do you know why I'm not willing?"

"Because you're a jerk?" she said.

"No. Because I'm not stupid. All I know about you is your name. Maybe. And that you're being chased by the state police. The only reason I took you this far is that you would have died out there."

"You're right," she sighed.

"So get out," he told her. "I'm already in enough trouble."

"There's no one around," Naomi pointed out. "The cops aren't chasing us. Maybe we can just go a little further."

"No."

"Please? I'm begging you." She clasped her hands together, giving him a truly pitiful face.

He looked away. "No. Get out of my car."

"*Please!* I'm not exaggerating when I say this is life or death for me. There are things you don't know."

He looked back. "Then tell me."

She paused. Staring at him. "Why? Will it help my case?"

"Depends on what you say. I might consider taking you somewhere else."

As he said it, he knew it was a mistake. But she reminded him too much of what he'd lost. Someone to protect. Someone who needed him.

Someone I failed, he thought.

"I'm going to need more than that," Naomi said.

"Too bad," Carver said. "This is life or death for me, too. If you recall, those cops were shooting at me."

"They weren't trying very hard. They knew I was in the trunk. They didn't want to hit me. For all they know, you're a kidnapper and I'm your victim."

Carver wasn't sure that was true. He wasn't sure about anything.

"Okay," he said, "tell me everything. And I promise to drive you until I find a gas station. This town doesn't seem to have one."

She thought about it. But not for long.

"Sounds good. I'll tell you, Carver. But maybe we should get away from the main road first. No telling when a cop might come through."

She was right. Carver reversed back onto the pavement, drove a little way up. He turned down a gravel side road, followed it through a curve and pulled off onto the shoulder, where the boughs of some dense trees hid him.

He turned the engine off. Unbuckled his seatbelt. Cranked the window down to let in some fresh air.

"Good," Naomi said. "Now here goes."

TWENTY-SIX

"Have you heard of a man named Morgan Unger?" Naomi asked.

Carver shook his head. "I know Stu Ungar. He played poker. One of the best of all time."

Naomi gave him a blank stare. "I don't know who that is. We're talking about Morgan Unger. *Senator* Morgan Unger."

"It rings a bell," Carver said. "I don't pay much attention to the news these days."

"Well, he's up for re-election this year," Naomi went on. "And I want to make sure he loses."

Carver settled in, leaning his seat back. "Is it personal?"

She nodded. "Up until a few weeks ago, I was in a relationship with him. Happily. I thought he was a wonderful guy. He treated me well. We got along perfectly."

"Politicians are good at that," Carver put in. "Appearing a certain way. Putting on a mask."

"Yup. Morgan was no exception to that. I thought I was dating a handsome, loving widower. His wife died five years before we met. Car crash. That's what drew me to Morgan in the first place. You see, my husband died that way too."

Carver felt a wave of empathy. "Car accident?"

"Drunk driver," she sighed. "It was three years ago."

"Sorry."

"Don't worry about it. It's not the point of the story. The point is, three weeks ago, things changed. I found something. I was cleaning up in his home office, putting things away. There's a desk drawer that's usually locked, but it was open. He must have forgotten.

"I looked inside. I felt guilty at first, digging around in things he obviously wanted to be kept private. I thought maybe he had things from his wife in there. Love letters. Birthday and anniversary cards. Things to remember her by. I was half-right."

"What was in there?" Carver asked.

"Receipts. Correspondence. Everything I needed to learn the truth. Her death was no accident. He paid a hitman to take her out and make it *look* like an accident. Instead of burning the evidence, he was sick and arrogant enough to keep it around. Probably pulled it out every now and then and had a good laugh."

She made a disgusted sound. Stared out her window. Carver waited for her to continue. A minute later, she did.

"She didn't want him going into politics. She wanted a simple, ordinary life. Kids. Privacy. Stability. There was a huge life insurance policy on her."

"Two birds, one stone," Carver said.

"Exactly," Naomi agreed. "He got to have his dream career, with a nice monetary boost to get him going. He used her untimely, tragic death to his advantage. Plucking on heartstrings across the state."

"I don't like this guy very much," Carver replied.

"Neither do I. Not anymore." She lifted herself off the seat, pulled the flash drive from her back pocket. "I have everything right here. Proof of what he did. I took pictures of everything with my phone. The only place they exist now is right here."

"No backups?" Carver asked.

"Not anymore, I'm willing to bet," she scoffed. "The pictures were also on my laptop. That's how he found out that I knew. It's what made me run away. I already had a plan to escape. I just had to put it into action a bit sooner."

Carver nodded. "You called on your old friend Zeke in Pomos."

"I didn't tell him anything," Naomi insisted. "I just told him I needed to get away. He asked what the plan was. You were never supposed to know I was in your trunk. Not until you were across state lines, at least."

"But someone blabbed."

"Sure did. I hope it was worth it." She shook her head. Then she turned back to Carver. "If I can get out of Nebraska, I should be safe from Morgan's lackeys. I can expose the truth and bring down an evil man. If you can at least get me somewhere with a gas station, I should be able to find a new ride."

Carver looked away from her. Through the windshield. He watched clouds skid slowly across the night sky.

"I hope Zeke's doing all right," Naomi muttered.

"He's not," Carver said.

"Huh?"

"I'll be honest with you, Naomi. Your friend is probably in jail right now. Or he's on his way. You're a fugitive. A powerful man is after you. They'll say you did something you didn't actually do. Something horrible. That way, they can undermine your chances of finding any help or sympathy. They'll put it on every news station in the state."

She looked horrified. "I guess... I saw that coming. I know what kinds of friends Morgan has. The influential kind."

She gave Carver a sad smile. Then she opened her door.

"What are you doing?" Carver asked.

"Leaving," she said. "I'll take it from here. You should get moving. I don't want you going down because of me."

He grabbed her arm, holding her back gently.

"I'm already in it," he told her.

She shook her head. "If they find you without me, you'll be fine. They don't care about you. You're a stranger."

"You're assuming they'll use rational thought. That's the wrong way to look at it."

He released her arm. She got out. But he joined her, stepping into the grass.

"You really want to help me?" Naomi asked.

"I'll sleep on it. Let's find a hotel."

TWENTY-SEVEN

Carver got his duffel bag out of the car. They walked together down the road, sticking to the white line by the shoulder. Single file. Carver stayed back, letting Naomi take the lead. Keeping an eye on her.

"I don't know if this place even *has* a hotel," she said. "We might end up sleeping in a hayloft or something. Just don't knock the lantern over and start a fire. Otherwise, we'll have to call the bucket brigade in."

"Sounds like you enjoy western movies," Carver said.

She shot a look over her shoulder. "You don't care what I like. At least, you shouldn't. The less you know, the better."

"We're past that phase. But you're right, I don't care."

They were silent for a moment, following the curve of the road. Trees to their right, thick with pine needles. Farm fields to their left.

"Quiet out here," Naomi muttered. "Not much of a nightlife in Elyria, huh?"

"These are rural people," Carver replied. "Up at the crack of dawn, in bed by nine."

She sniffed. "Sounds kind of nice. The simple life."

"It does," Carver agreed.

Once upon a time, he had been pretty close to having that kind of life. His days dedicated to working around the Carrol house, his nights dedicated to loving and caring for Annie, and maybe some kids.

He put all that out of his mind.

"There is a hotel here," he said. "I spotted it at the north end of town."

Naomi looked like she was about to complain about walking that far. Then she remembered the town was less than a mile long. She shrugged.

They reached the main road and turned right, onto State Highway 11. Two lanes of gritty blacktop. A dusty shoulder on either side.

At first, they stuck to that shoulder. It soon became clear the highway was deserted at this time of night. Carver walked out into the middle. After a moment's hesitation, Naomi joined him.

"This feels weird," she said.

"We'll get about a two-mile warning if any cars show up," Carver said.

They had to walk a good long way before they even reached the town proper. A small collection of buildings. Then more fields.

"There's the bar!" Naomi announced. "Looks closed."

"Too bad," Carver grunted.

She pointed at a sign. "Fort Hartsuff State Historical Park. Sounds exciting."

Carver frowned. "I've heard of Fort Hartsuff. It was an Army outpost in the late 1800s. But I thought Burwell was the nearest town."

"Oh my god," Naomi groaned. "Of course. I've never heard of Elyria, because who has? But Burwell I know. It's actually a real town. If we went left after that dirt road instead of right…"

"I see the hotel," Carver said. "We'll just lay low here for the night. Head to Burwell in the morning."

"If you say so."

"I do."

The place was called the Windy Lodge. It had six rooms and a tiny lobby. Nothing else. Unlike the bar, it was open. Or so the neon sign in the front window proclaimed.

"I'll go in alone," Carver said. "The news won't have my picture yet."

Naomi nodded. She waited in the parking lot as Carver went into the lobby. A bell rang over the door, making the old woman behind the counter startle awake.

"Goodness!" she said. "You scared me."

"Sorry," Carver said. "Just looking for a room."

"Well..." The lady reached for her guest book. "We've got... let's see here, two rooms free. Take your pick."

"Something with two beds."

"Okay. I'll give you room three. Right in the middle, all cozy and snug. What do you need two beds for? You're all alone."

"I like pushing them together and stretching out sideways," Carver said.

"Yeah, right," she snorted. "Here's your key. That'll be ninety dollars."

He handed the cash over, grabbed the key, and went outside. Naomi hurried over to him.

"Freezing out here," she said.

"Your fault for running away without a jacket. Didn't Zeke give you one?"

He unlocked the door. They went in, and Carver locked it.

Naomi rushed into the bathroom.

Carver sat on one of the beds and flicked through channels on the TV. There weren't very many, and the signal was bad. He settled on a John Wayne movie.

He heard the toilet flush. The sink turn on. That was his cue. He dropped the duffel bag at his feet, unzipped it.

"Ready for bed?" he asked when Naomi came out.

"So ready," she sighed. "I thought today would never end."

Carver pulled a pair of handcuffs out.

"What are those?" she asked.

"A precaution," he answered. "I don't know if what you told me is the truth."

"It is," she insisted.

"Maybe. Until I know for certain, I need to protect myself. It's either this, or you sleep outside."

She let out a huff of air. But she cooperated, lying on the bed and stretching her right arm above her head.

Carver locked her to the frame. Gave it a shake to make sure it was strong. He turned the lights out and crawled into bed.

"Does the TV bother you?" he asked.

"Kind of loud," replied Naomi's voice through the darkness.

He turned the volume down to a whisper. Drifting off to muffled gunshots and jingling spurs.

TWENTY-EIGHT

It didn't take Carver long to fall asleep. Staying that way was another matter. He was on edge. Every slightly louder sound from the TV woke him up. He eventually turned it off. The John Wayne flick was over by then, anyway.

After that, dreams kept him restless. None of them made sense. Annie was there. She was in trouble. He tried to reach her, but he couldn't move. No matter how fast he ran, he couldn't get to her.

When he woke up again, he was covered in sweat. Adrenaline filled his veins. He had a feeling someone was there. Nearby.

Of course someone was there. It was Naomi, in the very next bed. He saw her silhouette. On her back. Right hand up beside her head.She wasn't moving.

He heard a noise. A faint scuffing sound, like a shoe scraping across pavement.

He looked at the window. Saw a shadow moving beyond the curtains. Slowly. Bobbing from right to left, heading toward the door.

Naomi let out a snort. Followed by a soft breath. She shifted in her sleep, trying to scratch her nose with her right hand. The handcuff chain rattled. She used her left hand instead.

"Wake up," Carver said quietly.

Naomi was either a light sleeper, or she was just as on-edge as he was. She turned her head toward him. He saw reflected moonlight bouncing off her eyes. They were wide open.

Carver pointed toward the window.

She turned her head to look. Freezing solid.

Then someone pounded at the door, three solid whacks, making it shake on its hinges.

"Nebraska State Patrol! Open up!"

A woman's voice.

Carver got out of bed. He grabbed his bag, carrying it with him to Naomi's bed. He used a key on his keychain to unlock the handcuff, freeing her. She sat up fast. He held a finger to his lips.

Not that he had to tell her to be quiet. She hadn't made a peep since waking up.

He beckoned to her. Led the way into the bathroom. There was a small window inside. Carver slowly slid it open. He ripped the screen out and set it aside.

Outside, he saw a chain-link fence about three feet away. Nothing beyond it but open prairie.

He climbed out first, just to make sure he could fit before sending Naomi through. He managed to get into the debris-strewn alleyway. Reaching through, he helped Naomi. Guiding her feet to safe purchase.

"What now?" she whispered.

He was about to speak. To tell her the plan. Run to his car. Drive out of here as fast as possible. Assuming the spot he'd parked wasn't already swarming with cops.

Before he could talk, something rattled to his right. A can tipping over, spilling nails across the ground.

A flashlight flicked on, blasting Carver in the eyes. He blinked, holding up a hand. As his vision adjusted, he recognized the salt-and-pepper goatee.

Trooper Gibbs.

TWENTY-NINE

The trooper wasn't armed with a flashlight alone. He was holding his service pistol as well. Both were aimed at Carver's head.

"You want to try and run again?" Gibbs said. "This time, I'll shoot. You won't get far with a bullet in your brain."

Carver put up his other hand. Raising them above his head. Naomi flattened herself against the hotel wall, watching in shock.

She could get away. Gibbs was mad at Carver. All his focus was in one direction. If Naomi started running now…

Carver tried communicating this to her. Flicking his head toward the other end of the alleyway. But she didn't catch the signal.

"Back here!" Gibbs called. "Behind the building!"

Carver didn't move. Not even a single muscle fiber. But his mind was fully engaged, running through possibilities. Calculating. Churning.

Trying to land on the perfect scenario. Or at least one that kept both of them out of jail. And alive.

Scanning his eyes to the right, he noticed something. The fence. It was chain link, but in certain places, layers had been added. Corrugated metal plates, attached to the chain link with twisted bits of wire. He assumed they were there to keep dust off the windows. Or for privacy. Privacy against who? Cows, maybe.

At any rate, the metal plates were barely holding on. The twisted bits of wire were old. They were corroding. Rusting away. Getting loose. They were only in certain spots, which made more sense when he saw loose ones on the ground. They'd been falling off for a while.

It wouldn't take much effort to pull one away.

Carver knew he was faster than Gibbs. But Gibbs had his gun out this time. And Carver wasn't faster than a bullet.

Ten seconds had passed since he and Naomi entered the alley.

Too long.

It was time to make a move. Before the other cop showed up.

Carver slid his left foot to the side, nudging something. It rattled. Gibbs pulled his eyes away for a second, looking down at Carver's foot.

Carver grabbed the edge of the nearest metal plate. He ripped it off the fence, throwing it at Gibbs.

The trooper didn't shoot. He cursed, using his flashlight hand to bat the plate away, throwing the rest of the alley into darkness for a split second.

A split second was all Carver needed. He charged forward like a bull. Slamming into Gibbs. Putting him in the dirt. The trooper grunted, wheezing as the air left his lungs.

"Gibbs!" the female cop shouted. Her voice came through the open bathroom window.

Carver quickly disarmed the trooper, grabbing his gun. He tossed the flashlight away.

Still on top of Gibbs, he turned onto his back, aiming the gun at the window. Just in time for the other cop to stick her head and shoulders out. She was holding a pistol.

"Oh, dang," she said, putting her hands up.

Carver looked back at Naomi. He half expected her to be gone. Maybe she had finally recovered from her shock. Realized her best option was to make a run for it.

But she was still there. Her eyes were wide. Her chest rose and fell rapidly.

"Naomi, can you hear me?" Carver demanded.

She nodded.

"Take her gun away," Carver added.

THIRTY

"Hold up!" the cop said. "It's Naomi, right? We've been looking for you. All we want is to get you somewhere safe."

"She's lying," Carver said.

"The name's Sanders," said the cop, "and I never lie. I'm one of the good ones, Naomi. Now we've got to get that gun away from this guy. He's dangerous."

Naomi glanced at Carver.

"Don't," he warned her. "She might not know why she's out here, looking for you. But you know. And I know. Don't trust them."

Naomi nodded. She frowned at Sanders. "Give me the gun."

"You kidding me?" Sanders scoffed. "I don't know anything. All I know is you were kidnapped."

Carver smiled. "Cut the crap. Maybe you've never lied before tonight. I can believe that, because you're terrible at it."

Sanders looked at Gibbs. He had nearly three hundred pounds of muscle on top of him. He was incapable of speech. But he nodded. Letting out a little gasp that sounded like a tea kettle.

Sanders sighed. She let go of the pistol with all but her index finger, letting it spin around upside down. She handed it to Naomi.

"Don't do anything dumb with that," Sanders said.

Carver let up a little bit, giving Gibbs some air.

"You're in trouble," Gibbs breathed.

"So are you," Carver told him. "This is the second time you've failed to apprehend me. It's not going to look good."

"Give me a break," said Gibbs. "We both know you aren't some normal guy."

Carver shrugged. "How did you know we were here?"

"Screw you."

Caver raised an elbow, aiming it at the trooper's gut. "I could make you hurt, Gibbs. Badly."

"Good for you," Gibbs replied.

Carver gave him the elbow, using about twenty percent force. It still made Gibbs cry out, squirming in pain.

Carver wondered if he should go again. Harder. He didn't want to. Gibbs was just a man doing a job. But time was running out. This whole scuffle had caused way too much noise. By now, other guests were phoning the night manager, who in turn would be calling the cops.

Assuming Gibbs hadn't already called for backup before moving on the hotel. He'd be a moron not to. And Carver didn't think he was a moron. Just a bumpkin.

"The clerk!" Gibbs finally said. "She heard your description on the news. Recognized you."

Carver nodded. He could admire the old lady from the lobby. In any other circumstances, he would say she did the right thing.

"You won't get far," Gibbs added. "We'll be right behind you."

"Unless you plan on killing us," Sanders said.

"Would you shut up?" Gibbs snapped. "Don't give them any ideas."

Sanders shrugged. "Sorry."

"We aren't going to kill you," Carver said. "We're not the enemy."

"Then quit running," Gibbs told him.

"Quit chasing us," Carver responded.

"Not gonna happen."

Carver jumped to his feet. He turned to watch Gibbs struggle to a standing position. Using the fence to hold himself up.

"You're in trouble," Gibbs said.

"You already told me that." Carver looked at Sanders. "Come on out. Into the alleyway."

"What for?" Sanders demanded.

"So I know where you are. Climb on out. I'm not going to hurt you."

Sanders made a face. She grabbed the window sill, like she was about to start climbing out. Instead, she suddenly shoved herself back. Disappearing into the bathroom.

Naomi squeezed off a shot. Yelping in surprise as the gun kicked in her hand. The bullet hit the eave of the roof above her.

"Sorry!" she yelled.

"Nice shooting." Carver marched toward her, grabbed her elbow, and pulled her toward the end of the alley. "Let's go. Backup's definitely on its way now."

He glanced back in time to see Gibbs. Feet flailing as he kicked himself through the window after his partner.

THIRTY-ONE

Carver reached the end of the fence. He ran out and turned left, heading into the darkness. He didn't look back to see if Naomi was there. He didn't need to. He could hear her breathing.

"I can't believe it," she gasped. "I just shot at a cop. I didn't hit her, did I?"

"No," Carver said. "She's fine."

There was a low wooden fence at the edge of a farm field. He stepped over it easily, turned back to see if Naomi needed help. She vaulted over it with little effort, landing beside him. She was in good shape. Strong. Her breathlessness was from adrenaline.

Carver looked back at the hotel. They'd only made it fifty yards. He could already see police lights, flashing beyond the building.

"Time to move," he said. Without waiting for an answer, he started running again.

Naomi caught up. Running beside him.

"Where?" she asked.

"Doesn't matter," he grunted.

"What about your car? Shouldn't we have headed that way?"

Carver frowned, fighting back the pain.

"The car's gone," he replied. "They've found it by now. We'll have to survive with what we have."

"The clothes on our backs, and whatever's in that duffel bag," Naomi groaned.

"I still have my phone and wallet. A good amount of cash left. And we have two guns."

That made Naomi stop dead. Carver took a few more strides. Then stopped to look back. She was staring at the stolen gun in her hand. A haunted look on her face. She dropped the gun at her feet.

"This isn't who I want to be," she said quietly.

Carver looked over her shoulder, watching as flashlight beams played behind the hotel. Coming closer.

He walked back to Naomi. Kneeling, he unzipped his bag. He grabbed her gun out of the dirt, put the safety on, removed the magazine, and set the parts inside his bag.

"You don't need to do any more shooting," he said. "I'll keep Gibbs's gun with me. We should go now."

She nodded, but still didn't move. Carver picked up his bag and grabbed her hand. Gave her a tug. She broke free of the spell and ran again.

The field was broad. And as flat as everything else around it. They moved fast, driven on by the approaching lights.

On the other side, they came out onto a dirt driveway. A tractor was parked nearby, along with a bulldozer. A light burned outside a huge barn, but no one was around. All was silent, except for some distant voices, shouting near the motel.

Straight ahead was another segment of the canal they'd dealt with earlier. Luckily, the farmer's road had a bridge. They jogged across it, finally entering the wilderness.

It was the same hilly, lightly forested area Carver had driven through before. It proved easier on foot, but much slower. They paused once inside the trees, taking stock of their situation.

"Which way?" Carver asked. "North?"

Naomi shrugged. "Might as well. We're pretty much in the middle of the state here, far from any border. But at least things are more barren to the north. Less people."

He nodded and started walking.

"Carver?" she said.

He looked back. Waiting.

"Thanks," she told him. "And also… I'm sorry."

"We have a lot of distance to cover," he replied "Let's get started."

THIRTY-TWO

"Don't look at me," Gibbs snapped.

He was in front of Sanders, walking across the motel's parking lot. He couldn't see her, but he could sure feel her eyes. Boring holes into the back of his head.

"What?" she said defensively. "I'm just glad we're alive. Aren't you?"

"I got my butt kicked twice tonight, Sanders. By the same guy. And I had the advantage both times. How glad do you think I feel right now?"

"I dunno… not very?" she tried.

"You could say that," he grunted.

Backup had arrived. Two other patrol cars were parked nearby, lights flashing. The scene was covered. Gibbs was glad for that. He didn't want to stick around for another second.

A minute ago, they had gotten word via radio that a car had been found, matching the one Gibbs pulled over earlier. He and Sanders were on their way toward it. They headed south along the main road on foot, quickly crossing the tiny town of Elyria.

As the police lights faded behind him, Gibbs cooled down. Anger and shame faded. In their place, he felt terrified. He had failed yet again, after promising that he wouldn't. He didn't want to think what that might mean.

They found the car a little way down a side road. Hidden, parked tight against some trees. Two more patrolmen were standing nearby.

Gibbs paused by the rear of the car. Looking it over. Checking the license plate. He smiled, waving one of the patrolmen over.

"This the one?" the guy asked.

"It is," said Gibbs. "His car. Now the scumbag's on foot."

"Won't be long before we get him," the other man confirmed. "Whoever he is."

The trooper walked away, joining his comrade at the front of the car.

"We still don't know the guy's name?" Sanders asked. "That's hard to believe."

Gibbs looked at her. "I'm telling you, this guy's some kind of operator. A ghost. He's got to be."

"Then why is he working with Naomi Downes?"

"Beats me."

"I guess they're friends," Sanders suggested. "Maybe they go way back."

"Nah." Gibbs shook his head. "Naomi had a plan for making her escape: get in with a stranger who had no idea she was there. Somehow, she picked the biggest, scariest guy in the whole state."

"Lucky us," Sanders chuckled.

"But now the cat's out of the bag," Gibbs went on. "Mr. Big knows the deal. He's not an unwitting stranger anymore. So…"

"Why is he protecting her?" Sanders added.

"Exactly."

"Another good question, Gibbs." She turned toward him, hands on her hips. "How do you seem to know so much? Colonel Bell didn't mention any kind of escape plan in our briefing."

"I'm not sure I should be talking about that, Sanders. Or any of this, for that matter. In fact, I should probably shut my trap right now."

She smirked. "But you won't, because we're a team. And you happen to like me."

"I respect you as a colleague," he said.

"And as a friend."

"Of course."

"So you know I can keep a secret," Sanders prodded. "Come on. Tell me what you know."

Gibbs was silent.

THIRTY-THREE

Carver crouched by a fallen tree, resting his hand on the trunk. He was giving his legs a break. He was also watching the highway, a couple of miles away.

Headlights occasionally blazed in the night. Lone travelers, long gone by the time the next car appeared. None of them looked like cops. But at this distance, it was hard to tell.

Best to avoid the road altogether.

"Northwest," he said. "We'll parallel the road. Keep it in sight."

Naomi sat on the trunk, making it bounce. She sighed. "That way, we won't get lost. Right?"

He nodded.

"My feet are tired," she muttered. "I don't even know how long we've been out here."

"I do," said Carver. "It's been about an hour. We've covered no more than two and a half miles. Too many hills to make better time than that. And your feet hurt because you're wearing dress shoes."

She glanced at her feet. Frowning. "They're pretty comfy, actually. They just look fancy on the outside. I do a lot of walking at work sometimes."

"You're not at work," he reminded her. "You're on the run. You should have picked something better."

"Yeah? I should have done a lot of things," she snapped. "And how about you? You should have left me in Elyria. Or better yet, back in that clearing where you pulled me out of your trunk. You're no genius either."

He looked at her. Expressionless. "I think we're both fairly intelligent. It's easy to make mistakes in high-pressure situations."

"So, you do make mistakes. I was starting to think you were some kind of robot."

"Mistakes?" he added with a smile. "No. I was talking about you."

"Very funny. You don't make mistakes… but what do you call all this?"

She gestured around her.

"A decision to throw myself in the meat grinder," Carver answered. "That's what I call it. You offered me a mission. I accepted it. I aim to see it through."

She stared at him for a second. Then she laughed. It was a release of nervous energy, and it went on too long, becoming manic.

Naomi dropped off the log. She fell to the ground, flipping onto her back and holding her belly. She continued laughing. Carver waited, letting her get it all out.

She eventually fell silent, staring at the sky. Lifting her hand, she used the end of her finger to trace the constellations.

"Makes you feel small, huh? Looking at the stars?" she said. "Like your problems don't really matter."

Carver decided that was enough. He got up. Stood over her. Offered his hand.

"Let's go," he said.

She grabbed hold. Her fingers were cold. Carver pulled her to her feet and they kept moving. He let her go first. Occasionally steering her when she wandered off course. They cut straight across the landscape, heading north.

They walked for another hour. Naomi didn't complain, but he could tell she was suffering. Her legs began to wobble. She shivered, rubbing her arms. Hugging herself.

If he was alone, Carver would have walked all night. Gaining as much ground as possible under the cover of darkness. But he had perspective. The experience and training to contextualize things. A night spent walking wasn't so bad. He'd been through worse.

Naomi hadn't. Her worst night was years ago. The first night alone after learning her husband had died. Nothing could compare to that. Emotionally speaking, at least.

Physically, her low point was now.

"We'll find a spot to hunker down," he said.

He saw the relief in the sag of her shoulders. Carver felt a bit of it himself. He was willing to walk all night, but that didn't mean he wanted to.

Now, they just needed to find shelter.

THIRTY-FOUR

"How about one of those?" Naomi asked.

She was pointing down the hill, off to their northeast. Halfway between them and the highway, the land was nothing but farms. And barns.

"Farmers get up early," Carver said. "They aren't big fans of trespassers. And they normally have guns."

"Well, where else can we go?" she demanded.

"We'll find something," he told her. "I promise."

***

Ten minutes later, Carver saw something. The decaying remnants of a wooden fence, sprouting up in the middle of nowhere. Beyond, a few stalks of corn still grew among the tall grass.

An abandoned farm.

And in the center of it all was a dilapidated house. It looked like something out of a horror movie. Ghosts or axe murderers lurking within. Carver wasn't afraid. He had a feeling Naomi would have been, if she wasn't so tired.

They found the front porch. Carver climbed up carefully, testing the integrity of the structure. He waved Naomi up, and they went inside.

Carver grabbed a flashlight out of his bag. They looked around, taking in the sad sights. Faded family photos on the walls. A once brilliant chandelier corroding away to nothing. Hardwood floors left to rot.

"Pretty gloomy," Naomi said. "But it looks all right. Nice and dry. Thank god. It'd probably stink otherwise."

Carver dropped his bag in the middle of what used to be the dining room.

"We'll sleep right here," he said. "I don't want to risk climbing the steps to the second floor."

"Fine by me," Naomi yawned. "Got any pillows in that bag of yours? Maybe a blanket?"

Carver ignored her. He pulled his phone out and stared at the screen. After debating with himself for a moment, he gave Harvey a call.

"Who are you calling?" Naomi asked.

No answer came. Carver hoped the old man was just asleep. If anything else had happened…

He wasn't in a position to help. Not worth worrying about things he couldn't affect.

There was an old radiator still attached to one wall. Carver kneeled down, giving it a test yank. It was strongly attached. Tight connections.

"Come here," he said.

Naomi wandered over. "What is it?"

Carver opened his bag. Pulled out another pair of handcuffs.

"Seriously?" Naomi groaned. "I almost killed a state trooper for you."

"For yourself," Carver corrected her. "I haven't seen what's on that flash drive yet."

"I'd show you if I could."

"But you can't. I don't operate on hypotheticals. The truth is, I want to trust you. But I don't know if I can."

She folded her arms. "This is ridiculous."

He gave the cuffs a shake. "See it as a way of building trust. We've already been through this once tonight. And I'm tired."

"So am I," she scoffed.

"Then let's get this over with."

She sighed. "You're a boring guy, you know that? Annoying, too."

"And you're testing my commitment to the mission," he replied.

In the dark, her cheeks seemed to turn red. She dropped her arms. "You're right. I'm sorry. You're helping me, and I'm making things harder than they have to be."

Carver was surprised. And a bit amused. But he didn't smile. He attached one end of the cuffs to her left wrist. She sat down. He connected the other end to the radiator. She leaned against the wall, knees tucked up against her chest.

"This makes the Windy Lodge look like a luxury hotel in the French Riviera," Naomi grunted.

Carver looked around. "It beats sleeping under a log."

"That I can agree with," she laughed. "Kind of wish I could lay down, though."

He stepped away. Leaving a space of eight feet between them, he lowered himself to the floor. Using his duffel as a pillow, he closed his eyes. Resting his hands at his sides.

"Have you ever slept on a plane?" he asked.

"Yeah," Naomi answered.

"Then you can sleep here."

"Usually, plane seats have a bit more cushion. They also recline. By about two inches, but still…"

"I don't have any ginger ale or cookies for you, either," Carver shot back. "Sorry. We'll get moving again at first light."

THIRTY-FIVE

Gibbs paced along the road. He picked two trees to move between. Back and forth. Feet swishing in dead grass. There was a deepening chill in the air. He didn't feel it. His heart beat too fast. Pushing hot, nervous blood around his body.

The dirt road was awash with light. A flatbed had been brought in. Two mechanics were working on getting Mr. Big's car onto it. Two state troopers watched the progress, sipping coffee. Gibbs wasn't sure where they'd got it from. The nearest gas station was miles away.

Gibbs reached one of his trees. He turned around and paced back in the other direction. He kept his hands in his pockets. Now and then he pulled one out to wipe his mouth. Or pinch himself, just in case he was dreaming.

Suddenly, a shadow moved in the grass, striding toward him. Gibbs jumped, almost yelping in fear.

"Relax!" Sanders said. "What's got you so twitchy?"

"Colonel Bell's on his way," Gibbs sighed.

"Yeah, I heard it on the radio. So what?"

"So…" Gibbs stuck his hands back in his pockets, rocking back and forth on his feet. "Never mind."

"Come on. You going to tell me or what? I've been waiting ever since I first asked you. I can keep a secret, you know. Remember that time you accidentally left your gun at that burger joint for half a day? I never told anyone."

"Yeah, that was stupid. Thanks for covering for me. I would have lost my badge on that one."

"Uh-huh, you would have," she grunted. "I didn't say anything about it because we're partners. But not just that. I know you're a good cop. One mistake doesn't change that."

Gibbs smiled. "Now you're laying it on thick. I'm all nice and buttery."

"Like corn on the cob," Sanders laughed. "So, how about it? You want to let me in on what's freaking you out?"

Gibbs glanced at the other cops. They were fifty feet away. And the winch on the flatbed was screeching loudly. No way they would hear.

"Fine," he said. "Naomi Downes isn't just some random woman. She was working for Morgan Unger."

"The senator?"

Gibbs nodded. "She was an aide. Helped him on the campaign trail and all that. She was also romantically involved with him. She used her position to steal privileged information."

"Well, I knew that part." Sanders shrugged. "What kind of information?"

"I don't know. I wasn't told. I'm sure only a few people do know. Either way, it must be something juicy. Unger has been in contact with Colonel Bell, who in turn, enlisted me for a special operation."

"You?" Sanders said.

"Don't act so surprised," Gibbs snapped. "Like you said, I'm a good cop. Anyway, I was given some privileged information of my own. Someone in Pomos blabbed about Naomi's escape plan. I intercepted that car."

He pointed toward the flatbed.

"And Naomi was in the trunk," Sanders added.

"Yup. Mr. Big had no idea she was there. But whatever she told him afterward, he's now on her team."

"She must have lied," Sanders responded. "Told him whatever she wanted him to think. Some kind of sob story. Guys are suckers for a pretty woman who needs help."

Gibbs almost argued on behalf of his gender. Then he realized he had no way to refute her claim. She was correct.

"You could be on to something there," he eventually said. "All I know for sure is, I was supposed to catch her. I failed. Twice. As soon as Colonel Bell gets here…"

"You're going to get chewed out," Sanders finished for him.

"Majorly," Gibbs agreed. "This could be a career-ender for me."

"Well…" She put her hands on her hips. "We could just get back in your car and run. He can't yell at you if he can't catch you."

It was meant as a joke, to lighten the mood. But Gibbs took it a different way. He immediately took off down the road, moving at a fast walk.

Sanders ran to join him. They passed the flatbed, hit the pavement of the main drag, and headed back to the Windy Lodge.

"Are we really doing this?" Sanders asked. "We don't even have our guns."

Gibbs frowned. "*I'm* doing this. Catching Naomi is my only way of saving myself. I won't blame you if you don't come with me."

She clapped him on the back. "You can't make it on your own, Gibbs. Someone has to look out for you."

"You sure?" he asked.

"Positive. You're hopeless without me."

"That's probably not far off from the true," he sighed. "Thanks, Sanders. You're a good friend."

"Maybe even the best," she added.

Once again, he found no way to refute the claim.

THIRTY-SIX

Naomi couldn't get comfortable. Not for lack of trying. She did what she could, wiggling around on the hard floor. Searching for some perfect position that would keep her legs from falling asleep.

She wanted to scream. To stomp her feet. Rip the radiator off the wall and storm out. Everything hurt, especially her shoulder. The handcuff chain was so short, she had to keep her arm raised.

Carver was fast asleep. Lying there like a vampire in a coffin. Hands crossed on his chest. Feet together. Head supported by his mysterious duffel bag. He didn't snore. Didn't move at all, even to scratch his nose. He just lay there, breathing softly.

Naomi didn't make a peep.

She was waiting. Making sure.

An hour had passed since they had settled in. Maybe longer. It was hard to tell. Once, Naomi came close to falling asleep, a side effect of sheer exhaustion, but a howl from a nearby coyote woke her up.

Now she felt more awake than ever. The house made occasional rumbling sounds, the old structure creaking in the wind. It was unsettling.

"Carver?" she said quietly.

He didn't move. Just kept breathing.

"Carver," she tried again, a little louder.

Nothing.

All right, she thought. *He's definitely asleep.*

It was time.

She reached up with her free hand, poking around in her hair. She found the bobby pin and pulled it free. She jammed the end of it into the keyhole on the handcuffs. Jiggled it around, feeling for the right placement.

Come on. Don't tell me this is something that only works in movies.

She had picked locks like this before. She used to break into her parent's bedroom with a bobby pin when she was a kid. But that was a completely different style of lock.

Just when she was starting to feel doubt, she felt a click. Heard a ratcheting crunch of metal as the handcuff sprang open. She quickly grabbed it, silencing the mechanism.

Glancing at Carver, she waited. Watching his chest rise and fall. He didn't stir. She was still in the clear.

Naomi pulled her wrist out of the cuff. She left it dangling from the radiator and stood up. She stepped across the room, testing each foot placement, making sure to avoid any creaky spots.

Moving as slowly as a sloth, she finally made her way outside. She jumped off the edge of the front porch. As soon as her feet hit grass, she sped up. Hurrying to a safe distance. When she looked back, she could barely see the house. A faint shadow against the night.

She reached into her bra and pulled out a cell phone. She held the power button down to turn it on. As the operating system loaded, she prayed for a signal. Just one bar was all she needed.

As luck would have it, she got two.

More than enough. She opened a text conversation, the only one that was saved on the phone. She typed out a message and sent it along.

Heading north. Unknown which border crossing. Be prepared to move and meet me wherever.

She waited for confirmation that the text had been delivered. Then she turned the phone off and tucked it away again.

Just as slowly as before, she went back inside. Sat down on the floor. Clicked the cuff back onto her wrist. A little looser this time. Carver might notice, but she was willing to take the risk.

Her business was concluded. Some of the anxiety had been lifted.

And after another half hour of misery, she finally managed to fall asleep.

THIRTY-SEVEN

"Uh-oh," Sanders said.

Gibbs looked over his shoulder, back down the main road through Elyria. In the distance, he saw a fleet of police cars coming their way, lights flashing.

"That'll be Colonel Bell and his entourage," he grunted.

"Not good," Sanders replied. "We'd better get hustling."

They broke into a jog. It was about all they could manage. They were tired. Hungry. Sore. But they didn't have far to go.

A minute later, they were hurrying across the Windy Lodge's parking lot. They threw open the doors of Gibbs's cruiser and climbed inside. Gibbs turned the engine on and backed out onto the road.

He sped away, accelerating up past the speed limit and racing into the night. He left the lights off.

"Close one," said Sanders.

Gibbs breathed a sigh of relief. "Good thing I gassed up in Ord," he said. "Tank's still full."

The adrenaline of their getaway began to fade. Gibbs started to feel hot around the collar. Heart thudding. A sick feeling flooding through him.

"We may be doing the wrong thing here," he said.

Sanders stared at him. "Now you're having second thoughts? This was your idea."

Gibbs glanced in the rearview mirror. "I can let you out if you want. Not too late."

"Shut up and drive," she said. "I'm with you. I already told you that."

"Even though we're fugitives?"

"We're not, Gibbs. We're just… taking initiative."

"Feels like we're fugitives," he grumbled.

"Well, we're not," Sanders said forcefully.

"Not sure Colonel Bell would agree."

Sanders shrugged. "Yeah, he probably wouldn't. But results speak for themselves. If we find Naomi Downes, we're good."

"We have to find her now," Gibbs sighed. "There's no other option."

"Isn't that the whole point of this stunt?" she shot back.

"Yeah."

"Then shut up and drive."

"You already said that," Gibbs pointed out.

"I still mean it. And you didn't listen the first time."

Sanders put her hands on her knees, and began drumming with her fingers. To a stranger, it would be a sign that she was at ease. But Gibbs knew better. She only did that when she was worried.

"Where do you think they're heading?" she asked. "Naomi and Mr. Big."

"I thought you wanted me to shut up," Gibbs grunted.

"Shut up and answer the question," said Sanders. "And no, the ongoing irony of my words is not lost on me."

Gibbs smiled. It felt good.

"I don't know," he answered. "They could be headed in any direction, technically. But I'd say north is a good general direction. We're sort of north of Pomos, where they started. Stands to reason they'll stick to that vector."

"Unless they're trying to throw us off," Sanders suggested.

"They're rabbits on the run. They'll take a straight line until they can't anymore," Gibbs replied.

Sanders laughed. "Those rabbits kicked our butts. But I agree with your thinking. North it is."

The car radio suddenly crackled to life.

"Trooper Gibbs," a static voice came through. "Colonel Bell is here and would like to see you."

Gibbs grabbed the handset and put it to his mouth. "He's in Elyria? Shoot. I guess I just missed him."

"Your car was seen departing the Windy Lodge less than five minutes ago," the other cop replied. "Colonel Bell is requesting you return at once."

"No can do," Gibbs said. "I'm trying to do my job. Tell the colonel I'm going after Naomi Downes. I've caught up with her twice already. Third time's the charm."

"Trooper Gibbs, you must—"

"What? You're breaking up!" he shouted. "Just keep me in the loop on any new developments. I'll let Colonel Bell know when I've got her. Over and out."

He put the handset down and gave Sanders a scared look.

"You did pretty good," she said. "I bought it."
"I doubt Bell will."
"Results, Gibbs," she reminded him.

"Right. Let's go find these rabbits."

THIRTY-EIGHT

Usually, Carver didn't remember his dreams. They left minor impressions on him, nothing more. The ones he recalled were always about Annie. And they weren't exactly dreams.

They were memories, playing out the same way every time. He often worried if the memories were fading over time. Rotting away. Like a tape on its hundredth trip through a projector.

"*Ronan,*" she whispered to him.

He opened his eyes. It took a second to remember where he was. The abandoned farmhouse in the middle of nowhere, somewhere northwest of Elyria.

He was looking up at the underside of the second-story floorboards. A few bits of plaster remained, what had been the ceiling. The rest of it was scattered around on the floor. The gritty debris of the past.

It was still dark. But a hint of dawn light filtered in. A dull, blue glow. It was time to move.

He sat up, looking over at Naomi.

She was staring at him. The whites of her eyes caught the weak light. They seemed to glow.

"Sleep well?" Carver asked.

"Oh, yeah," she said sarcastically. "I thought nothing could beat silk sheets and a feather pillow. But here we are. Best night of rest I've ever had."

He smiled. "Just wait until you see the breakfast buffet."

She rolled her eyes. "Can you uncuff me now?"

He stifled a yawn. Pulling his bag onto his lap, he unzipped it. Looking around inside, he glanced at Naomi again.

"Well?" she asked.

"Just looking for the key," he said.

"Don't tell me you lost it," she moaned.

He reached into his pocket and felt the key. Pulling it out, he showed it to her.

"Great! Now let me out."

He got up, lumbering over on stiff legs. He bent down, unlocking the cuff. She immediately shot to her feet and hurried away.

"You didn't have to make it so tight, you know," she said.

"It felt pretty loose to me," he replied.

"Well… whatever. And how about you? Sleep well last night? Like a baby, I bet."

"I've trained myself to sleep in any situation, basically on command," he said.

"Good for you. Where'd you learn that? The same place that taught you how to be a huge jerk?" she grunted.

"More or less." He unlocked the other cuff, pulling it off the radiator. He then dropped the handcuffs in his bag.

"Is that it?" Naomi said.

He looked at her. Said nothing.

"Can't you tell me anything?" she added. "You're always going on about how you don't know if you can trust me. How about vice versa? How do I know I can trust you?"

"Our positions are different," Carver answered. "You need my help. I don't need to help you. It was a choice. You'll abide by my conditions, or you'll be alone."

She took a step back. Her face fell. Her expression changed. She looked scared, and completely defeated. For a second, it looked like she was going to fall down. But she caught herself at the last second, leaning on the old, dusty dining table.

"You can trust me," Carver said quickly. "I promise you that."

"I guess, I can," she said, her voice as quiet as a mouse.

Carver zipped the duffel bag up. He cinched the shoulder strap tighter.

"Carver is my last name," he said.

A bit of light returned to her eyes. She looked up at him.

"My first name is Ronan," he added.

She smiled. "Ronan? That's an interesting one."

"I had a teacher who liked to call me Ron. I hated it. But I never said anything about it, so I went by Ron for my entire school career. It stuck."

"That's ridiculous," she laughed. "But kind of cute."

He shrugged. "As soon as I left high school, I was never Ron again. I made sure of that. Most people just call me Carver."

"You go by your last name? Is that a sports thing, or a military thing? Looking at you, it could be either. But seeing you in action…" She shook her head slowly. "I'd guess military."

She was fishing for more information. He took the bait.

"You'd be right," he said. "Navy SEALs."

"That… makes perfect sense." She grinned. "I guess I'm in pretty good hands."

"Probably the best you'll find in Nebraska."

"Bit of a brag there," she added.

He shrugged again.

"Anything else you can tell me?" she asked.

"Plenty," he answered. "But I'm not going to. We should leave now."

THIRTY-NINE

The sky burned the color of blood. The rising sun spread its wings of light.

Carver watched the clouds as they climbed the hill. They were thin. Wispy. They moved slowly, curling around one another. A gentle ballet. There was no harsh weather on the horizon. But it was still cold. The grass crunched underfoot, covered in sparkling frost.

"Doing all right?" he asked without looking back.

Naomi let out a labored breath. "Yeah. Feeling kind of hot now, actually. Climbing these hills is hard work."

Carver wasn't having any trouble. He felt a little sore and achy, consequences of bad sleep and a lack of food. But his legs felt strong. This hill was nothing compared to some he'd dealt with.

Hills on the other side of the world. In another life. And under harsher conditions. Snipers taking shots. Shouting voices behind. Armed men chasing.

Carver looked back.

He saw only Naomi a few paces back. Hands on her knees as she powered up the slope. A half mile back, the abandoned house was barely visible. In its weathered state, it blended in with the skeletal trees and the overgrown grass.

"Remind me," Naomi huffed. "Why are we climbing up the biggest hill in Nebraska when there are easier ways around?"

"We need to get our bearings. The lay of the land," he answered. "We've got a lot of traveling ahead of us. Best to plan it out as much as possible."

"Sure, sure," she sighed. Sounding unconvinced.

But she kept on following. And Carver kept on climbing, setting a pace that she could keep up with. It felt slow. But he was confident they'd make it up later.

They reached the top of the hill. It wasn't very tall. A hundred feet above the farms below, maybe. It might not be the tallest hill in Nebraska, but it was the tallest one around. And they could see for miles.

Carver pointed north. "There. See that?"

"Sparkles," Naomi said.

"Reflections of the sunlight," Carver added. "Windows. Buildings. A lot of them. It's a sizeable town."

"Huh. Must be Burwell, which is where we would have ended up if we hadn't made that turn for Elyria."

"That's where we're headed," said Carver.

"You really want to go there? If some random old lady at a motel recognized us…"

"There's a risk," he agreed. "But the bigger risk would be dehydration and exposure. A town means stores. Food. Water. A jacket."

"How about a pillow?" she asked.

"Maybe."

"Looks pretty far away," Naomi groaned. "But I guess we should keep moving."

"Just a moment," said Carver.

He pulled out his phone. Checked the signal. Two bars, the elevation coming in handy.

He gave Harvey another call. Waited. And waited some more. Still no answer. Frowning, he ended the call and put his phone away.

"You told me your name," Naomi said. "And what you used to do for a living. How about telling me about those phone calls? Who are you trying to contact?"

"It's not anyone you need to worry about," he said gruffly.

"Is it someone who can help us?"

He started down the hill. "Don't ask. Don't talk at all. We should save our strength."

FORTY

Farm fields. Dirt roads. Remote homesteads surrounded by outbuildings. That was all Carver and Naomi saw once they left the hills.

Until they reached Burwell.

It was noon before their tired feet finally carried them into town. The quiet streets were lined with pickup trucks. After passing through several suburban blocks, they arrived at a main street. A broad avenue with business names like The Hitching Post.

They stood in the middle of the deserted field of asphalt. A woman in the window of a coffee shop seemed to be watching them. On second glance, Carver realized she wasn't looking at anything. Just staring into space.

"See a convenience store anywhere?" Naomi asked.

Carver shook his head. He turned right and walked further. He saw a police station dead ahead and turned on his heel.

"Wrong way," he said.

The other direction brought them to a grocery store. A half dozen cars stood in the parking lot. The only people they saw were two young kids and their mom, busy putting groceries in the trunk of her car.

They went into the store. Carver was happy to see a self-checkout. The less interaction with people, the better. They made a quick trip down two aisles. Grabbing a few boxes of granola bars, some beef jerky, and several large bottles of water.

Next, they hit the deli for something a little more substantial that they could eat right away. Some fresh fried chicken and potato wedges had just been put out. They opted for those.

Near the checkout was a magazine stand. At the top of it were a few maps of Nebraska. Carver grabbed one. Naomi scanned the items. Carver slipped some cash into the machine. Took his change. They put everything but the hot food and the map into his duffel bag.

Carver glanced around the store. He saw a couple of people. Neither was looking in his direction. Just going about their business.

"Let's find somewhere quiet," he said.

Naomi led the way back outside. There was a bar across the street. Not busy at this time of day. An alleyway ran behind it, with some benches inside. They sat down and ate.

"This is the best thing I've ever tasted," Naomi growled, ripping a hunk of meat off a chicken thigh.

Carver couldn't disagree. Objectively, it was far from the best. Harvey's fried chicken was superior. But a wise person once said that hunger was the best sauce. It made everything taste better.

The food was gone in no time. The containers were cleared out. Naomi even vacuumed up all the loose bits of breading.

"I kind of feel human now," she said. "What's next?"

Carver wiped his hands on a napkin. Then he unfolded the map of Nebraska.

"Looking for a border crossing?" Naomi asked.

He nodded and then stabbed a finger onto the map. "This one looks good."

It was a remote country lane between the 11 and the 281, at the northern edge of the state. It was barely visible on the map, which meant it was small. And it indeed crossed the border into South Dakota.

"Let's do it," Naomi agreed.

Carver smiled at her. He didn't want to be discouraging. But he felt daunted. Nebraska was a huge state. They had a long way to go.

FORTY-ONE

Not far away from their dining spot was an antiques store. Inside, they found a couple of hunting jackets for cheap. They smelled a bit stale, but they were cozy, and had built-in camouflage.

There was a coffee urn by the cash register, with a paper sign that read TAKE A CUP. Carver helped himself. He sipped his coffee as they left the store. And almost fumbled it when his phone rang.

"Finally getting that call back?" asked Naomi.

He got his phone out. Saw *H* on the screen.

"Yes," he said. "Wait here."

He left her standing in front of the antiques shop. Stepped down the sidewalk a bit, stopping in front of an empty newspaper dispenser.

He answered the call. "Harvey."

"How's it going, kid?" the old man chuckled.

Carver paused.

"Something the matter?" Harvey said. "I saw you called me twice. Sorry about that. Couldn't find my dang phone for about a day and a half. Guess it slipped out of my pocket when I was raking up leaves."

"I'm just glad to hear back from you," Carver said.

"Something wrong?" Harvey asked again.

Carver looked back. Naomi was still waiting, taking the opportunity to shrug her jacket on and zip it up. She saw him watching her, and smiled. Her cheeks were red from the cold.

"Things could be better," Carver admitted.

"Got yourself into some kind of trouble again?" Harvey sighed. "I figured you were done with that after taking care of things in Seattle."

"So did I. But something came up."

"Something?"

"Someone," Carver added.

Harvey laughed again. There was less spirit in it this time.

"Okay," he said. "Any way I can help you out?"

"Not on this one."

"Is there anything I need to be worried about?" Harvey asked.

Carver took a sip of coffee. It tasted sour. "It depends."

"On what?" Harvey snorted.

"On what kind of people I'm dealing with here. The picture isn't clear. But you might expect someone to show up at the house."

"Someone dangerous?"

"Maybe." Carver winced. "Maybe they'll just ask you questions, about me. Answer them honestly. I can take care of myself."

"Yeah, I noticed that. No one's shown up yet. But if they do, I'll manage. I can take care of myself, too. Just make sure you get back and see me some time."

"I will," Carver promised.

He ended the call. By the time he turned around, Naomi was headed toward him. He must have had a mean look on his face, because she immediately raised her hands.

"Don't worry, I didn't hear anything," she said. "You look relieved, though. Maybe at some point you'll tell me who you were talking to."

"I'm not committing to it," he grunted. "It's not anything you need to be concerned with. You have enough problems."

"More than enough. But at least I'm not cold anymore. Or hungry. Still exhausted, though."

Carver looked down the street. Scanning the storefronts. "I don't plan on leaving Burwell on foot. We'll never make it to the border that way."

"How are we going to get a car?" Naomi asked. "I doubt you have enough cash to buy one."

"I don't," he agreed.

She raised an eyebrow. "All right. I have a feeling it's time for me to play dumb and stop asking questions."

Carver drank the rest of his coffee, and crumpled the little paper cup in his fist. He looked around for a trash can, but didn't see one, so he put the cup in his pocket.

"Just follow me," he said. "And do exactly what I say."

FORTY-TWO

Colonel Bell didn't go down without a fight.

The radio harassment went on for most of the night. Every few minutes, the voice of dispatch would be hollering. Demanding that Gibbs return to Elyria. Once, the voice even threatened to send cars after him.

Sanders had to coach him through that one. Gibbs almost gave in. But he realized that he was already in the deep end. He was going to drown either way. But there was a ladder to get out. Just one. A ladder called Naomi Downes.

The messages from dispatch slowly petered out. By sunrise, they were down to once an hour. And they were even less frequent as the morning progressed.

Gibbs was glad for it. He already had a massive headache. It wouldn't go away, no matter how much caffeine he drank, or how many ibuprofens he popped from his glove box stash.

It was a little past noon now. He and Sanders were on their fourth cup of gas station coffee, feeling strung out. Burned out. Wrung out. Like dirty dishrags.

Burwell had been their first destination. But after cruising the silent streets for a time, Gibbs got antsy. He started overthinking, wondering if north was the right call.

"We can always check south first," Sanders had said. "They're on foot. If they're headed for Burwell, it'll take them hours."

So Gibbs took them south. They explored the towns of Ord and North Loup. Interviewing random people. Showing Naomi's picture around.

Hours later, with nothing to show for their trouble, they returned to Burwell.

The streets were quiet. Mostly. A few times, they had to dodge kids playing basketball or street hockey. At one such group, they stopped. Rolling down the window, Gibbs held out the photo of Naomi.

"Any of you saw this woman?" he asked.

The kids all took a close look. An older boy even reiterated the question, taking it seriously. But none of them had seen her.

Gibbs thanked them and moved on.

"Another dead end?" Sanders wondered.

"No," Gibbs said decisively. "They're somewhere. Nearby, I think. Back in Elyria, my gut was telling me to come here. And it's still singing the same song."

"Well, all right, then," she answered with a smile.

Gibbs had a strong feeling they were on the right track. But he didn't realize how quick his gut would be proven right.

Less than five minutes later, they were driving near a grocery store. They passed by an antiques store and saw an old man hurrying outside. He flipped the hanging sign in the door to CLOSED as he locked the store up.

The man turned, saw Gibbs's cruiser, and immediately started waving.

Gibbs slammed the brakes. Sanders opened her door. She put one foot out, leaning through.

"Sir, what is it?" she asked.

Gibbs nudged her, handing the photo over.

Sanders showed it. "Did you see this woman?"

"As a matter of fact, yes," the store owner said. "A half hour ago. I was heading to the local station to report it, but…"

"This woman," Sanders added. "Was she with anyone?"

"Yeah. Biggest old boy I've ever seen. Scary looking. But very polite, in all honesty."

"That sounds like our guy," Gibbs grunted to Sanders. "He beat me up twice, but in the friendliest way possible."

Sanders nodded. "Sir, did you see which way they went?"

The old man swept a hand vaguely eastward. "Off that way, I think."

"You think?" Sanders said impatiently. Then she smiled, a blush in her cheeks. "Sorry, sir. Thank you very much for the help."

She closed her door. Gibbs turned the cruiser around and headed east.

"Careful, Sanders," he said giddily. "You almost got mean back there."

"It's the pressure, Gibbs. Not only am I worried about myself, I'm worried about your sorry butt, too."

He grinned. "You're always worried about me."

"That's true." She knocked back the last of her coffee, wiping her mouth on her sleeve. "Do you think we'll find them?"

"They're here, Sanders. And I have the best partner any cop could ask for. We'll spot them for sure. The real question is, will we be able to do anything about it?"

FORTY-THREE

Carver and Naomi walked a loop around Burwell's small commercial district. They saw plenty of cars. But it was broad daylight. People were behind every window. Carver could hot-wire most cars, but not in a timely enough manner.

Especially not with the police station so close.

"What about there?" Naomi asked, pointing at a pizza joint further up the block.

"I thought you were playing dumb?" Carver asked.

"I got sick of it."

He shrugged. "Why the pizza place?"

Even before she answered, he could see where she was coming from. It was by far the busiest place around. Lunchtime. Cars came in and out in a steady stream.

"This is a small town," Naomi replied. "Everyone trusts each other, right?"

"They probably leave their doors unlocked at night," Carver added. "Are you suggesting we take advantage of that?"

"I don't see any other way. Maybe someone will run inside to pick up an order and leave their car running. Why not? It's cold out here. Maybe they want to keep things warm."

It was better than Carver's idea, which was to walk around and hope an idea actually occurred. He led them to the pizza place.

It wasn't an ideal spot. They were technically in view of the police station, though there were enough buildings in the way to provide a bit of a screen. Carver decided it was worth spending a bit of time on.

All they needed was a bit of luck.

They stood outside, backs to the wall, a few feet from the door. No one looked at them twice. In a town like Burwell, people weren't very suspicious.

Ten minutes passed. Then twenty. The cars kept coming. The customers kept running in and out with their lunch orders. They all left their cars unlocked. But not a single one left their keys behind.

Carver started to feel antsy. And so did Naomi, if her constant hopping from foot to foot was any indicator.

"This isn't panning out," she muttered.

Carver smiled to himself. "It was a good plan, but it might need to bake a little longer. Put it back in the oven."

"Was that a pizza pun?" Naomi groaned.

"A weak attempt at one," he agreed.

She shoved her hands in her pockets. "Kind of like my weak attempt at contributing something to this alliance. This partnership. Whatever it is. Thanks for trying to lighten the mood, though."

Carver wondered if giving her a playful nudge was too much. He decided it was. They still barely knew each other. And he was worried about getting too friendly.

It might cloud his judgment.

"Don't be hard on yourself," he said instead. "You've already shown a lot of bravery. And resourcefulness. Besides, it doesn't matter who comes up with the winning idea. As long as we make it out."

"You're right," she sighed. "Should we wait a bit longer?"

"We could. But standing in one spot is asking to be spotted. Let's try my idea."

She eyed him. "You had one? You should have said something before I wasted twenty minutes of our time."

"I just came up with it," he answered. "And it has no guarantee of working, either."

He started walking away. After a second, she jogged to catch up.

"What's your idea?" she asked.

"It's simple. Doesn't need to be explained. And you might be better off not knowing."

"Oh, no. I don't like the sound of that."

"You can dislike it all you want as we're driving out of here," he said.

The sound of passing traffic wasn't constant, but it was near enough. Cars went by in both directions on a regular basis. Some were old beaters that rattled and groaned. Others were new, letting out barely a whisper.

Behind them, Carver heard something in between. A powerful engine, well-tuned. It sounded familiar.

He looked back and saw the white hood. The light bar on top.

"Get down," he hissed.

He was already falling onto one knee, crouching behind a parked car. Naomi was a bit slower. She darted to where he was waiting and joined him.

Carver waited a second. He inched forward, peeking out from behind the car. For the benefit of anyone watching him, he acted like he was tying his shoe.

The state patrol cruiser went by at a steady speed. No brakes. No acceleration. No flash of its lights. It went around the corner and disappeared.

FORTY-FOUR

Sanders kept her eyes glued to the side mirror, even after the car went around the corner.

"Did you see that?" Gibbs asked.

"I think that was her," replied Sanders. "She either fell down, or she was tying her shoe."

"Or she was trying to hide," Gibbs suggested.

"But I think it was her," Sanders repeated.

"Yeah, I'm willing to bet on it," he agreed. "Hard to tell for sure. Any sign of Mr. Big?"

"Nope. Maybe he's inside one of the shops?"

"Maybe."

She finally pulled her gaze from the mirror and looked at her partner. "How do you want to play this?"

Gibbs didn't answer right away. His heart pumped fast, flooding his system with adrenaline. Along with a huge dose of bravado.

A big part of him wanted to march in. Guns blazing, figuratively speaking, since they had no guns. But what would it accomplish? Most likely, they'd end up embarrassing themselves again, in front of however many onlookers.

And the fugitives would be alerted. They'd get away again.

Gibbs kept driving out into the suburbs again. Slowing down, they cruised the streets.

"I think we'll do it the smart way," he sighed. "Radio it in, let Colonel Bell know."

"Whatever you say," Sanders said.

He gave her a troubled look. "How do you think we should do it?"

"Hard to say. If we were armed, we might take them by surprise. We could ask the local guys to help out."

"Burwell cops?" Gibbs grunted. "I wonder if any of them have even discharged their weapons."

"Probably not. Lucky them."

"We could borrow some guns," Gibbs added in a hopeful voice.

"Yeah, we could try," Sanders agreed.

A second later, they groaned and shook their heads. Going rogue was already a bad look. Admitting to local cops that they'd lost their weapons would make things worse.

They'd just have to hope that alerting Colonel Bell was enough to save them.

Gibbs took a deep breath and grabbed his radio handset.

"Elyria, are you still on this channel?" he asked.

The voice that had berated him earlier that morning replied. "We've moved on, Trooper Gibbs. But we're still patrolling the area."

"Good, good. How about the Colonel?"

"Colonel Bell is nearby."

"Tell him that Burwell is where he wants to be," Gibbs said. "We have a sighting of Naomi Downes here."

"Confirmed sighting?"

"Well…" He looked at Sanders.

She shrugged. Then nodded.

"Confirmed," Gibbs added. His stomach did a flip. It was one step short of an outright lie.

But "pretty sure" wouldn't cut it. Not this time.

"Acknowledged," the voice said. "Do what you can to keep her there. We'll head that way."

FORTY-FIVE

Carver stayed behind the car for a long moment. He re-tied both shoes, picked a pebble out of the treads. He waited and listened to each car that passed. The police cruiser didn't return.

"I don't think they saw us," Naomi whispered.

Carver stood up, adjusting his jacket. He smiled at a woman walking by. She smiled back, but increased her speed noticeably.

"I don't think so either," he said. "But let's play it safe, and act like they did."

Naomi seemed to think it was a smart play. She took off in the opposite direction of the state patrol car, heading south. The route would take them right past the police station. But they veered off down a side street, dodging the place to the rear.

"Keep your eyes open, but don't look suspicious," Carver said.

"How is that possible?" she asked.

"Act like you're looking for birds."

"Really? That's your advice?" she said.

"Try it," he told her.

She tried it. "Huh. This does feel better. Don't mind me, fellow Nebraskans. Just checking for grackles."

"Tell me if you see the cop car again," Carver said.

"Will do. Where are we going?"

There was a trash can behind the station. Carver pulled the crumpled coffee cup out of his pocket, finally disposing of it.

"I don't know yet," he said. "But I'll keep you updated."

She was silent for a minute, following him out into the residential areas beyond.

"Aren't you going to ask me what a grackle is?" she finally said.

"I know what they are. Nuisance birds that make a mess of parking lots across most of the United States."

"So, I guess you just know everything," she snorted.

"I don't know the winning lottery numbers," he shot back. "I wish I did."

"So do I." She pointed to a house. "If you had about ten thousand dollars in cash, you could probably go up to any of these places and offer it up. They'd hand their keys over in a heartbeat."

He laughed. "I have a better option. I'm going to get us a car for free."

***

They put a few blocks between them and the pizzeria. Soon, they were approaching the edge of town, where suburban streets gave way to farmland.

It was quieter out here. People were either at work or in the middle of town, shopping. It was as good a place as any to commit a misdeed.

Carver singled out one house in particular. A one-car garage, closed. A single car parked in the driveway. Curtains drawn on all the windows. The porch light was turned on, even though it was a sunny day.

Sure signs that no one was home. They were probably away on an extended trip. A day or two. Longer. It didn't matter.

The road was a dead end. Beyond the guardrail at the end were some bushes. Carver walked around the rail, leading Naomi into the brush.

"Wait here," he said. "Lay low. I'll be back."

"How long?" she asked.

"Five minutes," he said.

"Are you just rattling off a random number?" she sighed.

"Probably," Carver said.

She blew out her lips. Cheeks still bright red.

"Don't be nervous," he told her. "You'll be fine here."

"I'm not worried about me," she replied. "What if you get caught?"

"I guess, you'll have to get to the border on your own. But the chances of me getting caught are the same as us winning the lottery."

"You sure?"

He answered by giving her a level stare. She smiled.

"I'll be here," she then said.

FORTY-SIX

Carver had no way of hiding, except in plain sight. He acted natural, walking casually up the driveway. If anyone saw him, they'd think he lived there. Maybe he was a salesman, or an HVAC repair guy.

The front door was not the way to go. No matter how trusting a community this was, no one left their front door unlocked. Not when they were out of town.

So he went around. Opening a wooden gate, he slipped into the side yard and followed a cobblestone path to the backyard. It was a nice area. A gazebo. A water fountain. A set of expensive, comfortable-looking furniture.

Whoever lived here probably had good insurance. At least he hoped so. Maybe he'd find a way to pay them back sometime.

First, he approached the sliding glass door. The slats were drawn, but tilted just right so that he could peek inside. He saw a dark kitchen. Some mail piled on a granite countertop. A fruit bowl with a couple of apples inside. Not a dirty dish in sight.

He tried opening the door. It was locked. Next, he moved to a window. There was just enough of a lip at the top of the pane to get his thumbs on. He pushed up, felt something give way.

The window had been locked. But the latch was either designed badly, or the homeowner hadn't engaged it all the way.

It slid open. There was a screen, but that was easy enough to pull out. He leaned it carefully against the side of the house. Then he climbed inside. He was quiet at first, just in case he'd misjudged the place. Maybe someone was home after all.

Everything was dark and quiet. He heard nothing. No toilet flushing. No TV. No footsteps.

Carver moved through the house fast, exploring rooms. The third one he looked into was a home office. There was a set of car keys sitting on the desk.

He swiped them up with a bitter smile. He felt lucky and cursed all at once. Stealing the car was the last thing he wanted to do, but it was either that or end up in jail.

And it wasn't just him. If it was, he wouldn't care. Naomi was on the line, too. And if what she said about Senator Unger was true, her very life could be in danger.

They had no choice but to get out of here. As fast as possible.

Carver headed back to the window, making no attempt at stealth now. His feet fell heavily on the floor.

Suddenly, a man's voice rang through the house.

"Earl, is that you?"

Carver's blood ran cold. He moved faster, forcing his large frame through the tiny window. Slithering out like an eel. He quickly slid the screen back in place and closed the window.

He jumped over the railing of the back porch. Ran along the cobblestone path. He burst through the gate, swinging it closed behind him. Without looking back, he rushed for the driveway.

Any second now, the front door would open. The man in the house would see him. The cops would be called. His description would be spread around.

It was the moment of truth.

Should he grab Naomi and run?

Or should he commit himself fully?

Carver went for the car. As he opened the door, he glanced toward the bushes at the end of the road. They were too far away. Naomi wouldn't make it in time.

He made a hand signal, pointing to the east. Trying to indicate the next street over.

He had no idea if she even saw the gesture. But he couldn't wait around.

Carver got in the driver's seat. He slammed the door, turned the car on, put it in reverse, and backed onto the street.

He took off.

FORTY-SEVEN

"Hungry?" Sanders asked.

Gibbs tore his eyes away from the window. He looked at her, raising an eyebrow. He was about to tell her that food was the last thing on his mind. Then he started thinking about smothered steak and mashed potatoes, like his grandma used to make.

"Yeah," he said.

She pointed over her shoulder. "We could hit that pizza place. I'm sure we could get a couple of slices on short notice. Especially if it's supreme. Most people go for pepperoni or cheese."

They were parked just around the corner from where they'd seen Naomi. Or where they thought they saw her. They had cruised the streets for a while, trying for another sighting. But they came up empty.

Backup was on its way. It would be here any minute. All they had to do was wait. There was nothing much else they *could* do, except listen in on the local chatter.

Gibbs had his radio tuned. There wasn't much going on in Burwell. The whole time they were sitting here, all they heard were two deputies chatting about a runaway teenager.

"Pizza sounds all right," he said.

"I'll run and grab it," Sanders replied. "I guess, we'll need drinks, as well."

Gibbs pulled out his wallet. Handed her a twenty. "Napkins, too. Don't want all that grease on my hands."

She snatched the cash, pushed her door open and prepared to get out. The radio chose that moment to burst to life. The same cops who had discussed the missing teenager now sounded a lot more urgent.

They sat still and listened.

A car had been reported stolen from a house nearby. A white four-door sedan. As soon as the address was rattled off, Sanders looked it up, getting directions from her phone's GPS.

"Go!" she said.

"Shut your damn door first," he grunted.

"Oh." Sanders shut the door. "Okay, *now* go."

He checked for traffic behind him. Then he took off, hitting the lights but leaving the siren off. Stealth mode.

"Where to?" he asked. He saw a park up ahead. "Gonna run out of road here in a second."

"South," she answered. "Turn right wherever."

He turned right, startling a jogger who jumped out of the way. Gibbs gave him an apologetic wave and kept going.

"Up here," Sanders added. "Next street. Take another right."

He continued following her directions, ending up at a house on a dead-end street. An old man was outside, already talking to a local cop. Gibbs came to a stop and rolled his window down.

"What's the situation?" he called.

The local cop excused himself and sauntered over to the car.

"Homeowner says someone broke into his place," the cop replied. "He caught a glimpse. Big guy. Stole his car and headed that way."

The cop pointed back down the road, the only way a car could go.

"Was anyone else with him?" Gibbs asked.

"Doesn't seem like it," was the answer.

Gibbs scanned the area with his eyes. Thinking. Wondering. But not for long. It was time to take action.

"Much obliged," he said. Then he rolled up his window and turned around.

"They've been heading north so far," Sanders said.

Gibbs nodded. "How many ways are there out of this town?"

She checked the map. "A few. The 96 seems like the best option."

"Call it in. Get a roadblock set up. Let's hope it's not too late."

Gibbs had a feeling it was.

Mr. Big had been one step ahead of everyone so far. Maybe even two or three steps. He seemed to have fate on his side. Or something else.

Gibbs shook his head, dispelling his doubts. They would catch this guy.

They had no other option.

FORTY-EIGHT

If everything had gone according to plan, they would have been out of town already. Well on their way north, headed for the border.

But that wasn't the way it played out.

After leaving the dead-end house, Carver drove away as fast as he dared. He turned right at the very next opportunity, glancing in the rearview mirror one last time. He saw an old man lumbering into the road, shaking a fist and yelling.

Carver flew down the side street. Turned right again to get parallel to the dead-end road he'd just been on.

The cops would be on their way soon.

He had to be fast.

So he was. He had already stolen a car. In a moment, everyone in town would know, so breaking speed laws wasn't on his list of worries.

It was a short stretch to the end of the road. An eighth of a mile, maybe. Carver got up to fifty before slamming on the brakes, executing a fishtail turn. He ended up with his back to the end of the road, his front facing toward the way out.

He unlocked the doors and waited. Drumming anxiously on the wheel. He kept his eyes on the road ahead, dreading the sight of flashing lights.

Come on, Naomi.

He wasn't sure whether she'd seen his hand signals. Whether she would have the presence of mind to follow them. Maybe she had panicked and ran off in a random direction. He might never see her again.

All he could do was sit and wait.

But he couldn't wait forever.

He looked at the clock, giving her one more minute to appear. If he didn't see her by then, he'd have to leave.

He wanted to save her. To bring her to the border in one piece. It had been a while since he'd wanted anything this bad. It was redemption. It was proof he could protect those who needed protecting.

But he had to protect himself as well.

A minute passed. Naomi's time was up. Carver put his foot on the accelerator, getting ready to leave. The old man's car had a surprising amount of power. He could be gone in a flash, a white streak of speed racing away from Burwell.

He didn't leave.

He kept on waiting for another full minute. Sweat poured down his face.

Finally, he saw motion in the rearview mirror. A second later, the passenger door popped open. Out of breath, Naomi fell inside. She had some fresh scratches on her face and hands.

She shut the door. As she reached for her seatbelt, she looked at Carver and said, "Go."

Carver went.

He remembered the ways out of Burwell from the map they'd bought. The 96 seemed the most logical way, the fastest, as long as it was open. He had his doubts, but plowed ahead regardless. It had only been about three minutes since he stole the car. Maybe it would take longer than that for the local cops to organize.

"Are you okay?" Carver asked.

"Sorry I took so long," Naomi replied. "Getting through that brush was a feat."

"That's not what I asked."

"Yeah, I'm fine," she said breathlessly. "My lucky old jacket protected me pretty well."

Carver followed his mental map. It did not lead him astray. Pretty soon, they were turning onto the 96. It headed north along the west edge of town. But then made a westward curve. It went in that direction for a while. Eventually meandered north again.

Carver knew all this. But it soon became clear he wouldn't be seeing any of it.

A blockade had been set up. Three police cars were parked across the road ahead, lights flashing. Two local cruisers, and one state trooper. Carver wondered if it was Gibbs.

"That's not going to work," Naomi groaned. "Turn before they see us."

Carver was already on it. He took the turn casually, onto a side street, acting like any other motorist. As soon as he was out of sight of the blockade, he sped up.

"There's another way out of town to the east," Naomi suggested.

"The 11 road," Carver confirmed. "It'll also be blocked off by the time we get there. Look for something else."

"Where's the map?" she asked.

"My bag."

He had thrown it into the back seat when he got in the car. She rifled around in it, found the map and unfolded it on her knees. She leaned over, getting her nose about an inch from the paper.

"There's a back road near the 11 that heads north. Windy Hill, it's called."

"We'll head there," Carver said.

FORTY-NINE

Gibbs was moving along H street. He hit Highway 96 and turned right. Straight away, he saw the roadblock ahead.

"These local guys act fast," he said. "Color me impressed."

"Looks like one of ours made it there, too," Sanders added. "Wait… was that a white sedan?"

"Huh? Where?" Gibbs asked.

"Thought it just turned right up there. Never mind. I think I'm seeing things."

Over the years, Gibbs had learned to trust Sanders. He slowed down as they approached the next side street. Staring down it, they searched for a white car.

"Don't see anything," Sanders sighed.

Gibbs didn't either. No sense chasing ghosts. He continued on. His flashing lights got him up to the blockade. He had to dodge a handful of cars that were sick of waiting. Motorists started turning around, looking for an alternate route.

He pulled up by the roadblock. He and Sanders got out. They didn't recognize the state cop, so they approached the local guys instead.

"Nice work," Gibbs told them. "You got this set up in a jiffy."

"It sounded urgent," a guy named Welch said.

Gibbs put his hands on his hips, stealthily stretching his lower back. Too much driving.

"It is urgent," he confirmed. "We're after two people who are in possession of sensitive information. Government stuff. I can't say much more than that. But they need to be stopped."

Welch nodded. "Understood. We're already setting up another roadblock at the junction of 91 and 11. That'll block two other major ways out of town."

"Good. I don't suppose you have spare manpower?" asked Gibbs.

"No, sir," Welch replied. "If you want more roads blocked, you'll need to call in some backup."

"Already did."

Welch suddenly smiled. Shading his eyes, he stared at something past Gibbs. "Looks like they're here."

Gibbs turned and saw a convoy of six state patrol cruisers headed their way. Behind them, being escorted, were a few unmarked cars. Black with tinted windows.

"Who could those be?" Sanders muttered.

"No idea," Gibbs answered. "Probably someone important, though."

"Like Colonel Bell?" she wondered aloud. "I figured he'd be in one of the squad cars."

Gibbs nodded. "He will be. This is someone else."

FIFTY

It felt wrong to drive back through Burwell. Like every inch they covered was a mile on the road to oblivion.

Carver and Naomi kept their heads on swivels. Checking every car they passed, and every car that passed them.

It was cold in the car. But Carver refused to turn the heat on. The extra noise was bad. It would prevent him from hearing sirens. Or gunshots. Or voices yelling for him to stop.

So far, everything was fine. They saw no cops. No one looked at them twice. They were just a man and a woman in a ten-year-old car. Everyone in town was probably more curious about the rumors that must be spreading by now. *Did you hear they've got the highway blocked off? What's that about?*

"Crap, I've lost track." Naomi shuffled the map around, sticking her face close again. "Everything's so tiny. I don't know what road we're even on anymore."

"I do," Carver said. "We're still on G Street. It runs east to west all the way through town."

"Hard to see…" Naomi scanned the map for another moment. "Ah. Yeah, there it is. Sorry. I'm panicking a bit here."

"We'll be fine," he said. "What's our next step?"

He already knew. But he wanted to give her something to focus on. She wasn't used to this. The pressure. The fear. He was.

The way to handle it was to give yourself small tasks. Things that could be achieved. Make it to that next tree. Get your buddy over the next little hill. He may be bleeding out from shrapnel wounds. A bullet to the collarbone. But if you got him over that hill… and he was still alive on the other side… that was something.

Something to work with. To expand upon.

"Uh… this road dead ends pretty soon," said Naomi. "You'll have a choice to go left or right. You'll want to go left."

"Acknowledged," Carver said.

He drove a little faster. The lights were green ahead. No one in the way. He could afford a little extra speed. But he kept an eye on the crosswalks. In a town like this, people didn't always look both ways. They usually didn't have to.

The dead end came. Carver turned left onto 1st Avenue. They passed a laundromat and a butcher shop.

"What's next?" he asked calmly, checking the rearview mirror for flashing lights.

"This road will curve pretty radically to the right," Naomi replied. "That's where it turns into Highway 91. A little ways past that, it intersects Highway 11."

"But we don't want either of those."

"No. We want Windy Hill. Which is…" She clicked her tongue as she scoured the map. "Got it. It's right where this road starts to curve. It cuts off to the north."

That one Carver didn't know. Now that he did, he drove a little faster. The speed limit was about to increase, anyway.

The road started its curve. Carver dropped speed, ready to make the turn. He put his left blinker on. Alerting the sparse traffic behind him.

"Here it is on the left!" Naomi announced.

He turned onto Windy Hill. He was surprised to see that it was paved. But he was glad it was. It meant he could go faster.

Carver glanced to his right, further down Highway 91. But he couldn't see the roadblock. If it was even there at all, it would be at the junction of 91 and 11, the only logical place to put it.

It was beyond the curve, out of their sight.

Windy Hill was a quiet, narrow road. They blew past a couple of houses, and then it was just farmland. No one was working the fields.

"I think we might make it," Naomi said.

Carver just nodded, like everything was simple and easy. He didn't tell her how shocked he was. So far, they were very lucky.

It was about to run out.

Carver got his first hint of trouble when he looked in the mirror. He was checking to see if anyone had pulled onto Windy Hill behind them.

And someone had. A huge pickup truck. That wasn't out of the ordinary. It was a farm road. People around here had trucks. It was the vehicle of choice.

The problem was that this one was speeding up. Breaking through fifty miles an hour, then sixty.

The driver of the truck started laying on his horn.

FIFTY-ONE

Erick Foster always wanted to be a cop. But he had too many problems in his life. Speeding tickets. DUI charges. Bar fights.

There were probably some corrupt precincts out there that would still hire him. But not the Burwell Police Department. They hired only boy scouts. Choir boys. Not a bad thing, mostly. Not until real crime came to town.

And it just had.

Erick had two police scanners. One in his truck, one in his living room. He was at home when he heard about the stolen car.

He immediately ran outside, got in his truck, and started hunting. He had been driving around Burwell, checking out any white car he passed. Looking for a big guy who matched the description he heard on the radio.

Then he got to thinking. Stolen car. It was probably headed out of town. From his scanner, he knew roadblocks were being set up, at least on the main routes. But there were other ways out of town.

Erick had been scouring those, hoping to get lucky.

And he did. Just a minute ago, he saw a white sedan ahead of him, pulling off onto Windy Hill. As it turned, he got a good look at the driver. A big guy. Huge, in fact. He seemed to be all muscle.

There was someone else in the car, too. A woman who looked terrified. Had the guy taken a hostage?

Erick kept going. He used the next driveway he found to turn around. He drove back to Windy Hill and turned onto it. He could still see the white car, but it was getting away.

He accelerated, knowing he wouldn't get a ticket this time, because he was trying to help. Maybe, just maybe, if he managed to stop this guy… they'd finally let him in. He'd get a badge. A uniform.

Maybe the kidnapped lady in the car would be thankful, too. Erick would be a hero. An overnight sensation in the town of Burwell.

It was enough motivation to make a man do some reckless things.

He chased the car down. It started going faster, matching his speed. Exceeding it. Erick sped up. He punched on his horn, blaring it at the back of the stolen car.

"Stop!" Erick screamed, though the big man would never hear him. "Stop right there!"

To show how serious he was, he swerved a bit. Wobbling left and right on the road. He mashed the pedal down even further, surging forward. Almost hitting the back of the sedan.

He laid on the horn some more.

The car kept going. He saw the big man's eyes, staring at him in the rearview mirror.

"You son of a…" Erick reached for his phone and called the cops. "Hey! I got 'im right here. The guy who stole that car! He has a lady with him. I think he kidnapped her. I'm out on Windy Hill, northbound. He ain't getting away from me!"

FIFTY-TWO

Gibbs watched the convoy's approach. He stood rigidly, every muscle in his body taut. Sweat poured out of him, even in the forty-degree weather. His heart seemed to be pumping acid instead of blood.

"What do I do?" he said quietly.

Only Sanders heard him. She raised an eyebrow. "I don't, Gibbs. But we're in this together. Whatever Bell has to say, he can say it to both of us."

The convoy arrived. They fanned out as they pulled to a stop, spreading to block the road even more decisively. A few doors swung open. Several cops got out, grabbing shotguns from racks inside their cars.

Seeing that put things into perspective for Gibbs. This was huge. He probably didn't know the half of it. Whatever Naomi had, it was being taken very seriously.

One man who got out stayed unarmed. It was Colonel Bell. He must not have slept much either, but he looked as fresh as a daisy. His uniform was as crisp and shiny as ever.

He headed straight for Gibbs.

Gibbs tensed up even more. He made himself smile, tasting sweat on his lips.

"Colonel, good to see you," he said.

Bell smiled. He stuck out his hand, but said nothing. Gibbs wiped the sweat off his palm and shook with him.

"You're a stubborn man, Trooper Gibbs," Bell said.

"I just don't want to disappoint you, sir," Gibbs replied. "I did everything with good intentions. And it was my idea. Sanders just tagged along to make sure I didn't get myself killed."

"He's lying," Sanders snapped. "I'm fully involved. It's just as much my fault as it was his."

Colonel Bell held up a hand. "Shut it, both of you. What's done is done. Besides, you've done a good thing here. Naomi might have slipped away from us if not for the two of you. But we've got her now."

"You do?" asked Gibbs.

"Not quite yet," Bell answered with a smile. "But there isn't anywhere for her and her helper to go. You've done a fine job, Trooper Gibbs. And Trooper Sanders. Everything else is water under the bridge. We'll take it from here."

He looked back at the police cruisers behind him, and the black cars with tinted windows. Gibbs figured they must be private security. But for who?

It dawned on him. Senator Morgan Unger must be in one of those cars. He had shown up in person to make sure Naomi was caught. She had been his aide. She had stolen whatever she had under his watch.

This was very serious indeed.

It almost made sense. But Gibbs sensed something was missing. Of course, something was missing. He was just a state cop. He was never going to be let in on the whole truth.

But it didn't matter now. Gibbs sensed his involvement in the case was about to end.

"You two are dismissed," Colonel Bell added. "Feel free to return to your posts in Lexington. You'll have the next three days off to recuperate. Thank you again for your service."

He gave them a perfunctory salute and turned away.

He then headed back to his car.

FIFTY-THREE

"Come on, just *stop*," Erick Foster grunted to himself.

The stolen car kept going.

But it was driving funny. Not like it was broken or anything, just slow, as though the large man behind the wheel was in no hurry to get away. He had gotten up to fifty, but refused to go any faster, even though it was a paved road with zero traffic.

"What are you doing?" Erick sighed. "Stop or *some*thing."

Why wasn't he trying to escape?

Erick started having doubts. Maybe he'd gotten the wrong car. This was someone else, just trying to get home. He had scared them. They didn't know what to do. Maybe they wanted to slow down, let him get around them. But he was too close. If they slowed, he would crash into them.

It didn't seem possible. This *had* to be the right car. The description of it matched. So did the description of the guy driving. The only thing wrong was the lady in the passenger seat.

But hadn't she looked terrified? Back there before the turnoff onto Windy Hill? Before the driver knew he was being chased, she had already looked scared.

It was the right car.

Erick just had to stop it.

He drifted left, increasing his speed. The aim was to get beside the white car, try and force it toward the ditch. Then it would have no choice but to stop.

But the car drifted left too, right along with him, blocking him off. When he tried to go back to the right, it followed, mirroring him.

Now Erick was mad. He slammed the horn again, over and over. Short, annoying bursts of noise.

Something changed.

The white car finally sped up. Quick acceleration. It roared ahead, creating a gap of thirty feet or so. Erick pushed his pedal down, trying to catch up.

Then he saw brake lights. The white car zoomed toward him. Not going backward, just slowing down, while Erick was still speeding up.

Erick slammed on his brakes. His tires skidded. The rear end of his truck swung out to the right as he juddered to a stop less than ten feet from the stolen sedan.

Its driver-side door popped open. The thief got out. He was even bigger than he looked, six and a half feet tall. But it was his face that was scariest of all.

His expression was completely peaceful, even a bit friendly. Like he already knew what was going to happen, and wasn't worried by it.

He raised his right hand, pointing a gun straight at Erick as he stepped toward the truck.

"Oh, jeez!" Erick screamed, immediately putting his hands up.

The big guy shook his head. He shouted, "Roll your window down! We need to talk."

Erick rolled his window down, just a little bit. Then he put his hands up again.

The man with the gun came closer. Stepping out toward the middle of the road, getting a wider angle on Erick.

Suddenly, he pulled the trigger.

Erick heard a sharp *pop*, followed by a hiss. The air leaked out of his front left tire.

"Don't try and follow me," the thief called out. "I have more bullets, and it only takes one."

He nodded and smiled. An oddly polite gesture. Then he returned to his car and drove off.

Erick stayed where he was, trembling with his hands over his head.

FIFTY-FOUR

Carver started driving before his door was even shut. He was glad to have the guy in the truck off his back. But civilians were still the least of his problems.

"You okay?" Naomi asked.

"I am." Carver pointed his chin at the rearview mirror. "He's not. I scared him."

"That's fine. He was never in any real danger. Right?" Naomi asked.

"Not unless he pulled his own gun on me," Carver replied.

Naomi didn't like the sound of that. She curled up into a ball, pulling her knees to her chest.

"Don't sit like that," Carver warned.

She glanced at him. "Why not?"

"If we crash, the airbag will send your knees straight up into your jaw."

"Well…" She put her feet back on the floor. "That doesn't sound good. You think we're going to crash?"

"Anything's possible," he said.

They drove up a slight rise. Carver checked his mirrors again. He could now see over the top of the pickup truck, back toward the main road. What he saw surprised him.

No lights. No police at all. No cars to speak of.

Was it possible the guy in the truck hadn't called anyone in? Maybe he didn't have a phone with him. Carver didn't buy it, though. In this day and age, everyone had a smartphone of some kind. And satellite coverage was better than ever.

The cops must be all over Burwell by now. They were here for one thing only: to catch Naomi.

"Where are they?" he wondered aloud.

"Stuck in traffic?" Naomi suggested.

Carver smiled. "That must be it. Check the map. Where are we going next?"

She started looking. "This road goes for miles. You can follow some obscure back roads out into the middle of nowhere. Then we'll need to go offroad again."

"Does the terrain look rough?"

"Not any rougher than what we were driving through before Elyria."

Carver checked the gas gauge. The car had half a tank left. He wondered how good the gas mileage was. Probably not great. Then again, the car had been maintained well.

"What are the other options?" he asked.

"You can eventually take a side road that connects you back to Highway 11."

Carver nodded. He already knew the ideal path, the one that took him as far from main roads as possible.

"We'll go off-roading," he said. "But there's one thing we have to do before we get ourselves lost."

"What's that?" Naomi asked.

"This car is red hot. We'll need to switch it out for a new one."

Naomi shrunk again. But this time she didn't put her knees to her chin.

They came to a low spot in Windy Hill. A valley. As they climbed back out and came over a rise, Carver's stomach dropped.

There were flashing lights ahead of him. At least three cars, cruising in from the north.

"Oh no," Naomi moaned.

"They took that side road you mentioned," Carver said, "connecting from Highway 11. They're cutting us off."

She twisted around, desperately searching the road behind. "What do we do? Should we turn around?"

"That'll just bring us back to Burwell. No way out from there."

"Then *what?*" she asked frantically.

He was about to say something to try and calm her down, but she did it on her own. Taking a deep breath, she looked at the map.

"You should be able to turn left somewhere up here," she said. "We've got some country lanes. I don't know where they end up, but…"

Carver took the next left he found, a bumpy dirt track. It extended straight to the west, heading across farm fields. At the end, a tangled stand of trees was visible.

He had no doubt the police cars had seen him. There was no point in going slow. He poured on the speed, kicking up a dust cloud behind him.

FIFTY-FIVE

It was a shockingly short road. Before he knew it, Carver was approaching the end. It terminated at the top of a low hill, right at the edge of a forest.

A yellow sign stood at one side of the road. It was faded and full of bullet holes, but Carver could still read the letters.

DEAD END.

He pulled to a stop ten feet back from the trees. He looked left, then right. Searching for ways out.

"Let me see the map," he said.

Naomi handed it over. He draped the map across the steering wheel, studying it intently.

It didn't tell him much. To the north and south were more farms. They could go off-road, but it would be too slow. They would eventually reach civilization. By then, the cops would be ready to intercept.

They couldn't go back. Any second now, the red and blue lights would appear on the dirt road. If they were fast enough, maybe they could make it back to Burwell. But that was just delaying the inevitable.

Carver kept on studying the map. Glancing up every couple of seconds to check the lay of the land. There had to be a way out. There always was, if you had the guts to try it.

But he couldn't find anything.

"Carver," Naomi said softly.

He looked at her.

"It's all right," she added. "We tried our best. Let's just toss our guns and let them take us. It's not ideal, but…"

"I'll be sent to prison," Carver told her. "And you…"

He didn't say it. They both knew. Senator Unger wouldn't let her live. He'd find some way to make her disappear, just like he'd done to his wife.

Tears appeared in Naomi's eyes, but she kept on smiling.

She was doing this for him, Carver realized. To protect *him*. She was giving him permission to stop helping her, to look after himself instead.

It was the last thing he wanted to do.

But he saw no other option.

Unless…

Lights flashed behind them. The police were coming up the road. They'd be here in no time.

Carver looked at the map again. This time he wanted to know what was straight ahead of them to the west, past the trees and the end of the road.

What he found was a broad wetland. A section of the North Loup River, created by a dam at the north end of Burwell. It was wide, and probably fairly shallow.

He crumpled the map up in his hands, tossed it over his shoulder into the backseat.

The police were halfway down the road.

There was still time.

Carver looked ahead.

The trees were sparse here, spread far enough apart. The undergrowth was thin as well, bare and leafless in the cold.

He put the car in reverse, backing down the road. Getting another twenty feet away from the trees.

"Is your seatbelt on?" he asked.

"Yes," Naomi confirmed. "Yours?"

"Always," he replied.

He heard the first PA blast from the cop cars.

"*Stop the vehicle and step out with your hands in the air!*"

He put the car into drive, shoved the accelerator down. The tires spun in the dirt, tossing rocks and dust in a plume. The tires found traction and rocketed the car forward.

It was a rough ride. At this speed, every tiny rut and pothole was accentuated. The car bounced up and down, rattling until Carver was sure it would break apart.

But it didn't. They reached the end of the road. Whipping through the grass, the brush between the trees.

FIFTY-SIX

They were almost through. Sunlight shined through the trees, sparkling off the surface of the shallow water beyond.

The car hit a bump. The front end bounced upward. For a second, all they saw were sky and branches. One of the trees was too close. The passenger side mirror was obliterated. There was a terrible screech as the rear door was gouged and dented.

Carver didn't care, as long as the car kept going. He had already given up on the idea of returning it. After all this, it would be a miracle if it was even salvageable.

The front tires made contact. With the snaking roots and compact dirt beneath, they found plenty of traction. Carver never let off the gas. They managed to gain even more speed as they surged toward the river.

Suddenly, there was nothing under the tires at all.

They were drifting straight out, into the open air. The river glittered beneath them. Clods of dirt flew from the still-spinning tires.

Gravity kicked in. The car tilted downward, the heavier front end dragging it off kilter. Naomi braced herself, hands on the dash. Carver knew better. He stayed loose, taking his hands off the wheel.

The ground came up fast. They slammed into it at a thirty-degree angle, enough to dig a trench into the wet sand. They landed in a wide trickle of water, no more than three inches deep.

Carver put his hands back on the wheel. He hit the gas again, praying. The car managed to cough itself back to life, pulling them through the sand and up onto more solid ground.

Their leap from the trees had caused them to clear about ten feet of the river, landing closer to the middle. There were deep streams of water around, along with long, flat sand bars. The river formed many fingers, some clutching deeper into the earth than others.

It was worse than Carver imagined. He had been hoping for a marsh, something they could drive straight across. But that wasn't going to happen here.

It wasn't all bad, though. The sand bar they were on extended far down the river. Out of sight around its curves. Carver drove down it, staying in the middle. He was afraid of the edges. They might crumble away, erode beneath their weight, sending them into the depths.

He glanced down. Saw controls for powered windows. He rolled both front windows down.

"In case we go under," he said.

Naomi swallowed so hard he could hear it even over the groan of the engine.

"The flash drive!" she said.

"Check my bag," he told her.

She pulled the duffle bag out of the backseat and set it on her lap. Searching through, she discovered a resealable sandwich bag. It had some mixed nuts in it.

"I forgot those were in there," Carver said.

She opened the bag, gave it a sniff and made a face. She dumped them out of her window. She then slipped the flash drive into the bag and sealed it, leaving a little air in on purpose.

If they did go in the water, and she lost the bag, it would at least float to the surface.

Carver nodded to himself, feeling a swell of pride. Naomi had shown plenty of signs of buckling under the pressure. But so far, she was holding out. Getting stronger. Smarter.

Despite their current situation, he felt more confident than ever.

They were getting through this.

But the white car wouldn't be with them much longer.

He followed the sand bar as far as he could. But after less than half a mile, he was forced to stop. Not because he ran out of room, but because the sand was getting softer. The wheels sank into it, grinding the car to a halt.

He killed the engine, unbuckled his seatbelt, and opened his door. He grabbed his duffel bag.

"Let's not waste any time," he said.

FIFTY-SEVEN

Naomi got out. She dropped something. The flash drive inside the sandwich bag. Bending over to pick it up, she vanished from Carver's sight.

He looked past her, toward the trees on the east bank. The direction they'd come from. There was no movement. But he heard shouting voices. Cops on foot, trying to locate the fugitives.

"We need to move," he warned Naomi.

She finally stood back up. He saw the corner of the resealable bag sticking out of her jacket pocket. When she turned, he caught a glimpse of something she had added to it. Something larger than the flash drive.

He didn't mention it. Instead, he turned north and started jogging. Naomi followed.

The sand here was too loose and damp for the car. But on foot, it held up. Their feet sank half an inch into the gritty muck, but no more. The grains of sand locked together, compressed, forming a solid surface. But Carver already saw the end.

About fifty yards up, the sand bar tapered off into a narrow point. It was all water beyond that.

"We need to find a way off this river," he told Naomi. "Onto the west bank."

"I guess we're gonna have to swim," she said.

Carver slowed down. He approached the edge of the sand bar to his left, studying the water. It was clear enough for him to see the bottom was just a few inches down. This shallow section seemed to extend three-quarters of the way to the west shoreline.

"Here," he said. "Follow me."

They splashed their way through the shallows, kicking up spurts of icy cold water.

There were many things Carver had learned to tolerate through training, through mission experience. But there were certain things he just plain hated, that he could barely stand. Getting water in his shoes was one of them.

As soon as he felt the water flood over the tops of his shoes, he shook his head. He could already imagine wringing out his wet socks, trying to dry them. Failing. Having no choice but to pull them back on while still damp. An almost impossible task.

"You okay?" Naomi asked.

"Sure," he growled through clenched teeth. "I just hate wet shoes."

She apparently had no response to that.

Carver glanced down at his ankles. He realized he could no longer see the bottom. It was getting deeper. And the next step was going to be a doozy.

He held his bag over his head and jumped down into it.

He sank in up to his lower chest. Then his feet hit bottom again. He leaned into the current, trying to keep himself in one spot.

This water was almost too deep. If the current had been any stronger, he'd be swept away. Naomi might be tall for a woman, but she was still a good ten inches shorter than he was. She wouldn't stand a chance.

"Grab onto me," he ordered.

Naomi didn't need convincing. She leaped onto his back, wrapping her arms around his neck. Her legs around his waist. She let out a yelp. The shock of the cold. The force of the water.

With her weight on his back, it was actually easier. With a few hops and kicks, he got them moving toward the riverbank. He balanced his bag on one shoulder, trying not to let it hit Naomi in the face. With his other arm, he clawed through the water.

The shouting voices were closer now.

"What do you see back there?" he grunted, straining through the moving water.

Naomi turned her head. "Cops. They're running down from the trees. But I guess the water's too deep. They're just standing there."

"I assume they see us," Carver added.

"Oh, yeah."

He forged ahead. The bank was nearly within reach. With one last kick, and an outstretched arm, he grabbed hold of some grass. Pulled them in.

As soon as they were close enough, Naomi rolled off his back onto dry ground. She grabbed his bag, offered him a hand. He took it. She wasn't much help in pulling him out, but the gesture was appreciated.

He got to his feet, dripping water onto the grass. He looked to the east. Made eye contact with a handful of police officers on the far side. They turned and started running back through the trees.

"They'll try and meet us on this side," he said. "No time to rest. Let's go."

As he and Naomi hoofed it up the bank, Carver heard something that made the water feel warm in comparison.

It was the sound of a helicopter.

FIFTY-EIGHT

Gibbs and Sanders got back in his car. They waited for the convoy of police cruisers and black cars to move.

Meanwhile, things were happening on the radio. Communications were coming in. Apparently, a local man had located the stolen car. He called for backup.

All but one of the patrol cars peeled out, on their way to assist. The only one remaining was the car Colonel Bell had gotten into.

"We've got room now," Sanders said.

Gibbs nodded. But he didn't move. Not yet. He was laser-focused on his radio.

Over the next ten minutes, chaos ensued. It was hard to get everything, but it seemed Mr. Big led the police on a merry chase. There was even talk of him driving down the river.

"How do you drive down a river?" Gibbs grunted. "Who is this guy, James Bond? He's got some kind of aquatic vehicle conversion kit in that bag of his?"

"You want to go after him?" asked Sanders.

He motioned to Colonel Bell's car. "I don't think we're allowed. Reading between the lines, I'm pretty sure we've been benched."

"Hey," she replied brightly, smacking his arm. "At least he complimented us on a job well done, so we're all right, yeah? We can just head on back to base. No reprimands. No consequences."

"That's what it seems like." He shrugged. "If we head back to base."

"Where else would we head?" she asked.

"See those black cars?"

"Yeah. You think Senator Unger's in one of them?"

"Probably. But there's four of them. Why so many?"

"Private security," Sanders suggested. "They've got tinted windows, so no one knows which car the VIP is riding in. Standard stuff."

"Does a senator warrant that kind of caution?" Gibbs wondered. "Especially out here, where no one's expecting to see him? Not like he's on the campaign trail, making a scheduled stop."

"Where are you coming from, Gibbs?" she asked.

"I think something bigger is going on here," he told her. "Bigger than what we already know. We're being lied to."

"Or just kept in the dark for security reasons."

"I guess."

"Yeah, exactly," Sanders said. "Don't you think we should just go home? Call it a day? We've done our part."

"That's not what I'm talking about," he sighed. "I know my instincts aren't always the best, but…"

"You feel something," she finished for him.

"Yeah. It's the whole thing, Sanders. With Mr. Big, especially. How was Naomi able to convince him to help her so fast? And why are these cars here? Who's to say Senator Unger isn't the bad guy in all this?"

"A US senator being the bad guy? That could never happen," she said, rolling her eyes. She then paused and added. "All right, Gibbs. I think I'm with you on this. It doesn't make sense to me, either. But there's nothing we can do."

"We can follow the convoy," he said. "See what they get up to."

"Colonel Bell told us to get back to base," Sanders reminded him.

"No, he didn't. He told us to *feel free* to get back to our posts. That's not a direct order, it's a suggestion."

"Sounds like a technicality."

"Maybe, but still. We're officially off duty for the next few days, Sanders. There's nothing wrong with us following along."

"Just as long as we don't try to involve ourselves," she warned.

"I just want to know what's happening," Gibbs replied. "Are you still with me? If not, we'll head straight back to Lexington. And I won't mention any of this again."

Sanders thought about it. He saw the strain in her face. Finally, she nodded.

"I'm with you, Gibbs."

"You're not just saying it?" he asked.

"No. I'm in. I want to know what's going on, too. But we probably shouldn't be driving around in your car. Seems kind of obvious."

He nodded. "There must be a car rental place around. Let's find it."

FIFTY-NINE

Senator Morgan Unger was having a bad week. And it wasn't getting any better.

It all started one day when Naomi didn't show up for work. They were deep into their re-election campaign. Every day was crucial. A chance to get out there and blaze a trail of hope through the populace.

Naomi was the ace in his sleeve. His lover and his greatest supporter. A beautiful, charming face that did nothing but help his race.

Then she had betrayed him, destroying everything they'd worked to achieve. This was all her fault. He ought to be in Ogallala, Nebraska, by now. Shaking hands. Smiling. Holding babies and making them laugh for the camera.

Instead, he was here. Out of the public eye. Vanished from view while his opponent campaigned on. He was losing time. And if Naomi got away, he could lose a lot more than that.

He fidgeted in his seat. A glass of bourbon sat in the cupholder next to him, untouched. Unger loved bourbon. It took a lot to make him lose his taste for it.

He grabbed the glass. Tried a sip. Smooth oak flavor. A hint of vanilla. Right now, it tasted like cheap cough medicine mixed with dirt. It was the good stuff, too. A hundred dollars a bottle.

"How could she do this to me?" he groaned, swiping a hand through his greasy hair. "You can't trust anyone in this world, boys. You just can't."

The two men in the front seat sat stoically. They didn't look at him. They didn't say anything. They were statues of muscle and square jaws.

They were good at their jobs, but Unger wished they would talk. Anything to distract him. He was stewing in anxiety, incapable of getting comfortable. He sweated profusely.

For a while, he stared at his shoes. He didn't want to look anywhere else. But eventually he did, dragging his eyes to the window.

He gazed at the black car next to him, trying to see past its tinted windows at the person in its backseat. He couldn't see anything. But he could feel the presence. Huge. Looming. Intimidating.

Unger forced himself to look away. He turned and watched the road. The cars that approached honked their horns indignantly. Angry motorists wanted to get through. One of the local cops, a guy named Welch, turned them away.

It would have been funny, watching all those idiots who thought they were important but weren't, except Unger felt the same way right now. He felt like an insect.

It was a terrible feeling. And Naomi was to blame for it completely.

Unger grabbed the whiskey glass. He almost took a drink. Then his anger got the better of him. He chucked it as hard as he could across the backseat. The hefty crystal glass did not break. Instead, it cracked the plastic door panel, and fell to the floor, spilling its contents.

Now the whole car reeked of booze. And Unger didn't feel any better.

The two men in the front didn't flinch.

SIXTY

The smell of alcohol seemed to get worse somehow. It filled Unger's nose and throat. Made him want to throw up. His stomach rolled, twisting itself into a sick knot.

He reached for the handle. The door wouldn't open. He tried the window controls. Nothing happened.

One of the guys in the front finally spoke, without looking back. "You should stay inside the car, sir."

"At least let me open the window," Unger grunted.

"Sir, your orders were clear. You don't want anyone to see you here. It would raise too many questions."

"I know damn well what orders I gave you, but I'm about to vomit and I'd rather not do it in here!"

The man who had spoken looked at his friend in the driver's seat. The driver shook his head.

"We're just following orders, sir. The car can be cleaned."

There was a knock on the back door. The one opposite Unger. A face loomed beyond the glass, smiling toothily. It was Colonel Bell. There was a click as the door was unlocked. Bell opened it and got in.

The man's presence calmed Unger down. He swallowed back the bile in his throat. The nausea began to fade. The anger came back. He glared at his guards in the front seat.

I'll have to remember to fire these bozos. No severance.

Colonel Bell slammed the door shut. He sniffed the air. Noticed the glass on the floor.

"Too much to drink, Senator?" he asked.

"Not enough," Unger shot back. "I let my anger get the better of me. I apologize. I hope you have good news for me."

"A modicum," Bell replied. "But most of it is inconclusive at best."

"What about Naomi and our mystery man?"

"They've gotten away again."

Unger felt his face turning red, turning hot. "Colonel Bell…"

Bell spread his hands. "Don't worry. We know the general area they're in. And we already have a helicopter on the way. But if they should manage to keep eluding us…"

"How could they?" Unger laughed. "We have the entire State Patrol on their butts. There's no way they can escape."

Bell shrugged. "If there is a way, I think they'll find it."

Unger drew back. "What's that supposed to mean?"

For the first time in their working relationship, Colonel Bell looked uncomfortable.

"That'll make more sense in a minute, Senator," he said. "First, I'd like to make a suggestion. It might behoove us to call in some additional help. Perhaps the FBI."

Unger scoffed. "You want the feds sniffing our dirty laundry out here? No, thanks. We're taking care of this ourselves. No one has to know. Life goes on. For everybody."

Bell grinned. "Everyone except Naomi Downes."

"Well, that's the choice she made." Unger clenched his fists. If he had another glass, he'd probably throw it again. Maybe straight through the window so he could get some fresh air. "You said you had good news. What is it?"

Bell sat upright, back to looking in control. "We've identified her accomplice. His name is Ronan Carver."

"Huh." Unger shook his head. "I was almost expecting it to be someone I'd heard of."

"He was a Navy SEAL," Bell explained. "And he must have been involved in some major operations, because his records are sealed tight. Most of them, anyway. I was able to read about some of his exploits, and…"

"And what?" Unger snapped.

"And he seems to be an extremely resourceful and dangerous man," Bell went on. "We're up against a major adversary here, Senator. We may think we have the upper hand, but guys like Carver are on a different level. It's almost certain he'll find some way to turn the tables."

SIXTY-ONE

Carver reached the top of the bank. His feet sank into dense, wet foliage. It wasn't grass. It was something else. A spongy, scrubby plant that covered everything. It squelched with every footstep, murky water welling up around his feet.

"Come on," he told Naomi. "Don't look back."

But she already was. Staring over her shoulder at the cops. She was dripping wet. Her new jacket was meant to keep her warm, but it was a sodden mess. Carver realized the same could be said for him. But he wasn't worried about that.

"Naomi," he said forcefully.

She snapped back to reality, facing him. She tried to take a step, climbing up the final segment of the shore. She fell backward. The strength going out of her.

Carver grabbed her quickly by the wrist. Tugging her along. He'd carry her if he had to. But he didn't. Not yet. She picked up speed, regaining some of her composure.

They hurried across the marsh. The mushy ground ate a lot of their speed. They could only maintain a jog, five miles an hour. Carver stuck to that pace. When Naomi came up short, he pulled her.

"Are you with me?" he asked.

She mumbled something. He couldn't hear her over the sound of the approaching helicopter.

"Louder," he shouted.

"I'm with you," Naomi replied.

"Then act like it!" he commanded. "You're tired. You're cold. You don't want to be doing this. You're hurt and none of it's fair. But this is your reality. Fight through it. Keep breathing."

It was a variation on a pep talk he'd heard countless times. Sometimes from a buddy. Sometimes from himself when he was all alone in some dark corner of the world. You could even say it was a cliché. But it worked.

Naomi went faster. She pulled her hand away from his. She was wheezing. Out of breath. Stumbling every other step.

But she kept going.

Relieved, Carver put his mind to other matters.

He looked to the west. The marsh didn't go very far in that direction. There was a dirt road there. A field beyond. Easy terrain.

If it was easy for them, it would also be easy for their pursuers.

Carver looked north. The swamp extended much farther that way. He could see the end of it. Just barely. There were trees. Wild-looking areas.

"Is that... a chopper?" Naomi asked breathlessly.

He glanced over his shoulder, and saw it. One helicopter, a mile out.

It would be here in less than a minute. It would relay Carver and Naomi's position and stay on them like an annoying bug. Their chances of getting away would dwindle to nothing.

Carver slowed down. Came to a stop.

"What are you... doing?" Naomi gasped.

"Listening," he said. "Stay here."

"Are you crazy?" she asked.

He shook his head. "Trust me. We aren't going to outrun that thing."

"So we're giving up?"

"No."

She stared at him in disbelief. Then she shook her head and stepped closer to him. Waiting. Seconds passed. She became impatient. Tapping her foot at first, then hopping up and down. Overcome by nervous energy.

"Carver?" she said shrilly.

He was watching the helicopter. Studying it. Listening to the sound of its engine. Its rotor chopping the air.

"I have an idea that might work," he told Naomi. "Listen close and do exactly what I say."

SIXTY-TWO

Harvey Carrol considered himself a lucky man.

It was a funny thing to call himself lucky. He'd lost so much. His wife. His daughter. For a while, he'd even lost his sanity.

But he still had a lot to be thankful for.

The sky over Idaho, for one thing. It was a wide, majestic thing to behold, whether it was clear and blue or gray and gloomy. He could stare at it for hours, just watching time float past while he sat here. A rock in a river. Unmoving.

He was thankful for his house, too. The big porch he was sitting on right now, rocking back and forth in his favorite chair. A blanket over his lap to keep out some of the chill. A cozy flannel draped over his shoulders.

Everything was quiet. Just the wind, sighing through the trees. Carrying fall leaves across the fields.

Every few moments, he raised a mug to his lips. Taking a sip of tea. Chamomile, this time. He loved the real stuff. Black, green, oolong—it was all good.

"But I've already had my caffeine allotment for the day," he chuckled to himself.

The man sitting on the nearby bench turned his head. "What was that?"

The fellow's name was Einer. The sides of his head were shaved. The top sprouted long hair, which he'd combed back so that it looked like the rear end of a duck.

Harvey thought Einer looked like a fool. But he didn't say it, because Einer had a gun. A great big pistol that looked as if it kicked like a horse.

Einer had friends, too. Two other guys with assault rifles, scattered across the porch. Neither of them had said a word since they arrived earlier that morning.

"Just talking to myself," Harvey added. "Say, would any of you boys like a hot beverage? I've got all sorts of tea. Coffee, too. I reckon I've got some hot cocoa mix, as well. Maybe I could scrounge up some marshmallows. What do you say?"

"We don't need anything," Einer said coldly. "But thanks for asking."

"No problem at all." Harvey rocked back in his chair, smiling. "If you change your mind, just let me know."

"Just keep playing along, old man," Einer said.

"Play along with what?" asked Harvey. "I know your name, son, but not much else. I don't even know why you're here or what you want."

Einer smiled and made a show of polishing his gun, using the bottom of his shirt. His phone rang a second later. He stepped off the porch to answer it, moving away so Harvey couldn't hear.

He returned after a minute, hopping athletically over the porch railing.

"New plan, Harvey," he announced. "You'd better pay attention. If and when Carver calls back, this is what you're going to say."

SIXTY-THREE

Twenty years of flying had brought Dale to some interesting spots. For a while, he worked search and rescue in the Rocky Mountains, saving lost or injured climbers. Then he moved into the Coast Guard, where he did the same thing for those lost at sea.

He had also done a few tours of duty overseas. Extracting soldiers who found themselves in trouble. Making sure they got home in one piece, or at least back to base. It was a job he could feel good about doing.

Dale was born to help people. To serve his country in whatever peaceful way he could find.

When the call came in that a high-priority fugitive was loose in Nebraska, Dale started paying attention. When he heard that the fugitive was holding sensitive intelligence, he was already running for his chopper.

He stayed high in the air over Burwell. As soon as he was clear of it, he switched gears. With his hand on the stick, he let the old Huey float toward the ground. Dropping slowly. Gently. Like a feather.

A distorted voice came through his headset, coming from the woman in the copilot seat. Her name was Jen. He hadn't worked with her before. A new recruit. But he had a good sense for people. She seemed all right.

"Here's the river up here, right side!" she called.

Dale looked. The river was wide here, splitting off into a dozen little streams and then rejoining further down. He could see the stolen car, a white sedan parked right in the middle of the river, tires half sunken into sand.

From this bird's-eye view, certain other things could be seen. Things that were invisible on the surface.

"See that?" he asked, pointing to the west bank of the river. "There's a trail running straight up through the grass. Our fugitives went this way."

He swung away from the river, heading into the scrubby field beyond. The trail was still there, but it was harder to see. Visible only from right above. A pale line where the foliage had been smushed down.

Dale took it slow. Barely flitting along. He kept it high, a little over a hundred feet. He didn't want the downdraft of the rotors to mess up his trail.

It didn't take long to spot two figures lurking in the marsh.

"Got 'em!" Jen yelled.

"Call it in," Dale grunted.

Jen switched her radio frequency, relaying their position to dispatch. While she took care of that, Dale began circling the area. The plan was to follow the fugitives. Stay right behind them so they couldn't get away.

Except the two figures on the ground weren't going anywhere.

The big guy, recently identified as Ronan Carver, was lying on the ground. It didn't look like he'd assumed the position deliberately. He was in a twisted heap, as though he'd collapsed.

Heart attack.

Those were the first words that came to Dale's mind. The stress of the pursuit was too much for Carver. His body had given up. A sad end to a sad affair.

Naomi Downes was next to him. Tugging at his arm. Yelling. She turned her attention to the helicopter. Jumping up and down. Waving her hands.

Jen came back on, clicking her tongue. "He doesn't look good."

"He does not," Dale agreed.

"Wasn't this guy a Navy SEAL?"

"He was, yeah."

"What's he doing all this for, I wonder?" Jen asked.

Dale didn't know. All he knew was there might still be a chance to save the guy, so he started bringing the chopper down. Preparing to land.

He was about fifty feet above the ground when Carver suddenly stood up, pulled out a handgun, and started shooting.

Dale barely heard the burst of gunfire. But he felt the effects right away. The stick jerked in his hand. Lights flashed on the instrument panel. Alarms blared.

"Get outta here!" Jen screamed.

SIXTY-FOUR

The noise and the wind were relentless. Carver's ears rang as the gunshots faded across the marsh. Along with the helicopter. It spewed smoke from a couple of spots. But the rotors kept spinning, and the Huey managed to stay aloft as it fled the scene.

He had done what he could to minimize damage. But there was a chance the helicopter would still crash. A rough landing was inevitable.

Naomi held a hand over her eyes, watching the bird limp away.

"Are they going to make it?" she asked.

"It depends on the skill level of the pilot," Carver replied. "But the chances are good."

"I hope none of the bullets hit them," Naomi groaned.

"They didn't," Carver answered.

She looked at him. "How do you know?"

"Because none of my shots missed," was his simple reply. "You gave a good performance, Naomi."

"Yeah, sure." She rolled her eyes. "I probably have a future in acting."

"You got them to come in for a landing," Carver pointed out.

"I think that was you," she shot back. "Good job being a corpse. I was almost convinced myself."

Carver looked past her, toward the river. He didn't see anyone. But now that the chopper noise was gone, he could hear sirens. Getting closer.

"We need to leave," he said.

Naomi nodded. They took off running, feet squishing into the moist ground.

"How did you know where to aim?" she asked.

"Because I knew the model of the helicopter," Carver answered. "Army surplus. An older Huey model. I've seen plenty of them go down. I've also seen plenty of them *not* go down."

"Okay," she said. "Which means…?"

"The ones that didn't go down were patched," he added. "Armor plated. The sensitive areas covered up. This one didn't have the armor."

"Oh, thank *god* I got in your trunk."

Carver frowned. "Don't thank anyone yet. We still have a long way to go."

They kept on moving. As fast as they could through the wetlands.

Every few moments, Carver glanced to his left. Waiting. Hoping he didn't see a fireball rising into the sky.

But nothing happened. No explosions. No column of smoke. It seemed the Huey's pilot knew what he was doing after all.

SIXTY-FIVE

After another five minutes of running, they reached better ground. Solid and dry. They were able to increase their pace. Keeping to their north trajectory.

But there was quickly a problem.

They were next to a few different tracks. Rutted dirt roads used by farmers to get from one end of their fields to the other. These tracks connected back to the main road.

Suddenly, they heard sirens.

Carver glanced over his shoulder. He saw the lights coming up fast, bouncing around as the cop pushed his cruiser to unsafe speeds.

He nudged Naomi to the right. They ran down a slight incline. Back toward the river. There was a rusted horse trailer parked nearby. A few large bushes. They ducked out of sight, flattening themselves in the yellow grass.

They waited.

The siren wailed. Getting louder. Closer. Soon they heard the groan and screech of the car's frame, complaining as it jumbled over the uneven ground.

Carver belly-crawled to his left. Sticking his head into the open. He peered up the hill. Waiting and hoping.

If the cop had seen them…

It wouldn't be over. Not quite. He and Naomi were still armed. But the idea of shooting a cop was the last thing he wanted to consider. If it came to that, he'd rather turn himself in. This way, he'd distract the police while Naomi got away.

The car appeared, surging through a cloud of dust. Carver got a glimpse of the driver. He stared forward, jaw clenched. His body was a ball of tension as he fought to keep his vehicle under control. He didn't look to the right. Or to the left.

He hadn't seen the fugitives.

The car kept going, roaring out of sight.

"Let's go," Carver said.

Naomi jumped to her feet. They ran out of cover. Along the flank of the shallow hill. It was uneven ground, uncomfortable and slow-going. But it gave them a little extra cover.

"Where'd he go?" Naomi asked.

"No idea," Carver told her. "That track must loop around the other side of the field. Back to the main road. He'll probably go that way."

They heard more sirens. Getting closer.

The police were closing in. There wasn't much time. They had to get out of sight. Fast.

A minute later, they were approaching the river again. It curved west, cutting them off from their northern route. They ran right up to the edge of it, stopped, and stared across the wide expanse.

On the other side was salvation. Trees. A dense forest. The water directly in front of them was quite deep. Fast-flowing.

"See a way across?" Naomi asked.

Carver answered by turning left and jogging along the riverbank. She followed. A moment later, she tapped his shoulder and pointed.

An old telephone pole had been pushed out into the water. Maybe by local fisherman, or kids looking for a way across. It connected the bank to a shallow spot a third of the way across the river.

"It's a start," Naomi said.

Carver let her go first. He stayed on the bank, pressing down on the pole with both hands to keep it steady. There was no need. It had embedded itself fairly deep into the sand, holding strong.

Once she was down, Carver made his way over. Using the weight of the duffel bag to help him balance.

Balance had never been a strong point of his. He was too tall. Too top-heavy with muscle. It was slow going. Shuffling his feet over the rounded wooden surface. Cognizant that his weight could make it roll at any second, pitching him into the water.

It wouldn't be the end of the world. But he would like his feet to dry out at some point.

"Almost there!" Naomi called.

He could barely hear her over the rush of the water.

And there was another noise. A drone that blended in with the burbling water at first, but quickly grew until it became a separate thing.

It was the sound of another helicopter.

SIXTY-SIX

Carver jumped the last three feet of the telephone pole. He landed in the sand next to Naomi. His feet skidded. But he didn't fall.

Naomi was staring into the sky.

"Helicopter," she said.

Carver nodded. He followed her gaze and saw the black dot on the horizon. They had called in backup.

It could be on them in less than two minutes.

But Carver planned to be out of sight in a quarter of that time.

"Let's get to the trees," he said.

Naomi led the way. Any doubt that she was fully engaged was left in the dust. She moved swiftly. Decisively. Finding a path across the river with confidence. Carver was glad to see it.

Any challenge could be overcome if you had the right teammate.

Their final jump to the other side of the river was a wide one. But there was a tree branch extending over the water. A nice handhold. Naomi made the jump, pulling herself along on handfuls of pine needles.

"Toss your bag over," she shouted.

Carver made sure his duffel was zipped. He whipped it over with one hand. It cleared the water, and the bank, crashing into the trees and disappearing.

He got a running start and jumped. Landing easily in the grass without bothering with the branch.

"Showoff," Naomi said with a laugh.

Carver smiled. "Are you starting to enjoy yourself?'

"Not at all. But if I don't pretend like I am, I think I'll go crazy."

Carver didn't respond. But he didn't think she was telling the truth. He had a feeling there was a lot more to Naomi than she let on.

Maybe it was more than a feeling.

He moved ahead of her. Into the trees. He retrieved his duffel bag and forged ahead, finding a path through the tangled brush.

For a moment, they were safe. Invisible from all sides. The chopper was too far away to have seen them.

But Carver had no idea what lay ahead. Only a vague picture. A fairly wild stretch of land, sparsely populated.

But there would still be villages. Towns. Farms. And roads.

Like the road that was directly ahead of them.

Carver saw it as soon as he broke through the first layer of trees. He crouched down, signaling for Naomi to do the same. She walked on her knees, coming up next to him.

"See anything?" she asked.

Carver shook his head. Everything was still. Silent. The road was empty, as far as he could tell. Just a dirt track cutting through the middle of nowhere.

"Let's keep going," he said. "Slowly."

"Shouldn't we just run for it?" she asked.

"We will. Once we reach the road. But we can't see very far down it. We have no idea if anyone is coming."

She made an impatient groaning sound. But she stuck to his plan. They crept forward, gradually bringing more of the road into their view.

There was good news and bad news.

The good being the vast nothingness Carver saw beyond the road. A lot of trees. Hills and gullies to lose themselves in.

The bad being the two cop cars.

They were parked down the road to their right, lights and sirens off. Engines, too. They were sitting in the gravel lot outside a tiny cemetery.

Both cars were empty. No sign of the cops themselves. They could be anywhere. Behind them, maybe. Or directly ahead, ready for an ambush.

"Do we run now?" Naomi whispered.

"I don't know," Carver answered honestly.

SIXTY-SEVEN

Carver watched the cop cars.

He waited for movement. But there wasn't any. Straining his ears, he could hear muffled radio communications coming from inside the cars.

He was afraid to move.

Crouching down further, he peered around. Scanning the trees. The road. The bushes on all sides. He caught Naomi's eye. She stared back, wide-eyed.

She mouthed a question at him. *What do we do?*

He motioned back the way they came. Toward the river. She nodded. Together, they crouch-walked away from the road. Once they were back in the relative safety of the trees, Carver held up a hand.

Naomi drew to a stop. She was breathing heavily, face flushed. Sweat covered her forehead. He saw her jugular vein, taut as a rope. Pulsing with her rapid heart rate.

He knew he didn't look as nervous as she did. But he was feeling the pressure. Too much over too short a period. It was easier when you were in a foreign land. You were not beholden to enemy forces, people you had no loyalty toward.

But this was home.

The police were after him. Probably someone above the police by now too. The FBI. The CIA. Some private agency he'd never heard of.

Being a SEAL was hard work, but you were able to return home afterward. To a grateful populace at best, an oblivious one at worst.

This was light years outside the comfort zone. And that was where Carver shined.

He gave Naomi a reassuring smile, nodded his head, trying to remind her that he was here. That nothing bad would happen as long as they were together.

Then he looked back at the cop cars. He could barely see them now. Just a glimpse of white through the trees.

He started working on a plan. But his planning didn't last long. He was barely past the rudimentary phase when everything changed.

Someone new arrived, coming in from the east. A big, black car with tinted windows, its exterior waxed to a mirror sheen. It parked on the side of the road, close to the cemetery. The four doors opened in unison, and four men got out.

They wore black suits. Sunglasses. Wires in their ears. And they were carrying assault rifles.

Naomi gasped. The gasp was covered up by the four car doors slamming shut. The suited men took a few steps toward the cemetery and then stopped. They seemed to be waiting, watching something Carver couldn't see.

The police finally showed themselves, walking out of the cemetery to meet the newcomers.

An exchange happened. A badge or some other sort of credential was shown. A quiet conversation, barely audible.

"Who are these guys?" Naomi whispered.

"Mercenaries, maybe," Carver replied. "Or private security."

"Do you think…?"

He nodded. "I would say there's a good chance they work for your former boss."

Naomi's cheeks were no longer flushed red. All the blood seemed to have left her face. And the rest of her head, too. She went faint, teetering a little.

Carver shot out a hand. Catching her by the arm.

"Are you all right?" he said.

She took a deep breath. Nodded. "This is… a lot. But I'll be okay."

Carver gestured behind her. "Back to the river. We'll skirt the edge and look for a better place to cross the road."

Naomi turned, creeping through the trees. Carver stayed a mere foot behind her, ready to act in case she started to fall again.

He was entirely focused on her.

He didn't see the thick, snaking root. It draped across the ground, half buried by fallen leaves.

The toes of his left foot hooked under the root. He tripped. Without a sound, he quickly reached out and grabbed onto the closest thing he could find. A dead branch.

For a second, it seemed to hold, keeping him upright. A close call. Naomi didn't realize anything was wrong. She never even looked back.

Until the dead branch gave way with a sharp *crack*. The sound echoed through the quiet like a gunshot. Carver grunted, falling forward. Catching himself on the damp ground.

Naomi then looked back. Staring in disbelief.

"Run," she said.

SIXTY-EIGHT

Carver tried to stand. His foot was still tangled in the root. Reaching up, he grabbed onto a branch. A living one, this time. Pulling himself up, he got his foot free. He swung, launching himself forward.

He landed where Naomi had been standing a second ago. She was already on the move. But not fast enough. She was still trying to be quiet. To avoid being seen.

She clearly thought there was still a way out of this.

Carver was under no such illusion. He moved at a dead sprint. Giving her a nudge from behind. She glanced over at him. Got the message and increased her speed.

Behind, they heard the crashing sounds of four men in hot pursuit.

"*Stop right there!*"

Carver resisted the urge to look back. And the urge to run faster. He was already ahead of Naomi by a few feet. He didn't want to leave her behind.

There was a huge maple tree ahead. Carver moved behind it, put his back to the trunk. This gave Naomi room to get ahead of him. She blew past. He fell in behind her, shielding her with his huge frame.

"*Stop or we'll shoot!*"

Carver gave into his urge. He looked back. He saw flashes of black through the foliage. But there were too many trees. Too many low-hanging branches. No chance of a clear shot.

These guys were probably well-trained. They wouldn't waste ammo here. They'd wait until they had a good opportunity. A nice, wide-open area.

An area like the riverbank.

Which was where Carver and Naomi were headed. They were barreling toward their doom. Running onto a shooting range, essentially.

Even if by some miracle the bullets didn't get them, there was also the second helicopter. It must have gotten word from the cops at the cemetery, because it was swinging closer. Filling the air with sound.

Carver grabbed Naomi by the arm and pulled her to the side.

They made a right turn, heading deeper into the trees. But Carver could already see the trees thinning out on all sides. Their shelter wouldn't last much longer.

No matter which direction they went, they'd eventually break out into the open, where they could be shot down easily. Their two pistols weren't going to cut it, not against four automatic rifles.

There was only one option left. And it wasn't a promising one.

Suddenly, Naomi tripped. With a cry of fear, she went face-first into the ground.

Carver was going too fast. He stumbled right past her. Digging his heels in, he managed to stop. He turned around, heading back for her. By the time he reached her, she was already getting up.

But the fall had cost them a couple of seconds.

The gunmen were coming fast.

With no time to think or breathe, Carver shoved Naomi toward a fallen log. An old, dead tree. At least as big around as Carver himself. He jumped behind it, too.

Just in time for the shots to ring out, peppering the other side of the log with a solid drumming sound.

SIXTY-NINE

Naomi screamed.

Carver held his breath. Without thinking, he pulled her into his chest. Wrapping his arms and legs around her. Folding his body over hers.

Suddenly, the shooting stopped. Everything was quiet. Even the helicopter noise was fading away. Carver assumed it had been called off. Sent away so the hunters could work more efficiently.

For a long moment, nothing happened. The thicket was silent.

"They shot at us," Naomi whispered.

Carver nodded. The back of his head knocked against the log.

"Someone made a decision," he said.

"What does that mean?" Naomi demanded.

"It means they don't care about taking us alive. They just want that flash drive."

Naomi made a sound of despair. Carver held a finger to her lips. She went quiet.

They listened.

Finally, after an agonizing stretch of time, they heard it. Movement. Light footsteps crunching through the fallen leaves. The gunmen were coming.

Carver realized they were sitting ducks. Waiting to be surrounded. Captured. Killed.

It was time to make a move.

He pressed his finger to Naomi's mouth again, emphasizing his command that she stay silent. Then he disentangled himself from her. Pulling back his arms and legs.

Slowly, he rolled to his right. Onto his belly. He carefully unzipped the duffel bag, pulling out the gun he'd taken from Trooper Gibbs.

The log was being held up by a few stubby branches. There was a gap beneath it, about a foot high. But it was filled with tangled grass. A natural screen that prevented the gunmen from seeing the gap.

Carver crawled forward, shimmying his head and shoulder through the gap. He used the barrel of the handgun to part the grass, making a tiny gap to peek through.

Then he waited.

The mercenaries were smart. After their barrage of gunfire, they'd backed off. Repositioning. Coming up with a plan of assault. Maybe they knew Carver and Naomi were armed. Or they were just being careful.

Carver could hear them nearby, creeping around. But he couldn't see them. Not yet.

"Come on," he muttered under his breath. Then he clenched his jaw. Going silent.

His hand did not shake. The gun was steady. His body was motionless. Frozen in place.

Finally, his patience was rewarded. There was movement in the trees. Two mercs creeping closer, weaving through the undergrowth.

They did not look concerned. If anything, they seemed to be having fun. Each of them had a little smile on his face. They kept glancing at one another, enjoying the thrill of the hunt.

Carver planned on wiping their expressions clean.

Several times, he had a clear shot on one or both men. But he kept on waiting. Letting his breath out slowly through his nose. His heart rate slowed. His mind became as still as a glacier.

His two enemies came closer.

Carver lined up the first shot. He waited a second longer.

Then he squeezed the trigger.

The first gunman went down. His companion began to react. Falling to a crouched position, raising his gun. Searching for the attacker.

But Carver already had the guy's head in his sights.

The second shot landed between the mercenary's eyes.

SEVENTY

Two shots. Two hits. Two kills.

Two more bullets used.

Carver stayed where he was. He took in a breath, let it out again, relieving a modicum of the tension within him.

A rustling sound nearby almost made him jump. But it was only Naomi, belly crawling her way in beside him. She curled herself into the space beneath the log.

"Did you get them?" she whispered.

He held up two fingers. She nodded.

There were still two mercenaries lurking somewhere close. And now they knew for certain Carver was armed. They would be on high alert, posing an even bigger threat than before.

Carver itched to pull the magazine from his gun. To check how many bullets were left. It was just a nervous thing. He already knew the answer.

The pistol was a Glock 22. The magazine was the base model with a fifteen-round capacity. He had fired five of those rounds at the helicopter, and two at the gunmen just now, which meant he had eight left.

More than enough. For this encounter, at least. There could be a problem later on, if they ran into more adversaries.

He wanted to get his hands on one of those assault rifles. They were lying out there in the trees, next to the bodies of the two mercs. Fifteen feet away from the fallen tree.

Too far.

He looked at Naomi. She stared back. Every question she wanted to ask radiated from her eyes. *What do we do now?*

He didn't give her any kind of answer. The truth was too disheartening.

They couldn't do anything. The ball was completely out of their court. If they moved, they died. If they didn't move…

Waiting was the only option.

Carver held his hand out. Flat, palm toward the ground. He pushed the hand downward slowly. A gesture that meant *patience*. Naomi held her breath. Blowing out her cheeks.

A full ninety seconds passed. Through it all, Carver and Naomi stayed still.

Then they heard it again. Movement through the grass. Footfalls. So light and cautious they might have been from a baby deer.

Carver's heart beat faster. For a second, he assumed the worst. That the gunmen knew exactly where they were hiding. They were sneaking up, trying to get an angle. They had mere seconds before the shooting started.

Then he heard something else. Voices. The two men were muttering to each other. As they got closer, Carver could make out the words.

"Did you see where they went?"

"Nah. Shots came from somewhere around here… They're probably gone by now."

Suddenly, the footsteps became louder. The mercenaries were no longer going for absolute stealth. They moved closer.

Naomi tensed up, her face beading with sweat. But Carver could only smile, because the enemy had no idea where they were.

From somewhere to his left, there came a loud rustle. Followed by a thud. The log bounced, striking Carver's back. He sunk down onto his face, smelling dirt and decaying leaves.

The footsteps came closer. This time, they rang out with a more solid sound. One of the mercs was on top of the log, slowly walking along it.

Until he was right above the people he was after.

SEVENTY-ONE

The man on the log stopped moving.

Carver looked at Naomi. He wanted to communicate some kind of plan to her. A distraction. A decoy maneuver. But her eyes were closed. Her face looked shockingly serene. She'd retreated into her own world, hiding from the terror.

Maybe she had given up. Maybe she really didn't believe Carver when he said he wouldn't let anything happen to her.

That made him want to prove it to her even more.

The log jostled again. There were two more footsteps, heading to the left. *Clunk. Clunk.* Then another two, coming back to the right. The mercenary was pacing. Looking around, trying to spot something.

Carver couldn't see the guy. To get a good shot, he'd have to come out from under the log. It would create too much noise. It would take too long. He'd have a bullet in him straight away.

He needed that distraction.

Scouring the ground, he saw something. A pinecone next to his elbow. He pulled one hand off the gun to grab it. Holding the pinecone between his thumb and middle finger, with the finger tucked back slightly.

He waited.

The pacing sound came again. The man was walking to the left once more.

Carver flicked the pinecone to his right. It whizzed out into the trees, landing with a hearty crack against a trunk.

A series of heavier footsteps rang out. Carver used the sound to mask his own movement. Bringing his knees forward, getting them under his abdomen.

He launched himself forward, sprawling in the grass. He flipped over onto his back, spinning so his body was parallel to the log. He aimed up at a forty-five-degree angle.

The two men locked eyes. Carver and the merc. The latter's sunglasses had slipped down his sweaty nose. Revealing a set of blue irises. The whites were visible all around them.

He was scared.

He got off a panic shot. A bullet speared into the ground a foot from Carver's head. He felt dirt hitting his face. But he didn't flinch. Unlike his opponent, his shot was true.

The third gunman toppled off the log, thudding into the ground.

Naomi yelped and tried crawling forward. Sticking her head out through the grass. Carver motioned at her to stay put.

He scrambled back to the log. He grabbed Naomi's hands, forcing the handgun into them.

"If you see someone in all black," he muttered, "shoot them."

"Where are you going?" she whispered back.

"To try and make sure you don't have to pull the trigger," he replied.

Jumping over the log, he grabbed the assault rifle from the man he'd just shot. It was an M4 carbine. He pulled the clip, peeking in to make sure it had plenty of ammo. He slapped it back into place. Then he stood and went hunting.

He moved slowly at first. Tactically. There was a sound nearby. A car driving down the road.

He ran, covering the distance back to the cemetery.

The two police cars were gone. So was the black car with the tinted windows. The sole survivor of the assault had made his escape.

It was time for Carver to do the same.

SEVENTY-TWO

The young man behind the counter looked Gibbs dead in the face.

"Let me get this straight," he said.

He proceeded to fall silent. Staring blankly.

"Yeah?" Gibbs grunted. "Get it straight then. Go ahead."

"You're a cop," the kid said.

"I'm a Nebraska state patrolman," Gibbs replied. He chuckled, giving Sanders a can-you-believe-this-guy glance. "What's your point?"

"You're in uniform, sir. And I see your patrol car right outside. But… you want to rent a car?" The clerk shrugged. "Is that how it usually works?"

"It's not your problem, son," Gibbs grunted. "But I can change that, if you want me to. I'm a paying customer. How about you give me the car I'm asking for?"

The kid raised his eyebrows. "Can I see some ID?"

Gibbs showed his badge. As he held it out, he resisted the urge to give the boy a smack on the back of the head.

The young clerk's demeanor changed. He gave Gibbs a wide smile. "Well, that's a relief. I was worried you might be those two people who stole the car."

Gibbs stabbed a thumb toward his squad car in the parking lot. "Does that look like a white sedan to you?"

"No, sir. But you might have attacked a cop and stole his car."

"So, you think we live in an action movie?" Gibbs asked.

The young guy shrugged. Looking sheepish.

Gibbs thought about it. He recalled the events of the past thirty-six hours, replaying in his mind every gritty detail.

"I guess, maybe we do live in an action movie," he said. "Where do I sign?"

***

Ten minutes later, they walked out of the rental place that doubled as a tire store. Gibbs left his patrol car where it was, knowing no one would mess with it. He and Sanders headed toward their rental, an unassuming teal minivan.

"Who's driving?" Sanders asked.

"You," Gibbs sighed. He tossed her the keys. "I need to take a break."

"As long as you don't fall asleep on me," she yawned.

"Don't worry. I'll keep you company."

They got in. Sanders drove them back to the roadblock. A couple of the black cars were still parked there. But other things had changed. There were only two police cars left. One of the officers was on the road, waving people through one car at a time.

"Pull off to the side," Gibbs advised.

"Already on it," Sanders replied.

She came to a stop beside the shoulder. Traffic flowed past them.

"No one's looking at us twice," Gibbs said.

Sanders grinned. "They probably took one look at this van and assumed there's just some confused mom behind the wheel. I guess the disguise is working. Now what?"

"Now we wait," Gibbs replied.

"A stakeout?"

Gibbs glanced around. "Can't be. I don't see any coffee or donuts."

"That's a shame," she said wistfully.

And so they waited.

But not for long. The two remaining black cars moved as soon as there was an opening. They continued past the police cars, heading out of town on Highway 96, moving roughly north.

The roadblock dissolved. The cop who was directing traffic jogged back to his car. He fell in with the other patrol vehicle, tailing the VIP cars out of the area.

"Let's go," Sanders said with gritted teeth.

She coaxed the old minivan into motion. Soon, they were cruising along. Holding a safe distance behind the convoy. Not too close. Not too far.

Something big was happening here. And now they had a chance of finding out what.

SEVENTY-THREE

"We need to stop," Naomi said.

Her voice sounded far away. Carver looked back. She had fallen fifteen feet behind, leaning against a tree. There was a haunted look on her face. Carver knew that look. He had seen it on his own face, once, reflected in a stagnant puddle of water.

He looked away from her, surveying the land ahead. They had gone several miles since crossing the road by the cemetery, deep into the wilds north of Burwell.

But they were about to run out of trees. The land beyond was naked. A flat expanse of grass that stretched to the horizon.

As soon as they set foot out there, they'd be exposed. To helicopters. To an enterprising cop who decided to go off-roading. Maybe a farmer or a hiker. Anyone could see them. And while he'd stashed in his duffle bag the M4 he'd taken, even that would not be much help if they were caught in the open and then surrounded.

Maybe it was good to stop. Naomi might have the right idea.

Carver walked back to her. She watched him come, her eyes wide and glassy. As soon as he was within a foot of her, she suddenly collapsed.

He caught her. Lowered her carefully to the ground. She curled herself into a ball, pulling her knees to her chin.

Carver sat down beside her. He didn't touch her. He didn't look at her. He just talked.

"I've been through it," he said. "It's not easy for anyone."

She didn't move or make a sound. But he had a feeling she was watching him.

"They died because of me," she slowly said.

"No." He shook his head. "They died because I shot them. The only reason we were in that spot at that moment was because I've been calling the shots."

She sniffed. "You're trying to help me. It's my fault."

"You're smarter than that," he grunted. "You know whose fault it is."

She paused, but then she said, "Morgan Unger."

"That's right," Carver replied. "He sent those men. All we did was run from them, and they shot at us. They made the first aggressive move. As soon as they did that, they forfeited their right to live."

"You really believe that?" she groaned.

"I do."

She was silent for a moment. She let out a deep breath.

"Does it get easier?" she asked. "Killing people?'

"It does," he confirmed. "But it won't for you. You haven't killed anyone. And I don't plan on letting you. I'll get us through this, Naomi."

She let out a dry laugh. "I feel like dead weight."

Carver sighed. He got to his feet. Offered her a hand. "Enough self-pity. Get up."

She grabbed his hand. He helped her to her feet.

"Okay, I guess I'm ready to keep moving," she said.

"We aren't going far." Carver pointed across the wide field that awaited them. "Crossing that in daylight is a bad move. We'll find somewhere to get some rest. We'll move once it's good and dark."

Naomi shrugged. Waving for him to go first.

"No," he said. "I'll follow you. Pick a spot."

She tried on a smile. "I guess it doesn't involve shooting at people, so I can handle it."

She started walking. Carver hesitated a moment, looking at her pocket. The one she'd stuck the sandwich bag into, holding her flash drive. And whatever else she'd stashed in it. But he no longer saw the bag.

"Still have the drive?" he asked casually.

She fished it out of her back pocket, showing it to him. "Nice and toasty dry."

"Good," Carver said. "Just making sure."

He watched her closely as they walked through the woods.

SEVENTY-FOUR

When it came to lodgings, Carver wasn't expecting much. A flat spot under a pine tree, maybe. A shadowy pocket under an overhang. Maybe an old hunting blind, if they were extremely lucky.

But Naomi led them to gold.

"What is that?" she asked.

Carver stopped next to her, gazing into the trees. He saw it right away. Something rectangular. A set of straight edges and lines. Obviously manmade.

"It's too small to be a house," he said.

"But it's something," Naomi responded.

"It is. Let's check it out."

"Okay." She took a tentative step forward, biting her lip. "Uh… do you want to go first?"

Carver chuckled. He got in front of her and led the way. As he walked, he unzipped the duffel bag. He stuck his hand inside, and held the pistol. Keeping it hidden, but at the ready.

"Anyone there?" he called. "Hello!"

A blackbird cawed in a tree. A distant plane engine droned through the sky. There was no other sound.

The object turned out to be an RV. It was on the small side, old and faded. Leaves and pine needles were stuck all over it. A thick layer of grime obscured the vehicle's true color.

"Random," Naomi muttered.

Carver pointed at a heap of rotting, mossy wood. "I think that used to be a picnic table. This used to be a campsite."

"And someone just left a whole RV out here?" Naomi shuddered. "Hopefully, they aren't still inside."

"I doubt it," Carver said. "It probably just broke down. They walked out of here and never bothered to come back."

He approached the RV.

Grabbing a handful of leaves from the ground, he scrubbed at one of the windows. Scraping away years of algae and muck. He put his face to the glass, cupping his hands around his eyes.

The interior seemed to be orderly. It had been left in good condition. But it was stuck in time. Based on the plaid pattern of the couch cushions and the shag floor, it was at least thirty years old.

But there was no way it had been parked here that long. Four or five years at most. Which meant there was a chance the inside was livable.

At least for a few hours.

"I'm going in," he announced.

"Careful!" Naomi called out. She then busied herself, kicking at the remains of the picnic table.

Carver tried the door. The handle was a bit sticky. But with a little extra force, it popped open. He pulled his shirt up over his mouth and nose. Not that it helped much. The fabric reeked of swampy river water.

He stepped up into the RV. The air was cold and stale. It smelled like a thrift store. The aroma of old fabric that had been sitting in someone's closet for years. There was an underlying tang of animal waste.

That was no deal breaker for Carver. The whole forest was one big toilet. He'd seen and smelled worse.

"Come over," he called to Naomi.

She approached cautiously, sniffing at the air. "Smells a little off."

"It's the best we're going to find," Carver told her.

She shrugged. "As long as I don't have to cuddle with any raccoons, I'm down."

SEVENTY-FIVE

She climbed aboard. Carver shut the door and immediately hurried around, opening windows. He pulled the curtains open as well, letting in a bit of light.

All in all, the place wasn't too bad. The bed was even made. But they sat on the couch instead. Carver unzipped his bag, handed Naomi a bottle of water. He grabbed one for himself, too. They started chugging, pausing only to let out a belch.

"Wow, that was good," Naomi sighed. She peered at the bag. "What else do we have? I forget."

He divvied out some of the food. Granola bars and beef jerky. They didn't speak at all for the next ten minutes. They were too busy stuffing their faces.

"That's weird," Naomi finally said.

"What is?" Carver asked.

"I ate, and now I feel a lot better. All I need now is a cup of coffee. Or a cold beer."

He leaned back, interlacing his fingers behind his head. "I'll buy you one as soon as we get to South Dakota."

Naomi picked at her teeth. Her eyes were glazed over, staring into space.

"You still think we'll make it?" she asked. "We don't even have a car anymore."

Carver closed his eyes. "I'll get us there."

She took a deep breath, fidgeting around on the couch.

"That beef jerky was good," she said.

"Teriyaki flavor," Carver muttered.

"Any left?"

He handed her his bag. There were a couple of shreds of dried meat left inside, which she devoured in seconds.

"Any more granola bars?" she added.

He nodded. "A few. Here."

He offered her the box.

"No, that's all right," she said. "Just want to make sure I didn't hog all the food. Save it for yourself."

"I'll be fine," Carver replied. He tossed the box into his bag. "It can be a midnight snack."

"I thought you'd have more of an appetite," said Naomi. "A guy your size."

He closed his eyes again. "I'm worried."

"About us?" she said cautiously.

"No. We're in control of our situation. I'm worried about what I don't know. About Harvey."

He kept his eyes shut. But he sensed her leaning closer.

"Harvey? Is that who you've been trying to call?" she asked.

He nodded. "He's the father of a woman I used to know."

"Like… in a romantic way?" she pried.

"Yes. She died. Harvey and I have stayed close. Your enemies have become my enemies, Naomi. They might go after him to get to me. To get to you."

She shrank away again. "Sorry. Where does he live? Can we get to him?"

"No."

"Well, where does he live?"

"Idaho."

"Oh. Well, maybe you can call him again. Make sure everything's okay. Right?"

Carver pulled his phone out of his pocket. He gave it a shake. A trickle of brown water poured out of it.

"I don't think you'll be making any calls with that," Naomi said. "Sorry."

He smiled. Shrugged his shoulders. "Maybe I can borrow your phone, the one you were hiding in your bra."

SEVENTY-SIX

There it was. An almost imperceptible change in her expression. A widening of the eyes. A quickening of the pulse.

"My phone?" she said incredulously.

"Yes. The one you used last night, after you sneaked out of that abandoned house. You thought I was fast asleep. I wasn't."

"Oh… Well…" She swallowed hard. Grinned to hide her fear. "You saw everything, huh?"

"I did."

"So, what are you going to do about it?" she asked.

He kicked off his shoes. Then he started on his wet socks, peeling them off slowly. Cringing the whole time.

"I want to see what's on that flash drive the first chance we get," he said. "Until then, I'm going to keep on trusting you. As long as you tell me who you were texting."

"My contact," she said. "The guy who's going to pick me up once I'm past the border."

"Who is he?"

"I'd like to tell you, but I can't. He's someone I trust. I don't want to spoil that."

He stared into her eyes. She stared back. Carver saw nothing to distrust. But maybe she was a good liar.

"Why doesn't he just come into Nebraska?" he then asked. "And extract you directly?"

Naomi laughed a little, brushing hair out of her eyes. "He's not like you, Carver. He's a smart and accomplished guy. But he's no action hero."

"Neither am I," Carver replied. "Last question. Why did you try and hide this from me?"

"Because..." Naomi looked away. Her eyes moved around the room for a moment. Then they settled on the floor. "I thought it better to keep you in the dark. Not to protect you. Just for my own selfish reasons."

Carver said nothing. He kept looking at her until she explained.

"I'm already asking him to do too much," Naomi added. "It was hard enough getting him to help me as much as he is. I didn't want..."

The breath went out of her. She hid her face in her hands.

"I know what you're going to say," Carver said. "You didn't want me to know the details, because then I might ask for your friend to extract me as well. You were worried he'd get scared off. That you'd be on your own."

She nodded slowly. He could only see a sliver of her face. It went beet red.

"How did you envision this going?" he asked. "Were you just going to wave goodbye to me once you were in South Dakota, and disappear?"

"I don't know, Carver. I really don't know."

She showed her face then. It was streaked with tears. He grabbed her hand, held it gently.

"I can take care of myself," he said.

"Yeah," she croaked. "I did notice that about you. But I feel awful."

"Don't," Carver urged. "Even if your contact could help me, I'd turn him down. I have my own places to be."

"Like Idaho?" she asked.

He nodded.

She reached into her shirt, pulled out the hidden phone. "Do you want to call Harvey?"

He shook his head. "They're probably watching his line already. No reason to put all three of us in danger. If Harvey fails to get in contact with me, they'll have no reason to hurt him."

"If they have him at all," Naomi added.

"I like your optimism. But I don't share it."

Suddenly, Naomi let out a big yawn, which made Carver yawn, too. He pointed toward the bed.

"There's enough room for two people," he pointed out. "I'd take the couch, but…"

"But it's about four feet long," Naomi laughed. "Sure, we can share the bed. Are you going to cuff me again?"

He thought about it. "No. I trust you."

SEVENTY-SEVEN

"Shoot, all these channels and there's never anything good on." Harvey tossed the TV remote down. A soap opera played on screen. A businessman had just come home to find his wife in bed with his brother.

"Who watches this crap?" Einer barked. He was sprawled out in an armchair, drinking a beer and munching his way through a bag of chips. His shock of blond hair looked goofier than ever.

Harvey looked around. One of Einer's meathead companions was in the door to the hallway. Holding his rifle in one hand, picking his nose with the other. The other guy was in the bathroom.

"I used to keep up with the soaps," Harvey sighed. "My wife was big into them. But it hasn't been the same since she passed on."

Einer snorted, tossing a chip at him. "Shut up, old man. I don't care about your damn wife. Check your cell again."

Harvey pulled his smartphone out. He still barely knew how to use the thing. But he knew enough to see that he had no missed calls.

"Nothing," he said.

Einer let out a growl. He sat forward, slopping beer onto the floor. "Try calling him back again."

"He won't answer, son," Harvey chuckled. "You're not dealing with a dummy here, you know."

Einer stared straight at him. "Actually, I think I am. Didn't you hear me? Call him back."

Harvey went into his call history, dialed back the number Carver had called him from. It didn't even ring. It went straight to a robotic voice, telling him the number was unavailable.

"See? He's too smart." Harvey bent down, scooping off the floor the chip Einer had thrown. He set it on the coffee table. "I'd thank you to mind your manners in my house. I understand you fellas are here on business, but there's no reason we can't be civil."

Einer took another swig of beer, draining the bottle. He lifted the empty above his head. Harvey tensed up, thinking he was about to get a bottle to the head. Instead, Einer let his wrist go limp. The bottle fell, bouncing off the arm of the chair.

"Sure, we can be civil," he said. "For now. But Carver's costing you, old man. For your sake, you better hope he calls back. I was going to get you to convince him Naomi Downes can't be trusted. To turn her in. Then you'd both be free to go. But I guess we're doing it the hard way now."

One meathead came back from the bathroom. That was Einer's cue to get up and head for the toilet himself. Before leaving the room, he glanced at Harvey.

"The hard way," he repeated. "And the bloody way."

Harvey sat back. He reached for a sudoku book he'd been working on, and grabbed his reading glasses from his pocket.

He figured there was a better-than-average chance he'd die today, one way or another. But he only had a few puzzles left in the book, and he hated leaving things unfinished.

SEVENTY-EIGHT

Darkness came fast. The sun fled out of the sky like it was scared for its life, casting Nebraska into a somber dusk.

Gibbs was in the driver's seat of the minivan now. They'd switched spots. Sanders was nodding off in the passenger seat, occasionally mumbling jokes about the towns they passed.

But the towns were few and far between. And so were the jokes. North of Burwell, there was just about nothing until you got halfway through South Dakota. A boring drive. Monotonous.

The only thing that kept Gibbs awake was the thrill of the hunt. He kept the taillights of the convoy firmly in his sights.

Things got interesting around the town of Bassett when a few other cars came out of nowhere and joined the group. More of those black sedans with tinted windows. At the same time, one of the two remaining police cars drifted away, vanishing from the group.

Nothing much happened after that.

Now they were driving down dirt roads. Getting further and further from civilization. The convoy must have noticed they were being followed by now. But they didn't seem to be worried.

Why would they be? They were the law. It was Gibbs and Sanders who were doing something strange. And they were the law, too.

It was all starting to get confused, Gibbs thought. The chain of command. The chain of consequences. With every mile he drove, he felt more like a fool. A fool who should be back home right now, watching funny internet videos and eating a TV dinner.

"Verde chicken enchiladas," he said.

Sanders snapped to attention. "Huh? What was that?"

"Verde chicken enchiladas," Gibbs said again. "It's my favorite flavor."

"Flavor of what?"

"The frozen dinners I buy."

"Frozen food will kill you faster than anything," Sanders said. "That's what my mom used to tell me. But I can't say no to a microwaved bean and cheese burrito."

"Well, I'm glad you aren't eating any of those today," Gibbs snorted. "I have to share a car with you."

They had a good laugh. But it was cut short when they saw a sea of red brake lights glowing up ahead.

"We're stopping," Gibbs said, almost in disbelief.

The convoy started to turn, headed down a gravel driveway toward a big barn.

"Check your phone," said Gibbs. "Where are we?"

Sanders scrambled to open her GPS. "Just a few miles shy of the border. Other than that, it's the middle of nowhere."

Gibbs slowed down, uncertain what to do. The last of the convoy's cars pulled off into the driveway, leaving him alone on this desolate road.

"What do we do?" Sanders asked.

"I'm gonna keep going," Gibbs told her. "Drive right on past, all inconspicuous. Then we can double back on foot."

"If you say so," she said uncertainly.

Gibbs did as he said. As soon as they passed the driveway, he saw a sign that made his heart skip a beat: DEAD END.

"Uh oh," he said.

"Just keep going," Sanders hissed. "Can't turn around now."

Gibbs drove on, and they had a lucky break. The road they were currently on had a dead end. But there was an intersecting road, heading east. They pulled onto it, parking beside a stand of trees.

"I doubt anyone'll come this way for hours," Gibbs said. "I think we're okay here."

Sanders nodded. She rolled her window down, and stuck her head into the cold evening air.

"Not full dark yet," she said. "Let's just wait a little while."

"Sure," Gibbs agreed. "We probably don't want them to see us coming."

SEVENTY-NINE

After ten minutes of waiting, night had truly fallen. Gibbs and Sanders got out of the van. The temperature outside had dropped fast. They shivered, pulling their jackets tighter.

"Nice night for a walk," Sanders said.

"Yeah," Gibbs grunted. "Real nice. Couldn't be nicer. Let's go."

They shut their doors and walked down the road. Trees loomed over them on either side. The road was narrow and dark. Everything was silent. The moon was a mere sliver. After thirty seconds of walking, they could no longer see the minivan.

They could barely even see each other.

Stumbling through the blackness, they found their way past the trees. Now all they had to do was cross a field. About as long as a football field. Then they'd be at the barn. It glowed in the near distance. Its doors were open. At least a dozen parked cars were visible. But they saw no movement.

"What's going on in there?" Gibbs whispered.

Sanders was about to answer. Instead, she ran into a waist-high fence and fell onto the other side. She jumped to her feet. Brushed herself off.

"There's a fence here," she said. "So look out for that."

Gibbs climbed over. He nearly topped when his shoe got stuck. Sanders caught him. He thanked her. They moved on.

Crossing the field was a breeze. No obstacles. No issues. Soon, they were approaching the barn. There was another fence, separating the field from the driveway. They crept along it, trying to get an angle on the inside of the building.

It didn't take them long to find one. They were close enough to see everything. To hear everything. But no one was talking. Not yet. There was a hushed silence in the barn.

Two dozen men and women were sitting inside, all wearing dark clothing.

The men had thick necks and buzz-cut hair. And bulging muscles beneath their coats.

The women wore their hair short as well. There was no shortage of neck tattoos and battle scars. They had an air of toughness and bravado to them. Radiating an energy that, as far as Gibbs knew, you only got from one place.

"They're ex-military," he whispered to Gibbs. "They got to be."

"Mercenaries?" she asked.

"Maybe. Or just soldiers that got hired up to a bigger position."

As they stared into the barn, Gibbs and Sanders both noticed the same thing. It looked a lot like the talk Colonel Bell had given them at that other farm, back near Pomos, where this whole mess started.

Their feelings were confirmed when three men stepped into view at the front of the crowd. The first was Colonel Bell, once again.

The second was a clean-cut fellow with a winning smile. Gibbs recognized his face straight away, but he couldn't quite place the name.

"That's Morgan Unger," Sanders said. "Nebraska senator."

Gibbs nodded. He didn't say what he was thinking. He didn't need to, because Sanders said it.

"He's actually here in person, Gibbs. Holding a secret conference with a band of mercs? This has got to be some major business. I mean *serious*."

Gibbs couldn't agree more.

But Senator Unger wasn't even the most shocking face on display. The third man who stepped into view earned that prize.

He lagged behind the others. Moving slowly. Deliberately. Dragging an air of utmost seriousness with him.

This time, Gibbs knew the face as well as the name.

The third man was William Lamay, the Vice President of the United States of America.

EIGHTY

"Is that who I think it is?" Sanders hissed.

"Do you mean if that's the Vice President?" Gibbs asked.

"Yeah."

"It's definitely who you think it is." Gibbs wiped the sweat from his face, shaking his head. "This is above our pay grade. Way above."

"Ya think?" Sanders grunted. "Are we still gonna stay and watch?"

"You bet we are," Gibbs replied. "Because I'm too dang scared to move now."

Inside the barn, things were settling down. VP William Lamay stood off to one side of a makeshift stage. Colonel Bell stood on the other side. Senator Unger took the podium. He rustled some papers beneath the mic. Cleared his throat.

And started to speak.

"We all know why we're here," he said, "and there aren't any TV cameras, so I'll cut to the chase. We're hunting two high-level targets, Naomi Downes and Ronan Carver."

At the mention of Carver's name, a brief disturbance passed through the crowd. Dirty looks. A few sad ones. Some muttered words.

"Many of you have heard of Ronan Carver," Unger went on. "Some of you may have worked with him. It goes without saying he's a dangerous man. Highly dangerous. Which is why we have the best of the best in this room."

The mood changed yet again. This time, the gathered mercenaries smiled and pumped their fists. They were getting stirred up. Primed and ready to blast off. And Unger knew just where to aim them.

"So far, the targets have been heading north. We have no doubt they will be attempting to cross state lines. Ladies and gentlemen, we can no longer afford to take chances. This is sudden death. Both Naomi Downes and Ronan Carver are to be shot on sight."

A sober air settled over the crowd. They were all business now, nodding and frowning. Some were even taking notes.

"This is a potential stain not only on my senatorial campaign, but also on the administration which Vice President Lamay serves. As such, we want to downplay this as much as possible. Keep it out of the public eye. Which is another reason you're all here.

"The FBI and the CIA are being kept out of this," Unger went on. "And so are the state police from now on. All hopes for an easy, painless solution are long gone. People, your country is counting on you to get this done. Let's get to work. Any questions?"

A few mercs raised their hands. As Unger called on them, Gibbs hunkered down further in his hiding place. He turned to Sanders.

"No state police," he whispered. "So why is Colonel Bell here?"

"Why is the Vice President here?" Sanders shot back. "How deep does this go?"

Gibbs shrugged.

He was famous in the Nebraska State Patrol for having an unreliable gut. His instincts got him into trouble as often as they got him out of it.

Right now, his gut was telling him something fishy was going on. That Senator Unger may be up to something.

It was a fifty-fifty shot.

He just had to decide which way to go. And whether finding out the truth was worth risking everything.

EIGHTY-ONE

"Annie, I thought I lost you," Carver said.

He'd also thought he was somewhere else, a smelly old RV in the middle of nowhere. With someone else. But now he was in a grassy field. A warm sun overhead. A soft breeze floating past.

And Annie was there. Head on his belly. Smiling up at him.

"You thought wrong," she said.

"Where's Harvey?"

"Oh, he's probably working on that junky old car again," Annie sighed. "He'd probably have you working on it, too. But he won't find us out here."

Carver lifted his head to look around. "Where are we?"

"I don't know," she said. "And I don't care. Do you?"

Carver considered it. He didn't have to think for long. He laid back down. Ran his hand through her hair as he stared up at the clouds.

He was happy.

He was also asleep, dreaming of this place once again.

A second later, he woke up. Found himself surrounded by darkness and that stale, mildewy stench. The RV. It was dark now. Maybe that was why he'd woken up.

It was safe to keep moving. The helicopters could still spot them with searchlights, but it would be much harder. And it would be easy to see the choppers coming. Plenty of time to hide.

"Naomi," Carver said, reaching out to nudge her. "It's time to—"

But she wasn't there. The other half of the bed was empty.

Carver felt something close around his wrist. Cold metal. He knew what it was even before he heard the click of ratchet teeth.

"Sorry," Naomi said from somewhere nearby. "I don't know if we'll ever be able to fully trust each other. And there are too many ways for that to go bad."

He sat up. Or tried to. The handcuff chain came up short, yanking him back. He felt for the other cuff. She had attached it to the metal frame of the bed, right beneath where it was bolted into the wall of the RV.

"I trusted you," he growled.

"And I took advantage," she said. "You were sleeping pretty deeply. I don't think I could have snuck out of bed otherwise."

He saw her then. A silhouette in the dark. He lunged, trying to grab her. She jumped out of the way. Then she bent down, grabbing something big and heavy off the floor.

His duffel bag.

"Sorry," she said again. "I hope for both our sakes, we never meet again. Goodbye, Ronan Carver."

With the bag and all of their guns with her, she ran out of the RV. Slamming the door shut behind her.

EIGHTY-TWO

It wasn't often that Carver lost his cool. He knew what having a temper could lead to. The hot-headed guys always washed out, or ended up dead. Even worse, they often got good men killed.

Carver was all alone now. He couldn't get anyone killed. And he was a dead man if he didn't get away. So, in some unconscious area of his mind, he gave himself permission to go berserk.

He flipped face down on the bed, his cuffed hand pinned under his chest. Then he pushed himself up on his knees and started yanking on the cuff with all his might, thrashing and growling, sweat flying off of his face.

He screamed. He cursed Naomi. He cursed himself for letting any of this happen. For trusting someone. There was only one person he could trust, and it was an old man waiting for him back in Idaho. He should have known that. He should have remembered.

Everyone else was dead.

And if he caught up with Naomi, she had better watch out.

Out of breath, he took a break from his freakout. And noticed that his wrist was killing him. The cuff had torn into his flesh. Naomi had cinched it tight. He was starting to lose circulation. His fingers going purple, swelling up with blood that couldn't escape.

He took a deep breath and calmed down.

It was time to think of a smarter way out of this. Something that didn't involve ripping his own skin off.

As he sat in contemplation, he heard something. A distant, tiny voice. Sounding urgent. His first thought was a megaphone, echoing from miles away. A search party?

They had found him. They were coming now. Closing in.

But that wasn't it. If they were coming, why would they want to advertise to him where they were? Why use a megaphone at all?

He looked around the RV and saw a faint glowing light a few feet away from the bed, shining against the floor.

He scooted himself to the edge of the bed. Stretching the handcuff chain as far as it could go, he reached out with his foot. He used it to drag the glowing object toward him. He picked it up.

It was a phone. Naomi's. The one she'd been hiding in her bra. It was in the middle of a call, and the caller ID of the place she had phoned was right in the middle of the screen.

The Nebraska State Patrol.

Carver put the phone to his ear.

"Sir or ma'am," a voice said. "I heard screaming. We're going to send help. Just stay where you are."

He ended the call and tossed the phone away. Thinking back, he felt his stomach churn. Naomi had said his full name out loud. *Ronan Carver*. The State Patrol would have heard it. They would have had plenty of time to triangulate the phone's position.

They were already on their way. It wouldn't take long for them to find the RV with Carver cuffed inside. A sitting duck.

The spot was obscure. But it wasn't quite remote. He and Naomi had traveled on foot to reach it, straight out of Burwell. It was a few miles into the countryside, no more.

He figured he had ten minutes before a chopper showed up, at most. Not much longer before cars arrived.

He had to be away from here in five.

EIGHTY-THREE

Five minutes.

He had to be out of the RV by then.

It would be better if he could do it faster.

Carver got back onto the bed. Kneeling, he stretched the handcuff chain tight. The cuff on the other end slid up the rail it was attached to. Clanking to a stop when it reached the attachment point between the rail and the wall.

He breathed, and closed his eyes for a moment. The image of Annie flashed in his mind. The sunlit field. The soft breeze. He went there again, filling himself with the peace and confidence of that place.

It was time to get out of here.

He reached down, grabbed the metal rail with both hands. Slowly, he bore up on it. Stretching every muscle in his body tight. Transferring the strength of every single cell of his being into his hands.

He didn't jerk or tug. He just pulled, leaning back, clenching his jaw. Sweat poured down his face and trickled down his back. He let out his breath in a slow, hydraulic hiss.

The metal dug into his fingers. The rail was like a dull knife, threatening to flay his skin. He dug deeper. Pulled harder. The rail was his only hope. He knew the handcuffs. They were his. They were the type of cuffs used in prisons to secure dangerous, violent offenders.

They would never break. He had to attack the structure they were attached to, and even that was an extremely tall order. The RV was old. It was made back when things were built to last. If it had been kept clean, it would still be road-worthy.

He kept on pulling. His hands screamed in pain. His muscles shook uncontrollably. Every vein on his face and neck popped out, swelling like fat worms. His lungs were empty. His vision was going black.

In a moment, he'd pass out.

If he woke up before the cops arrived, he'd try again.

He thought of Annie.

After killing the man responsible for her death, he had thought his duty to her was over.

But he was only half right. He may have avenged her, but that wasn't what she would have asked him to do. She would have wanted him to live on. To find happiness. Or at least, a sense of purpose.

Up until a few minutes ago, his new purpose had been to save Naomi.

Now his purpose was to get out of this RV so he could hunt her down.

Something happened. A popping sound, followed by a screech of twisting metal. The welds holding the rail to the screw plate gave out. The rail popped free.

Carver fell forward, gasping with exhaustion. He let himself breathe for exactly ten seconds. Then he got back up and pulled the cuff free from the broken end of the rail.

He got off the bed, the cuff jangling from his wrist. He had a minute or so to spare. Enough time to look for anything that might help him. Perhaps the RV's owners had left something behind.

He found Naomi's phone on the floor and used it for light. Shining it around the interior of the camper. There wasn't much left. A baseball hat gathering dust on a table. A few old cans of food that had long since rusted through, the stuff inside eaten by critters.

Inside a cupboard, he finally spotted something. Something he almost missed. It was a bobby pin, left behind on a shelf.

He had heard a lot the other night when Naomi broke out of her cuffs and left the abandoned house. Seen a lot, too. Despite his background, he'd never known if the bobby pin trick actually worked, or if it was just a movie thing.

Naomi had made it look easy enough.

He jammed the pin into the lock on his cuff. It took a moment to feel his way around. But he felt a click, and pulled the handcuff free. Dropping it on the floor.

Rubbing his wrist, he gave himself another second to breathe. And then he heard the choppers in the distance.

He slid the bobby pin into his pocket. He turned Naomi's phone off and pocketed it as well. And then he was through the door, sprinting into the night.

EIGHTY-FOUR

Vice President William Lamay was a regal man. His dense snow-white hair was swept back in a perfect wave, not a single strand out of place. His wool suit was immaculate, completely free of lint, as though it had been kept in a clean room.

He stepped onto the center of the stage, taking the spot from Senator Unger. He smiled at the crowd. Adjusting his tie. Pulling at his lapels. He cleared his throat.

He opened his mouth to speak. Looking at him, you might expect some aristocratic accent to come out. Posh British, maybe, or transatlantic. Instead, he spoke with a southern drawl.

"Well, this isn't how my nights usually go," he began with a smirk. "But maybe we can fix that. Does anyone here happen to have a snifter of brandy on hand? No? I'd settle for a beer, too. Or even a diet cola."

People in the crowd laughed.

"Maybe I'll buy you all a round when this is done," Lamay went on. He paused, letting his eyes travel over the people before him. "And that's why I went into politics instead of comedy. I'm going to make this short. I just want you all to know that you have the full support of the US government in your current endeavor."

A few people pumped their fists. Someone whistled loudly. Everyone else just nodded. Their jaws were clenched. Their eyes burning sharp. They were ready to go, just waiting to hear the word.

Off to the side, Colonel Bell was distracted. He pulled a phone out of his pocket and looked at it. Then he answered a call and stepped off to the side, turning so Gibbs couldn't see his face.

"You are all professionals," Lamay said, "so I won't bore you with talk of rules and limitations. You know what you're doing. It's ugly work, but someone has to do it. So, I thank you all for taking that burden on."

Colonel Bell suddenly rushed toward the VP. He leaned in, whispering something in the man's ear. Lamay nodded. Bell took a single step back. Waiting.

"With that," said Lamay, "I'll turn you back over to Colonel Bell."

He moved away. Bell swooped in, clutching the edges of the podium.

"We've got a lead," he said. "A phone call just came in from a rural area a few miles north of Burwell. It seems to have come from Naomi Downes and Ronan Carver. Further details will be provided in transit."

That was apparently the magic word. Chairs slid back as all the mercenaries got to their feet. They flooded out of the barn. Not quite running, but moving steadily with focused looks on their faces.

Instead of heading toward the fleet of parked cars, they turned and disappeared around the corner of the building. A second later, Gibbs and Sanders heard the telltale whine. Helicopter rotors spinning up.

"There they go," Sanders said. "I guess, Naomi and Carver are pretty much screwed now. Serves 'em right."

Gibbs grunted, shrugging his shoulders.

She grabbed his arm, turning him around and making him face her.

"I know that grunt," she remarked. "You're about to do or say something stupid. Maybe both."

"I'm just not sure Naomi and Carver are the bad guys here," Gibbs replied.

"They almost shot me," Sanders hissed.

"*Naomi* almost shot you, the untrained one of the pair. And we both know that was a reflex squeeze. She didn't mean for it to happen."

"Maybe. But she's still guilty. She stole sensitive documents. State secrets."

"How do we know that?" Gibbs asked. "Because Senator Unger said so? Guys in his line of work never lie, huh?"

Sanders just stared at him. He knew the look. She was annoyed—and ready to blow up on him.

She took a deep breath and said, "There's nothing we can do either way. Let's get back to the car before someone sees us."

She was right, and Gibbs knew it. He looked back at the barn. Bell, Unger, and Lamay were all gone as well. Only a couple of armed guards remained, strolling around inside.

He pulled the car keys out, handed them over. Sanders grabbed them.

"Gibbs, let's go," she whispered.

He glanced over his shoulder, saw her creeping away into the dark.

She disappeared.

But Gibbs didn't follow.

EIGHTY-FIVE

He would have liked the backup. But Sanders was already gone.

And Sanders was also smart. She knew getting even this close was harebrained, let alone what Gibbs was considering now. He couldn't ask her to join him. Not this time.

Even if he did, convincing her to do something so stupid would take way too long.

Without looking back for her, he got to his feet and hurried along the fence. Staying inside the field for now.

He stayed low. Bent almost in half to avoid being spotted. As soon as he could no longer see the barn's front doors, he hopped the fence. Ran to the wall of the large structure and put his back to it.

He looked both ways. Breathing fast as the helicopters buzzed into the sky above him. They turned, tipping forward and racing south.

As the sound of the choppers faded, things got deathly quiet. Gibbs could hear his own heartbeat. It wasn't too late to leave, to jump back over the fence and chase after Sanders. But he wasn't going to do that.

Gibbs was afraid. He was also a fool. But he wasn't a coward.

He looked left and right to see if there was a side door. There wasn't. He went all the way to the back of the barn and checked there as well. There was a door, but it was chained shut.

The only way in was through the front. Through a giant garage door. Wide open. Plenty of light spilling out.

Sneaking was no longer an option. If he wanted to get inside and learn anything at all, it was time for a different tactic.

There had to be something. A genius idea that could get him into the barn. But he was drawing a blank. His adrenaline-soaked brain refused to give him anything.

So he decided to go on instinct.

He returned to the front of the barn. Pausing by the corner to catch his breath. To compose himself. Then he put on a meek smile and marched right inside.

"Hello, excuse me?" he called. "Anyone here?"

Right away, two men with submachine guns rushed to intercept him, knocking over folding chairs.

"This area is off-limits!" one of them shouted. "Identify yourself immediately."

He threw his hands in the air. "Trooper Gibbs, Nebraska State Patrol!"

"What are you doing here?" the guard demanded.

"Well, I heard that those fugitives might be heading this way," Gibbs answered. "I've been looking for them. I guess I was focusing a bit too hard, because I ran out of gas. Could someone here give me a ride?"

He moved to his left. Peeking around the two guards. He got a brief look at the rest of the barn's interior. Things he hadn't been able to see from his spot by the fence. Including a bank of laptop computers that was set up by the left wall.

Then the guards were on him. They turned him around to face the door. Then they each grabbed a wrist and marched him outside.

"Sheesh, sorry if I walked in on something," Gibbs barked. "I saw those helicopters take off and figured this was some kind of official business. I guess I can just leave."

"You aren't going anywhere," the man on his right said. "Not until our superiors get back and tell us what to do with you."

"What's going on here, anyway?" Gibbs asked. "I'm a cop. You should be careful."

"No questions," the guard snapped.

They ran him straight out to one of the parked cars. A rear door was opened. Gibbs was shoved inside. Before he could even breathe, a handcuff was on his wrist, locking him to the door handle.

The two men left, returning to the barn. And Gibbs was alone.

"I guess that was a pretty dumb idea," he sighed to himself.

EIGHTY-SIX

Carver ran for twenty minutes straight, as fast as he could go. Which wasn't as fast as he would like. It was dark, and there were too many hazards. Trees. Low branches. Twisted clumps of grass.

He outran the sound of the choppers and the stench of the old RV. He lost his pursuers. Using the stars he could see as a guide, he headed roughly north. Making a safe assumption that Naomi would stick to the plan.

He figured she must be feeling pretty good about herself right now. She had outsmarted and outplayed the Navy SEAL. A boost to her confidence. She had a good head start on him. She was also smaller, more capable of snaking through the foliage.

And she had light, if she was smart enough to dig into his duffel bag and find the flashlight.

She was probably moving much faster than he was, even with the extra weight of the duffel bag. She might have found his compass, too, used it to head straight north, whereas his tack was much more vague.

He didn't know whether he'd be able to catch her or not.

After twenty minutes, he stopped to rest for a moment. He leaned against a tree, hot breath steaming from his mouth. Vapor from drying sweat billowed out of his shirt.

Right away, the chill started to assert itself. Goosebumps prickled along his arms. He shivered. Running had made him heat up, but his sweat was now causing him to freeze.

He stripped off his damp shirt, tucked it into his waistband. As he was doing so, he felt Naomi's phone in his pocket. He wondered if he should turn it back on. Check her text and call history. See if he could get any clues.

She had been communicating with her contact. They must have a specific rendezvous point and time picked out. Now that she had no way of making further contact, these plans would be set in stone.

If he managed to get out of these woods and get himself some transport, he'd check the messages. But not before then. The police would be watching this phone closely. It wasn't worth the risk. Just carrying it in its off-state was bad enough.

He started moving again, further into the frosty darkness.

Soon, he broke into a clearing. The night sky was a wide tapestry above him. The stars a glittering ocean. He was mesmerized for a moment. Then he realized those distant pinpoints weren't the only source of light.

Straight ahead, through the trees, an orange glow flickered. He headed toward it.

It was a campsite. There were two tents, but only one car parked nearby. Four people were huddled by the fire, looking sullen. They were passing a bottle of liquor between them. When Carver approached, they gave him a bleary glance.

"What's going on tonight?" a blonde woman slurred. "It started off so fun."

Carver stepped forward. The four campers scrunched closer together, watching as warily as they could in their drunken state.

"Good evening," Carver said. "Did a tall, dark-haired woman pass through here?"

"She did more than pass," a guy with a mop of curly hair replied. "She stole my frickin' car, man."

"And my phone," the blonde woman added.

"We'll get the car back, Johnny," another guy replied.

Carver focused on Johnny, the guy with curly hair. "What kind of car is it?"

"Huh?" Johnny mumbled.

"The car that was stolen," Carver said patiently. "Can you describe it to me?"

"Yeah, I guess. It's red."

"Four door?"

"Yeah. It's a Ford."

Carver nodded. "Are there any other distinguishing features you can tell me about?"

The blonde woman stood up, wobbling a little. "Excuse me, but who are you?"

"Uh… it's got a dent in the hood," Johnny added. "I fell on it. From a roof."

It sounded like an interesting story. But Carver didn't have time. He pointed at the remaining vehicle. "Whose car is that?"

"Mine," the other guy said.

"I have to take it from you," Carver told him. "I'm sorry. Please hand me the keys."

The guy scoffed. "Seriously? At least that lady had a gun. You don't have anything. Get out of here before we call the cops."

Carver looked around. And listened. He then smiled. "None of you have a phone, do you? If you did, you would have called them already. And since I know they're already in the area, they would have been here by now."

"So?" the guy with the car grunted.

Carver stepped around the fire.

He didn't do much. Just picked the guy up off the ground and stared at him. He had the keys in his hands less than five seconds later.

He thanked the campers, apologized again, and drove off.

EIGHTY-SEVEN

Before meeting Naomi, Carver had never stolen a car. Now he was at two. The most recent one was a generic hatchback, but it had a pretty good engine. It had no problem pulling him through the windswept grass, away from the campsite.

He glanced in the rearview mirror once. Watching as the glow of the fire faded. He no longer felt bad. This was what had to happen. The four campers would be fine. They could spend the night in their tents. Walk back to civilization in the morning.

There were faint tire tracks in the grass, left over from the campers' journey out to the site earlier. Carver followed them. They soon curved to the west, and joined up with a narrow dirt road.

A sign flashed by. Some kind of placard about local wildlife. Just past this was a small parking area, jutting off of the road. There were no cars there. Certainly no red Fords.

But Carver knew he was on the right track. Naomi had been through here just a little while ago.

And she had a new phone, stolen from one of the campers. With it, she could make contact with her secret helper. Formulate a plan. Organize a rendezvous.

Carver was now in the dark. Whatever information existed on her old phone was outdated. It was no longer worth the risk to carry it around. He rolled the window down and chucked the phone out.

Cold air flowed in. He let it come, welcoming it. Not because it was pleasant, but because it kept him alert. Despite the anger and adrenaline, he was getting tired. The nap inside the RV hadn't been enough to recharge his batteries. Not nearly.

If he felt this rough, he could imagine how haggard Naomi must be. She was an office worker. She wasn't used to this kind of tension. She was running on her last fumes.

He didn't think she would stop. She was too smart for that. But chances were high she would make a mistake. He had to hope she would.

It was now his only chance of catching up with her.

But should he even be trying? There was no practical reason for him to chase her. The logical thing would be to make his own run for it, to get out of Nebraska and disappear.

But she had betrayed him. Tricked him. He had to know why. He had to know if it was worth it—and whether she was lying about more than her supposed trust.

There were lights up ahead. A thin scattering. He soon reached the main road. Highway 96. He stopped just before driving onto it. He killed the engine and the headlights. He sat, listening to the wind.

Thinking.

A big wooden sign to the right declared the name of the Calamus Reservoir, a state recreation area. It was all around him. Through some trees to his right, he spotted some RVs. Saw people walking about in their campsites, laughing. Fetching beers and hotdogs from coolers.

He turned the engine back on, nudged the car onto the road.

If he turned left, he'd be on his way back to Burwell.

If he went right, he would be heading north. The way Naomi was going. It had to be. She wouldn't be heading back to the scene of the crime. It was all about getting to the nearest border, and that was still South Dakota.

Whether or not he tried to pursue her, going north was also in Carver's best interest. He was unlikely to catch her now. With any luck, she'd disappear into thin air. Never to be seen again.

Carver turned right and kept going.

EIGHTY-EIGHT

An hour had gone by, and Gibbs was getting scared.

No. That wasn't right. He'd been scared since the beginning. Now he was completely terrified. He was handcuffed in the back of a strange car, outside a barn where a top-secret briefing had just been delivered by the VP himself.

He was in some major hot water right now. Deep in the hole. And he was only starting to realize it now. He had plenty of time to think. The two guards didn't come back to check on him. Everything was quiet. The choppers were long gone.

And so was Sanders, if she remotely knew what was good for her.

Gibbs had tried to grab his phone. The last he knew, it was in his left pocket. But the guards had snaked it from him without him realizing it.

He was alone, isolated, and probably not too far from oblivion. The more he thought about it, the more certain he became that death was around the corner. These people were above the law. They could do what they wanted. They had no idea what Gibbs had seen or heard.

It would be easy to simply make him disappear. If he was lucky, that would entail a quick death. A bullet to the back of the head.

But maybe they'd take a different route. Drop him into a deep, dark prison cell. Somewhere off the grid, where no one would ever find him.

"Oh, man," Gibbs groaned.

He missed when the thought of losing his job was his biggest problem.

His bravado was long gone. The only thing left was the sick realization that he'd been a complete idiot. He never should have gone after Carver and Naomi like this. He should have listened to Colonel Bell back in Burwell, and returned to his post.

A long line of bad decisions had led him to this point. He could have stepped away at any time. Saved himself. But he didn't.

Maybe he could still get away.

He tugged at the cuff. It was attached to a handle on the door. Just a bar to grab onto when you were pulling the door shut. It was plastic on the outside, but he imagined the structure within was something sturdier.

It was unlikely he'd ever be able to break it. But he had to try.

He crawled across the backseat as far as he could go until the chain was taut. Then he started to pull as hard as he could, straining with all his might. He kept it up for ten or fifteen seconds. He stopped right before he passed out, catching his breath.

He slid over to check the handle. He had succeeded in scuffing the plastic a little, but nothing else.

"Carver could probably break it," he sighed. "I should never have canceled that gym membership."

An idea occurred.

If he could get outside, onto his feet, he'd have much more leverage.

Enough to break the handle? There was only one way to find out.

Ducking his head, he peeked through the windshield. He didn't see the guards. They were probably back inside the barn, a good distance away. As long as he was quiet, they'd have no idea what he was doing.

With his free hand, he popped the door open. Moving with it, he got one foot out on the ground.

Then one of the guards was magically at his side, shoving him back in.

"What do you think you're doing?" the guy grunted.

"Just getting some fresh air," Gibbs said.

"Yeah, right. Just sit back there and don't mess around. You're in enough trouble."

Gibbs winced. "Look, I don't know what's going on here, but I'm a state cop. You should let me go."

"Not up to me," the guard replied.

"Who is it up to?"

"You'll find out for yourself."

"Any idea what's going to happen to me?" Gibbs asked.

For the first time, the guard's expression softened. "I don't know. But it probably isn't gonna be pretty."

He slammed the door shut and walked away, leaving Gibbs to contemplate his words.

"This is it," he said in disbelief. "It's over. I'm done for."

He had to accept it. There was nothing else to do. This was the darkest moment of his life. He could at least face it with some kind of dignity.

The inside of the car suddenly lit up like the Fourth of July.

He turned, squinting through the back window, and saw several sets of flashing lights flying toward him.

Police cars.

EIGHTY-NINE

"What in the world?" Gibbs muttered.

Four state police cruisers swung onto the property. They screeched to a halt, throwing up clouds of dust, fanning out to either side.

Straight down the middle came a civilian car, a teal minivan. The car Gibbs had rented back in Burwell. It came to a stop as well. More clumsily, almost fishtailing into a fence.

The doors of all five cars popped open. Ten cops flooded out of them, including Sanders.

The guards reacted immediately. They appeared at the front of a car closer to the barn. They each fell to one knee on either side of the front bumper. They tilted their SMGs sideways, aiming over the hood.

Nine of the state troopers fell into position. They stood behind their open doors, resting the barrels of their handguns on top. Most had the standard Glocks, but Gibbs saw a couple of .357 magnums as well. He couldn't help but holler out, pumping his fist inside the car.

"Surrender now!" one of the troopers yelled. "We have you outnumbered!"

He was answered by a few submachine bullets that smashed into the door he was hiding behind. The glass shattered. Holes were ripped in the metal. The cop ducked down. A second later, Gibbs saw him scrambling toward the back of his car.

His partner on the other side opened fire, sending a full clip toward the guards. They shrank back, putting their heads down.

While they were suppressed, Sanders made her move. Staying low, she dashed toward Gibbs. Yanking open the back door on the other side of the car. She tossed herself in, spilling over the backseat.

"Here!" she cried, handing him a handcuff key.

Gibbs stuck the key into his handcuff. It went in less than a quarter inch. He yanked at the cuff, but nothing happened.

"Not working!" Gibbs shouted back.

"Dang." Sanders blew out her cheeks, which were red from exertion. "I guess we'll need to get the key off one of—"

Her next word was drowned out by the sound of the windshield shattering. Gibbs heard something whistling past his ear, like a supersonic insect. Then the rear window exploded as well, showering him in chunks of glass.

"Dagnabbit!" he screamed.

Sanders gave him a funny look. Probably from his choice of words. Then the reality of what had just happened sunk in. She screamed in fear and wormed her way out of the car.

"We're catching strays over here!" she yelled.

While a handful of troopers kept the guards pinned down, two more ran up to assist Sanders. The three of them pushed forward, making it ten feet closer to the barn. Then the guards jumped back up, sending a fan of bullets their way.

The guy on Sanders' right took one in the shoulder. Blood sprayed. The force spun him around. Sent him to his hands and knees. Sanders turned back to help him.

That was when the guards decided to push.

They came out spraying wildly, counting on all the troopers to duck and cover.

It didn't happen. Instead, the police also pushed. Rushing to help Sanders and their fallen friend. And they had superior numbers.

While the submachine guns fired haphazardly, the pistol shots were deliberate. And accurate. The guards went down, one after the other.

Silence fell. Gunsmoke was thick in the air, but quickly lifted. Blown away by the cold wind.

"What in the name of God," Gibbs said in awe.

Someone outside called, "I'm hit!"

"Where at?" another cop asked.

"Leg!"

"Is it bad?"

"I don't think so. I'll be all right."

"Let's get medics out here ASAP!"

Gibbs opened the door. He stepped outside, standing awkwardly due to the handcuff chain. He stared around in a daze. Then Sanders appeared. Smiling, she unlocked his cuff, freeing him.

"Found the key," she said.

"What just happened?" Gibbs asked.

"What happened is I watched you get nabbed," she answered. "Then I went for help. Didn't take too long to rustle up a little posse. As soon as they heard one of their own was being held against their will, they were game."

Gibbs pointed to the cop who'd been hit in the shoulder. "Is he gonna be okay?"

"After some stitches and some R and R, sure," Sanders told him.

"We got lucky," Gibbs sighed.

She just winked. And he knew what that meant. Luck had nothing to do with it.

Another patrolman came running up. "Trooper Gibbs! Glad to see you alive. What exactly is going on here?"

Gibbs grimaced. "If I told you, you might regret coming to save me."

"Huh? Sanders, I'm going to give Colonel Bell a call."

"No!" she and Gibbs snapped in unison.

"Why? What's the problem?" the trooper demanded.

"Those guys you shot were working for him," Gibbs answered. "Or he was working with them. Or for the same guy they were working for. Whatever, it's a whole mess."

"So, you don't have any answers?"

"Not as many as I'd like." Gibbs gestured to the barn. "But we'll probably find some in there. We should be quick about it, though."

NINETY

96 soon merged with Highway 183. Carver jumped on and followed it north. He kept his eyes open. Prairie grass rippled in the wind, lit by dim moonlight. There were no other cars. No lights to speak of.

The posted speed limit was 65. Carver got as high as eighty, pushing his luck. But not by much. There was no one around.

He saw a sign for a place called Rose. Nothing seemed to change. There were a few extra trees on either side of the road. Then he was past it, back into the middle of emptiness.

For a while, the road seemed to be headed nowhere. No cities. No towns. No podunk gas stops. And no offshoots. He felt certain he was on the right path. All he had to do was look forward.

Maybe he'd see her taillights, fading red into the night. She would look back, see a car pursuing her. She would know the fear that people always felt when Carver almost had them.

He did see lights eventually. But they were from the town of Bassett. It was much smaller than Burwell. He drove through it slowly, scanning all the houses with wide eyes. Checking driveways. Side streets. Back alleys.

He didn't see a red Ford sedan. It was possible Naomi had hidden it somewhere and she was now lying low in Bassett, but it was unlikely. They were close enough to the border that she would have pressed on.

Carver didn't waste much more time. As soon as he was past most of the houses, he sped back up. Approaching ninety as he left the town behind.

He gave the town a final look in the rearview mirror. That was when he saw the flashing lights.

They came racing out of Bassett. Surging up behind him. He was going almost ninety. They must be well past a hundred.

There was a slim chance they were after someone besides him. But those odds died when the cars slowed down, closing in around him like a clamshell.

Carver cursed, reflecting on his own bad decisions. Back at the campsite, he had assumed none of the drunkards had a functioning phone. But he hadn't taken the time to verify his theory.

One of them must have called.

Or maybe some cops searching the abandoned RV had found the campers afterward, and heard about the stolen car in person.

Either way, Carver was on their radar.

The road was straight as an arrow. And flat as a pancake. Out here, farms lined either side of it. Fenced off. There was nowhere to go. And he doubted the little hatchback could outpace the police cars.

He was unarmed. Alone.

But he knew there had to be a way out. There always was.

The cruisers were keeping their distance on the two-lane road. They must have heard about his previous antics. They were trying to prevent themselves from being rammed.

There were wide gaps between them, including one almost straight ahead of Carver. Not wide enough to fit the car through. Not unless he wedged it through, shoving his pursuers out of the way.

As Carver pondered the chances of success, something else was happening.

The passenger side window of one of the patrol cars rolled down. The man inside leaned out a little, holding a megaphone to his mouth.

"Ronan Carver!" his voice boomed. "We know you're alone! We know none of this is your fault!"

NINETY-ONE

Carver almost laughed. They were pulling cheap tricks, trying to get him to turn himself in so they could lock him up for life. They thought he was dumb. Weak-minded.

Apparently, they hadn't done much research.

He ignored the guy with the megaphone. He saw something up ahead. An opportunity.

There was a car coming down the road from the north. It was about a mile away. They'd be on it in no time. The troopers would have to dodge.

Carver would have his way out.

"Ronan Carver!" the amplified voice came again. "Pull over! We'd like to talk! Peacefully!"

This time, he laughed out loud. He wasn't going to pull over. In about thirty seconds, the car would be here. He'd snake his way through the whole mess. Come out the other side, clean as a whistle.

For a moment, he'd be safe.

After that, he had no idea what would happen.

Or maybe he did. It was almost inevitable, after all. This car couldn't compete with the souped-up cruisers. He could try and go off-roading again, but they'd still catch him. He would have to go on foot again. Or steal a different car.

If he made it long enough.

Carver wasn't one to give up. But there was a difference between throwing in the towel and accepting defeat.

Fifteen seconds before they reached the other car. It had stopped driving, parking itself along the shoulder. Trying to stay out of the way. But the road was narrow. Farm fences on both sides. The police cars would still have to change positions to prevent a crash.

Carver licked his lips and adjusted his sweaty grip on the wheel.

Am I really going to do this?

"Ronan Carver!" the cop with the megaphone bellowed. "Colonel Bell wants to speak with you and make a deal!"

Colonel Bell. The man who held the highest position in the Nebraska State Patrol. If anyone was able to make a deal, it would be him.

They reached the parked car.

The police cruisers reacted. Hitting the brakes and backing off. They fell in behind Carver, nearly crashing into one another. They were forced to come to a complete stop.

Carver kept going.

He watched in the mirror as the flashing lights fell further and further back.

Then he pumped the brakes, carefully, bringing the stolen car to a gentle stop. He didn't want to damage it. It wasn't his. He'd perpetrated enough destruction over the past couple of days.

All to help Naomi Downes. A liar. A traitor.

Maybe she hadn't told the truth about anything. Maybe, all this time, Senator Unger was the good guy.

It was time to find out, one way or another.

He unbuckled his seatbelt and got out of the car. Holding his hands in the air. The cops were already on their way again. They arrived a few seconds later. Jumping out onto the road. Running toward him.

"I need answers," Carver said to one of them.

"Maybe that'll be part of the deal," the cop said. "Give me your hands."

They were kind enough to cuff his hands in front of him, but not before one cop had slapped a couple of large band aids on his cut wrist.

Carver let them drag him to a car and shove him in the backseat.

NINETY-TWO

The Rock County Sheriff's Office was located on a dusty patch of land in the middle of Bassett. It was surrounded by houses and trees. Carver sniffed the night air as he was led across the parking lot, savoring what might be his last taste of freedom.

For a little while, anyway.

"Thank you, gentlemen," he said.

"For what?" Officer Stenberg grunted.

"For parking so far from the building. The air feels nice."

"You're a weird guy," Stenberg replied.

"Do you think I got into this situation by being normal?" Carver shot back.

Everyone laughed at that.

"Ah, man, you're so lucky," Stenberg said. "You've been a real pain in the butt for us. But you haven't hurt any cops. Not too badly, anyway. Maybe we can all forgive and forget."

"It's not up to any of us," Carver reminded him.

"Yeah, I guess not. But anyway… Thank you for your service."

Carver gave him a nod. "And for yours."

***

Officer Stenberg was with him all the way into the station. They finally parted ways once Carver was secured inside an interrogation room.

"He'll be with you shortly," Stenberg promised as he left the room.

By *he*, Carver figured he meant Colonel Bell. He hoped so. Otherwise, this was a big waste of time. And he'd have to find a way to break out. He hoped it wouldn't come to that. He was a little tired.

It was about twenty minutes before the door opened back up. A man came in. The first thing Carver noticed about him was the two cups of coffee he held. The second was the impressive display of commendations on his shirt.

The third was the name tag. COL. PAUL BELL. He was a man of average height and above-average chin size. His eyes were tiny and black in a large, craggy face. Giving him the look of some kind of clay golem.

"Ronan Carver!" he announced like he was greeting an old friend. "How the heck are ya?"

Carver shrugged. "I'll take my coffee now."

"You think this is for you?" Bell chuckled, holding up one of the cups.

"It had better be," said Carver.

"Or?"

"Or we're done here."

Bell's grin widened. "You think you're in a position to make demands?"

"I'm here because I want to be," Carver told him. "I could be somewhere else an hour from now. Who knows?"

Bell slammed the door shut with his foot. "Is that a threat of some kind?"

"I just want you to understand what's going on here," said Carver. "I'd like to be peaceable. Some coffee would help."

Bell sat down. He took a sip from one of the cups, set the other in front of Carver.

"Drink it quick," he advised. "We won't be here for long."

Carver drank some coffee. It was too hot. He blew on it.

"What do you want to talk about?" he then asked.

Bell smirked. "Despite your arrogance, I'm glad you saw reason, Mr. Carver. I guess it was only a matter of time. You're a very intelligent man, on top of your numerous other assets. I think you deserve to know the truth about who you've been associating with."

"I'm glad we agree," said Carver. He drank more coffee. "What can you tell me?"

"I won't tell you anything, really," Bell replied. "But I'll take you somewhere and show you the truth."

"That works for me."

Bell raised his cup in a toast. They drained their cups simultaneously.

Then Bell stood up. He opened the door and leaned into the hall. "Let's get him out of here!"

NINETY-THREE

Bell stepped out of the room. Three burly men with bushy beards replaced him. Carver recognized them right away, not by name or by face, but by profession. Mercenaries. Former Navy SEALs, maybe. Like him.

"Get up, princess," one of them snorted.

Definitely SEALs. Carver stood, sizing them up. They were intimidating guys. He thought he could take them on one at a time. But all three together? Probably not.

Good thing he didn't have to.

The mercs led him back out of the station. Bell led the way. Other than the colonel, there was no more state police presence. They were outside of that domain now, onto something more serious. And more secretive.

Two choppers were parked in the lot behind the station. A few more muscle-bound guys in tactical vests stood outside one of them. At the sight of Carver, they hopped back in. The rotors on both helicopters spun up.

Carver was brought to the other chopper. He climbed aboard, sandwiched amidst the three mercs from the station. Colonel Bell joined them. They clipped themselves into their jump seats and waited.

Bell gave Carver the thumbs up. Carver just stared at him until he looked away.

The rotors whined overhead. The engine rumbled. The volume inside the copter grew to a nearly deafening level.

"Hey there!" a voice shouted to Carver's right.

He looked into the sun-damaged face of a red-haired mercenary. "What do you want?"

"Just wanted to say!" the merc yelled. "I know about you! All the stuff you've done. Boo-yah!"

He held up a fist. Carver bumped his own fist into it. They nodded at each other. Carver resisted the urge to do something else with his fist. He was starting to get into a bad mood. The coffee hadn't done much to wake him up.

Neither did the chopper ride.

Colonel Bell grinned like an idiot the whole time. It was apparently still a novel concept to him. But Carver had been on plenty of more exciting rides. He had slept through most of them. He was tempted to do the same here.

But he didn't want to miss anything.

The two choppers headed north, separated by a couple of hundred feet. Along the way, they were joined by three others. Presumably packed to the gills with more dangerous men.

Soon, they were well beyond civilization. Flying over a black nothingness. Occasionally punctuated by lights from scattered farms.

The buildings got a little denser as they approached the border. But the brightest property by far was a farm lit up with a dozen floodlights. The helicopter started to descend, letting Carver know that the farm was their destination.

Something was wrong, though. The place was full of cops. Their lights flashed. They swarmed everywhere. As soon as Bell saw this, his face fell. He jumped out of his seat. Stumbled into the cockpit and yelled something at the pilot.

He got back in his seat quickly. The choppers began an aggressive descent, plummeting toward the ground behind a huge barn.

NINETY-FOUR

"Hey, Gibbs," Sanders said. "How's it going in here?"

She had been outside for the past few minutes, securing the area with their comrades. Now she was in the barn, watching her partner expectantly.

It wasn't going well. Gibbs wasn't good with computers. He knew how to send an email. Or play solitaire. That was about it. And these weren't regular computers. They had security. Passwords that needed to be entered.

"Not good," he sighed. "I don't think we'll be able to crack these things."

"Then we should think about getting out of here," Sanders urged. "Before they come back."

Gibbs nodded. Sanders was right, as usual. They wouldn't be able to fight a whole army of mercs. Best to leave this place behind. Call it a stalemate. It was unlikely anything would come of this now. To punish Gibbs and his compatriots, Unger and Lamay would have to admit to what was going on here.

And that was unlikely.

Gibbs reluctantly turned away from the screens. "How are the guys doing outside?"

"Just fine," said Sanders. "Someone had a first aid kit in their car, so wounds have been tended. We didn't find any other guards. But we're a bit antsy to go home."

Gibbs was just about ready. He gave the computers a longing gaze. The truth could be hidden inside. Something he wasn't supposed to know. But that made him want to know it even more.

He became aware of a humming sound. It seemed like the fans in the computers were spinning up. Like the machines were overheating.

It kept getting louder.

And closer.

Gibbs and Sanders realized the truth of the sound at the same time. They ran outside, just in time for a few other troopers to stumble into the barn. Scared looks on their faces.

"Choppers inbound!" one of them yelled.

Gibbs got outside first. He ran away from the barn, past the parked cars, all the way to the road, where he could get the clearest view.

He could see the lights. A cluster of them in the southern sky. Five sets, at least. Five copters. They were coming fast, sweeping low as they prepared for landing.

By the time Gibbs sprinted back to the barn, he already felt the wind from the rotors blasting down on him.

The choppers drifted over the barn, falling toward the ground beyond it.

"We gotta go!" Gibbs screamed, gesturing wildly at Sanders.

She came to meet him. Searching her pockets for the keys to the rental car. She couldn't seem to find them. They must have fallen out during the shootout, Gibbs figured.

Not that it mattered. The helicopter sounds died rapidly. Everything fell into an eerie quiet.

"What do we do?" someone asked. "Run?"

"Too late for that," Gibbs announced. "You all just keep calm. Let me do the talking."

"You sure?" Sanders asked.

Gibbs smiled. "If I'm the only one who opens my mouth, they'll figure I was responsible for the whole thing. I'll say you all were assisting an officer in distress. Which is true. You were just doing your jobs."

The other cops nodded appreciatively. But Sanders didn't look so sure. She was about to make a complaint. Gibbs didn't give her the chance. He left the barn, stepping around the corner to meet whatever was coming.

Among a small army of mercenaries, he saw four familiar faces.

Colonel Bell, looking as insect-like as ever.

Senator Morgan Unger. His clean-cut facade was starting to show some cracks. His quaffed hair was in disarray. His clothes were wrinkled. His face was pale. But he smiled nonetheless.

Vice President Lamay was as calm and regal as before.

And then there was Ronan Carver. The big man had seen better days. He was filthy, especially his shoes. His hands were cuffed in front of him. He seemed to be a defeated man. At least until you looked into his eyes.

Then you realized something about the guy. Even now, he was in control. Or thought he was. Gibbs almost felt bad for the former Navy SEAL. He had lost, but he wasn't willing to accept it.

Same here, pal, Gibbs thought.

"Fancy seeing you here, Trooper Gibbs," Colonel Bell called. "Last time I saw you, I was giving you a direct order to return to your station. You want to tell me what you're doing all the way out here?"

NINETY-FIVE

Everything was quiet.

Gibbs stared at Colonel Bell. He tried to speak. No sound came from his mouth. If there was a good answer, something that would get him out of trouble, he'd never find it. He was marooned. Nowhere to go.

"We're just passing through, sir," Sanders answered for him.

Bell smirked. "I wasn't talking to you. I know you aren't responsible for this mess, Trooper Sanders. Only one person on the force is stupid enough to have gotten involved in government business."

All eyes turned to Gibbs. Even the eyes of VP Lamay. It was a terrible feeling. Gibbs prayed that he'd burst into flames, fall into a sinkhole, or just cease to exist.

There was no way out.

So he might as well go further in.

Gibbs made himself smile. "Yeah, it was my idea. Dumb old Gibbs. Sanders was just saving my skin. Being a good cop. Same with the others. But I managed to find this place, and I'm ready to help."

Bell looked at Unger. Both men stifled laughter.

Lamay gave Gibbs an appraising look. He seemed both impressed and pitying.

"Help?" Bell grunted. "You've disobeyed several direct orders from me already. And you've put the lives of your fellow state troopers at risk for no good reason. You can help by handing over your badge."

On cue, a couple dozen mercs marched up behind Colonel Bell. They swept in, disarming the cops.

Gibbs licked his lips. "Colonel Bell…"

Bell raised an eyebrow. Stared at him.

Gibbs went on. "You're the one who's in the wrong here. I know something fishy's going on. All I want is the truth."

Bell looked enraged. He stepped forward. Senator Unger put out an arm, blocking him.

"You're a man with an overblown sense of worth, Trooper Gibbs," Unger said. "You have no leverage here. Do you understand? Or do I need to remind you who you're speaking to?"

"I'm speaking to an elected official who only has power because people like me give it to him," Gibbs shot back. "My taxes pay your salary, Senator. Maybe you should give me some respect."

There were some stunned looks. Except for Carver. The big man just smiled to himself and looked up at the sky, like he had nothing better to do than stargaze.

Unger recovered quickly. He laughed and shook his head. Turning to one of the mercenaries, he gave his orders. "Keep them out here until we decide what to do next."

Then he gestured at Carver. Two of the mercs grabbed the big man by either arm, pulling him toward the barn. The senator followed, along with Bell and Lamay.

NINETY-SIX

Carver kept playing along. He walked between two guys who probably benched four hundred apiece. They had beards and battle scars, a couple of tough hombres.

He looked down at his cuffs, still smiling. Then he glanced over his shoulder. Saw three important men following behind. Past them, Trooper Gibbs stared with a dumb look on his face.

Carver felt bad for the guy. He also felt a new sense of respect. The state cop fit the definition of the word *bumbling*. But he was here. He was acting fearless, even though his pale face and pit stains told a different story.

He didn't think Gibbs was going to make it. If the guy was lucky, he'd lose his job, along with the ability to work in any kind of law enforcement again. But Carver wouldn't be surprised if it went further than that.

When you messed with the bull, you got the horns. Unless you were quick enough to dance out of the way. Or ruthless enough to stab that bull right in the throat.

Gibbs didn't seem to fit in either camp. He had no weapon and no leg to stand on. He was lucky to still be breathing.

The bearded mercs pushed Carver into the barn and stepped away. He looked around. Saw a bunch of chairs. A stage. Some laptops and monitors off to the side. A hastily rigged field headquarters, of sorts.

"Very quaint," Carver said. "You boys planning on having some kind of *hootenanny* out here?"

"Where I'm from," VP Lamay replied, "we call it a *hoedown*. But no. That's not what all this is for. We simply needed a secure site near the border from which to launch our final attempt at capturing Naomi Downes. One of the men we've hired happens to own this property."

Carver jerked his head to the side. "What are the computers for?"

"We've been using them for communication and planning. But they only have one real purpose," Unger explained. "You."

Carver stared at the senator. "Me?"

"Yes. You. As soon as we identified you as Naomi's accomplice, we figured we were sunk. No way we'd catch a guy with your set of skills," Unger chuckled.

"Well, you caught me," Carver replied.

"You let yourself be caught," Unger said. "You saw reason. That was the first step in our plan. We wanted to appeal to your logic. It never would have worked if Naomi hadn't ditched you."

"No, it wouldn't have," Carver grumbled. "Keep talking. I don't have all night."

Unger laughed again, cocking a finger pistol at Carver. "Good one. You're a clever man, Mr. Carver. And we knew you'd always doubt us unless you had concrete proof. On those computers is a copy of everything Naomi stole from us."

"From you," Lamay reminded him.

"Yeah, well…" Unger cleared his throat. Wiping lint off his coat.

Carver stared at the computers. They were twenty feet away. The monitors were stuck on lock screens, showing a prompt to enter a username and password.

"What did she steal?" Carver asked.

"Something the enemies of our country would pay top dollar for," said Unger.

"Just tell him," Lamay broke in.

"Fine. Naomi stole a huge chunk of information. Fake names and identities. Locations and mission parameters. The identities of thousands of American covert operatives across the planet. If you were still serving, Mr. Carver, you would probably be in there, too."

Carver felt his heart skip a beat. All at once, everything caught up to him. He stumbled over to the rows of chairs and sat down. His handcuff chain rattled against the seat.

NINETY-SEVEN

"If this information gets into the wrong hands," Unger went on, "things will happen. I don't need to explain to you the kind of damage this could do. The amount of lives that could be lost. The important missions that could be destroyed."

Carver shook his head.

Unger came over. Sat in the chair just ahead of Carver, facing backward. He spoke softly.

"We believe her contact is a foreign intelligence officer. Possibly a mole who has been working in the USA for years, looking for a good reason to come in from the cold. The kind of person who knows what to do with information like this. And who to take it to."

"We can't let her get away," Carver said.

Unger gave him a sad smile. "There's no 'we' in this, Mr. Carver. You've already helped us enough by getting out of the way. We can capture Naomi on our own. Would you like to see what's on the computers?"

Carver swallowed his anger. He looked over at the monitors. "No. I don't need to see it."

"Good!" Unger stood up fast, nearly knocking the chair into Carver's knees. "We can save some time, then. If you would follow me…"

Carver got to his feet. Followed Unger and the others back outside.

Bell approached. Leaning close to Carver's ear, he talked quietly.

"You deserved to know the truth," he said. "It was the least we could do, given your stellar service record. Consider it a final honor rather than an act of forgiveness."

"I understand," Carver answered. "Where am I being taken to?"

"We'll put you on a chopper," said Bell. "You'll be taken back to the station in Bassett and held until this business with Naomi is wrapped up. Then we'll figure out what to do with you."

As they passed the disarmed state cops, Carver gestured to them. "What about them?"

"Gibbs is going with you. The others… that's up to me. And I'm inclined to let them go. They're not guilty of anything, as far as I can tell."

Carver nodded. He didn't really care what the Colonel had to say about anything now. The guy kept talking, but Carver tuned him out. He looked up at the stars again. The weather was clear. The air was cold but windless.

It was a fine night for flying, even if it would be a short ride. He had to wonder what would happen to him after his stay at the station.

Nothing good, he was sure.

NINETY-EIGHT

"Get in," a gruff mercenary barked.

Carver climbed into the helicopter. He fell into a seat. He planted his feet, corkscrewing them into the floor. The same thing a powerlifter did before performing a bench press. Stability and power, tightening up every muscle in the body.

It helped keep you balanced when you were in a chopper, flying and darting all over the place. He wasn't planning on staying in this particular seat. In fact, he'd probably be out of it before the chopper even took off. But it was good to be prepared for everything.

He sat and watched as the rest of the mercenaries flooded into the other helicopters. They took off one by one, moving across the night sky in formation, leaving Carver's chopper alone on the ground.

Across from him, a guy with a long beard and an angry face sat, staring. Carver met his eyes, and stared back. He was curious who would look away first.

"How you doin', sweetie pie?" the merc asked.

"I'll be better in a few minutes," Carver replied.

"Yeah? How's that?"

Carver smiled. "Nothing you need to worry about."

The merc burst out laughing. "You're real cocky, huh? I'd like to see you try something. I know guys like you. All talk. You won't do anything."

"What if I did?" Carver asked.

"I'd put you on your backside double-quick," the guy said. "Give you a nice slice of humble pie. I think you could use one. Maybe, I'll add a little whipped cream for ya. How's that sound?"

"I prefer pumpkin," said Carver. "But I'll take the whipped cream. Thanks."

"Room for one more?" another gravelly voice rang out.

Carver looked. A second mercenary hopped aboard the chopper, dragging Trooper Gibbs along. The cop looked depressed. He wasn't even cuffed. The fight was gone from him, and everyone knew it.

Gibbs was plunked down in the seat beside Carver. The two armed men sat across from them, keeping watch. Not very carefully, though. They kept looking at their phones. Chatting. Joking around.

The rotors began to spin. A steady *thwup-thwup-thwup* that grew in pitch and frequency. Carver waited, tuned into the sounds of the helicopter.

It lifted off the ground, going straight up at first and then turning slowly. Carver watched the two grunts the whole time. Neither of them had any kind of reaction. They looked bored. This wasn't new to them. Just another day at the office.

They did not believe anything could go wrong. It was an easy assignment: deliver two unarmed men to a nearby police station. One of them cuffed, the other completely demoralized. No big deal.

They weren't paying attention. Why should they be?

The chopper started moving, leaning forward. The tilt caused Carver's weight to strain forward. That was good. It meant he'd be able to get across the passenger cabin faster.

He pushed against the floor with his feet, lifting his rear off the seat slightly. Giving him a better angle. He snaked the middle finger of his left hand into his pants pocket, found the bobby pin he'd taken from the RV.

The chopper was filled with noise. Dimly lit by a red glow that created deep shadows. No one noticed when Carver slipped the bobby pin into the lock on his cuffs.

NINETY-NINE

Carver worked the bobby pin around, holding his hands between his thighs to conceal his work. Meanwhile, his face was a mask of hopelessness. He tried to look as depressed as Gibbs. By the way the mercs grinned when they looked at him, he was succeeding.

He felt a click. A release of tension. One wrist was free of the handcuffs. He went to work on the other. It took another minute. Precious time was wasting away.

The helicopter was heading south. The opposite direction he wanted to go.

As soon as both hands were free, he dropped the bobby pin. Then he lunged out of his seat.

Only six feet separated him from the armed guards. Tight quarters. Both men held assault rifles, too large and unwieldy for such a small space. Neither of them had time to aim before Carver was on them.

First, he went for the guy who'd offered him a slice of humble pie. He saw fear in the man's eyes, but it only lasted for a second. Then Carver's knees slammed into his chin, knocking his skull against the steel bulkhead behind him.

He ripped the gun from the merc's limp hands. In the same motion, he twisted and stepped to his right. Used the butt of the gun to clobber the other guard in the side of the head. His lights went out. He slumped in his seat.

Carver fell into a crouch, ducking to one side. He peeked through into the cockpit. The pilot and copilot were oblivious. They stared forward, calmly flying.

Neither of the two unconscious mercs had secured themselves in their seat. The next time the helicopter took any kind of turn, they would slide out into the night, and plummet a few hundred feet to the ground.

Carver cursed to himself. More time was about to be wasted. But it had to be done. One by one, he pushed the men back into their seats and clicked their harnesses into place.

Then he grabbed both rifles and turned to Gibbs.

The trooper was watching with wide eyes. As soon as Carver looked at him, he started shaking his head. He looked scared.

Carver rushed to his side. He pushed a gun into Gibbs's hands. Leaned close to speak to him.

"Watch my back."

Gibbs nodded. He still looked unsure. Carver figured he needed a moment to collect himself. That was fine. Their two guards wouldn't be a problem for a while.

With the other assault rifle in his hands, Carver marched forward into the cockpit. He tapped the copilot on the shoulder. The guy looked around, annoyed at first, then terrified when he saw the gun barrel aimed at his face.

The pilot noticed something was wrong and also looked over. His eyes went wide. But he was a professional. He immediately looked back at his instrument panel—and also at the radio handset that was wired into it.

Carver leaned over, ripping the handset out and tossing it away.

"Land!" he shouted. "Right now!"

The pilot nodded. He gave his copilot a reassuring pat on the arm and brought the chopper toward the ground. Touching down lightly in a grassy field.

"Do you want me to kill the engine?" the pilot called back.

"No," Carver told him. "Get out."

The two men nodded. They undid their harnesses and stood up. Carver reversed into the passenger cabin, letting them walk toward him.

"Get those two!" Carver commanded, gesturing to the unconscious mercs.

His orders were followed. The guards were removed from their harnesses. Lifted carefully out into the field. Carver waited until all four men were at a safe distance. Then he fired a warning shot, making them go faster.

Carver ran back into the cockpit. Ready to head north.

ONE-HUNDRED

Carver fell into the pilot's seat. He quickly buckled himself in, scanning the controls at the same time. The stick. The throttle. The pedals. He didn't know this exact model of helicopter, but the basics were the same.

Plus, the engine was already running. The rotors spun slowly. That took some of the work out of the equation.

Carver grabbed hold of the controls. Taking a deep breath, he throttled up the rotors and took off.

It was a shaky ride at first. The controls were finely tuned and sensitive. Every tiny movement of his hands resulted in a huge movement. There was no time to get the hang of things. He checked the compass on the instrument panel, angled the chopper north, and started moving.

He let his breath out and smiled. This was going well. Now he had to face his next problem. He wanted to find Naomi, put a stop to her plan, but he had no idea where she was going. All he had was a vague direction.

Or maybe there was something more.

He thought back to his conversations with her. The loose plans they'd formed. It had been in Burwell, right after they'd polished off the fried chicken from the grocery store.

A border crossing had been chosen. A remote road in the middle of nowhere, between Highway 11 and 281. At the time, Carver had figured it was their best bet. Their only chance at getting into South Dakota without being spotted.

Things hadn't changed in that regard.

Naomi might have settled on a different crossing point. But why would she? It would take her too far out of the way. A waste of precious time.

As far as she was concerned, she had already beaten Carver. She no longer needed to worry about him. And he was the only one who knew the plan.

Carver was certain she'd stick to the same country lane.

He kicked the helicopter into a higher gear, flying forward at near top speed.

He'd almost forgotten about Trooper Gibbs, until the man stumbled into the cockpit. Grabbing onto the copilot's seat, he hauled himself into it with great effort. Buckling the harness down over his chest.

"Two questions!" Gibbs shouted. "First of all, why the heck didn't I get out of this helicopter while it was still on the ground?"

"Your second question?" Carver replied.

"Can you fly this thing on your own?" Gibbs asked.

"What does it look like I'm doing?"

"Good." Gibbs used the sleeve of his jacket to mop his forehead. "Because I've got no idea what any of these buttons and sticks do."

"To answer your first question," Carver went on, "you're here for the same reason I am. You want to catch her."

Gibbs gave Carver a nauseated smile. "She made us all look pretty dumb, didn't she?"

Carver nodded. "She did. But we can turn it around on her. I know where she's going. She has a big head start on us. But we can go a lot faster than she can. I think we'll make it."

ONE-HUNDRED ONE

Naomi kneeled on the gravel at the side of the road. She held her stomach, pressing in on it with her arms. Trying to get this over with so she could get back to moving.

She looked both ways. She was in the middle of nowhere. But a set of headlights was approaching from the south. A tractor-trailer. The same one she'd just seen at a rest area a couple of miles back. It was here a bit sooner than she expected.

Come on! she urged herself.

Then it came up. Mostly bile. She spat a few times, trying to get the taste out of her mouth. She felt even worse than she had a minute ago, but at least the nausea was gone.

She stood up and waited by the shoulder of the road. Jumping up and down and waving a hand. She wasn't wearing the most visible clothing, but the semi-truck driver still spotted her.

It took him a few seconds to come to a stop, air brakes squealing and hydraulics hissing. She jogged along the road, duffle bag in hand, reaching the truck in time for the driver to lean over, popping the passenger door open.

"Hop on in!" the guy announced cheerfully.

Naomi sized him up. He looked like the typical truck driver. In his fifties. Out of shape and bearded. He was most likely harmless. And she couldn't afford to be picky.

"Thanks!" she replied, jumping into the seat and shutting the door. She set the duffle bag at her feet, and put her seatbelt on.

The truck rolled forward, gathering speed.

"You all right?" the driver asked.

"Yeah," Naomi said.

He gave her a curious glance. "The name's Lonnie, by the way."

"Thanks for the ride, Lonnie," she said.

"Don't mention it. Did you have some kind of car trouble?" he asked.

She hadn't, except for the fact the car she had been driving was stolen. She made sure the owner couldn't call the cops on her, but by now he must have found a way to report the incident. The car was hot. It had to be gotten rid of.

It was currently parked in some trees not far from the spot where the trucker had picked her up. It was low on gas, but undamaged. Best of all, it would take the police a day or two to find it. Maybe longer.

By then, she'd be on the other side of the world.

She looked around the truck. It was cozy. Personalized with knick-knacks and a fuzzy steering wheel cover. It was much more comfortable than her plan of hiding in a trunk, and it would get the job done.

A sneaky way of crossing the border.

"I don't have a car," Naomi said. "My whole life's kind of a mess right now. There's a guy who's mad at me. I need to get away."

"I hear ya on that," Lonnie sighed. "Part of the reason I took this job was to put some distance between me and… well, you don't need to hear my drama. Where do you want to go?"

"I have a friend who can meet me right past the South Dakota border," Naomi replied. "It's kind of a remote road, if you don't mind going out of your way."

ONE-HUNDRED TWO

Carver spotted a silver line cutting through the tapestry of night. It was a paved road. He dropped toward it. Saw the markings, the yellow dotted line in the middle.

"This must be 281," he said.

Gibbs had his phone out. Sanders had found it on one of the guys back at the barn and returned it to him. Gibbs clutched it tightly in one hand, while using the other to paw at the screen. His map was open.

"We're going too dang fast!" he cried out. "The GPS can't keep up! There we go. The little dot just jumped. Yeah, this is 281. What road are we looking for again?"

"487th Avenue," Carver answered.

"Sheesh, they've got a lot of avenues out here. Looks like that's a couple miles to our west."

Carver nodded. But he didn't turn. He kept following Highway 281, toward some far-off lights.

The chopper covered the distance in no time. Keeping high, Carver swept around the scene in a wide circle, leaning toward the side window to get a better look. He saw a half dozen police cars, a couple of SWAT vehicles, and, nearby, a parked chopper. One of the others from the barn.

"Roadblock," Carver said.

"I guess that would be the border," Gibbs grunted. "Not our crossing, though. Shouldn't we get out of here before they send that helicopter up after us?"

It was a legitimate concern. Especially, if the original pilot and copilot had found a way to alert their compatriots.

Carver eased the chopper out of its loop and faced slightly southwest. He took it slower now, flying out over the night.

The road he and Naomi had picked was less than two miles away.

She might have already gotten across, but the chance was low. She probably would have switched cars. Or caught a ride with someone else. The smart way to do it. But it was also the slower way.

No. She hadn't crossed yet. Carver knew it. He *felt* it. He was going to find her.

No matter who she was with or where she had gone.

ONE-HUNDRED THREE

"You sure this is where your friend said to meet him?" Lonnie asked. "Ain't nothing much out here."

Naomi looked through her window. The inside of the truck was dark. But the emptiness outside was even darker. All she could really see was her ghostly reflection.

They had just turned onto 487th Avenue. It was one of many dirt roads in a grid that cut through northern Nebraska's farm country. It was night. Winter was approaching. The area was as desolate and empty as it would ever get.

"This is where he told me to go," Naomi said. "His place is just off Highway 81."

"That don't make sense," Lonnie grunted. "This fellow might be yanking your chain, Miss. 81 is way out east of here. Unless you meant Highway 18. That's right over the border here."

"Yeah. That must be it," Naomi chuckled.

Her heart skipped a beat. She even had the map in her stolen duffel bag, and she was still getting details wrong. Flipping numbers. Highway 18 meant nothing to her plan. It was just a detail. Window dressing to sell her lies to guys like Lonnie. But it was still important. She couldn't afford to screw stuff up.

She took a breath and calmed down. Everything was fine. In just a little while, this would all be over. She just had to hold it together until then.

It wasn't easy. Getting things right. Forming plans and putting them into action. Certain people made it look like a breeze.

People like Ronan Carver.

Thinking about him made her stomach lurch again. Shame and guilt clawed their way up her gullet. She felt awful for what she'd done to Carver, after all the help he'd given her.

He's resourceful. He'll figure it out.

She had no doubt. Carver would survive this. He'd probably come out of it even better than she did. But that didn't make her feel much better. He'd go the rest of his life hating her.

Would he track her down? Chase her to the ends of the Earth?

Maybe. She could only hope so, because Unger surely would. And when he caught up, she'd like to have Ronan Carver at her back.

If he could ever find it in himself to help her again. It was unlikely. The man was too smart for that, even if he did have a soft spot.

"How far to the border?" she asked.

"Oh, five or six miles from here," Lonnie answered. He glanced at her again. "You really just want me to drop you off as soon as we cross over? In the middle of nowhere?"

"Yes," Naomi said. "My friend is going to pick me up. Everything is going to be fantastic from here on out."

Lonnie said nothing.

In the quiet, Naomi heard an approaching sound that brought back bad memories. Visions of the river just outside Burwell. The chase. The shootout in the trees.

It was the sound of a helicopter.

Naomi bit her lip to keep from crying out. She resisted the urge to shout at Lonnie to drive faster.

Unger's men must have found her, and they were coming fast.

ONE-HUNDRED FOUR

It was almost impossible to see the dirt road. It was only visible as a faint streak down below. More of an impression than anything tangible.

"Are you sure that's 487th?" Carver demanded.

"I'm looking right at it!" Gibbs protested. "See? The blue dot... that's us, right?"

"Yes," Carver confirmed. He didn't look. He kept his eyes forward, staring down the barrel of the last road out of Nebraska. So far, he didn't see anything.

"The blue dot's right over 487th Avenue," Gibbs added. "Not much of an avenue, I guess. There's nothing out here."

"This is your home state, Gibbs. Don't act surprised. I'm going to take us a bit lower. You can put your phone away now. Help me look."

Gibbs tucked his phone in his pocket. He leaned forward against his harness, peering out of the windshield as Carver gently dropped them by another fifty feet.

"Watch out for power lines," Gibbs barked.

"I'm not that low," Carver grunted. "Do you see anything?"

"Not yet."

Carver flew straight north. The same direction as the road. They were closing in on the border. Less than five miles to go, give or take.

"There's something!" Gibbs exclaimed.

Carver saw it, too. A faint set of taillights. Some reflectors, too.

"What is that, a semi-truck?" Gibbs scoffed.

Carver brought them a little nearer. Close enough to prove Gibbs's theory. As soon as Carver saw that it was a semi, he pulled back, lifting high into the sky.

"This is a dirt road in the middle of nowhere!" said Gibbs. "What's a semi doing out here?"

Carver didn't answer. But it was a very good question. As far as he could tell, there was only one answer.

Keeping his altitude, he accelerated again. Chopping the air ferociously as he hurtled toward the border. Gibbs squeezed his eyes shut and clenched his fists.

"Carver!" he cried out. "Slow down! My skin's gonna peel off!"

"Just a moment longer," Carver replied.

He dropped speed. And gave Gibbs another thrill ride as the chopper dropped out of the air like a rock. The trooper screamed in terror. Carver braced, gritting his teeth. He gave the engine a bit of juice, teasing the throttle.

At the right moment, he pushed the chopper forward. Speeding along barely twenty feet above the ground. Gibbs kept screaming, at a much higher pitch.

Soon, Carver saw a sign flash by. Big and rectangular. WELCOME TO SOUTH DAKOTA.

He brought the helicopter higher, leaning back to eat some speed. Then he swung over to the left, touching down in some tall grass a little ways off the road. He killed the engine, already unbuckling his harness.

Carver looked over at Gibbs. The state cop looked like he'd just run a marathon. He was covered in sweat, breathing hard. And he looked like he was about to puke. Or pass out.

"Why didn't you just park in the road!" he yelled.

"This chopper could be our only way out of here if things go wrong," Carver replied. "I don't want to risk getting it rammed by an eighteen-wheeler. We can stop the truck just fine with these."

He grabbed at his assault rifle. It slipped from his grasp. He leaned out of his seat, catching it.

Something came through the windshield. Punching its way through the glass.

Carver flinched. A split second later, the sound reached him, a sharp *crack*. He dropped the rest of the way out of his seat, hitting the floor.

Looking up, he saw the bullet hole. Right in front of where he'd been sitting.

ONE-HUNDRED FIVE

"Sniper," Carver said calmly.

Gibbs tried to jump out of his seat. The harness caught him. He let out a shriek, grabbing at the latch and jerking it around.

"*Carver, help!*" he shouted.

Carver reached up and around the trooper's chest. He found the latch and clicked it open. Gibbs seemed to hit the floor faster than the bullet that had nearly popped Carver's head like a balloon.

Carver studied the bullet hole. It was big. He'd heard and felt the impact. The thunderous *crack* of the shot. It was a high-powered rifle. A big caliber. A .50 BMG, maybe. The kind of bullet you shot when erasing people was your goal.

"Okay," Carver said.

"What's that supposed to mean?" Gibbs demanded.

He could have explained his whole thought process. The fact that Gibbs was only alive because the gun that was shooting at them was unwieldy. Relatively slow to operate. But that would be a waste of breath. All he needed to do was keep both of them alive.

"We're going to start crawling," Carver said. "Follow me."

He twisted around, belly-crawling his way into the passenger cabin. Gibbs was right behind him, bumping into his feet.

"What kind of gun is that?" the trooper whispered.

"Not the kind you want to be thinking about. Keep moving."

"Can it shoot through the sides of the helicopter?"

"Do you want me to answer that?" Carver replied.

"Uh… yeah. No! Yeah, actually. Wait! Never mind."

Carver reached the open side door. The next part had to be fast. He didn't know exactly where the sniper was. No way of knowing what kind of angle the guy had. Whether he and Gibbs would be exposed at any given moment.

He hesitated.

Another bullet struck the chopper, making it shudder. The gunshot came rolling after it, an evil echo.

Gibbs lost it. Jumping up, he screamed and nearly stumbled over Carver as he raced out of the chopper. He fell out into the grass. Shot to his feet. Sprinted directly away from the door, parallel to the road.

Carver cursed. He crawled forward, sticking his head out through the door. He looked across the road. Waiting.

There was a third shot a couple of seconds later. This time, he saw the muzzle flash. It came from the other side of the road, in a stand of trees beyond a fallow cornfield.

Carver looked back at Gibbs. Saw Gibbs drop to the ground.

ONE-HUNDRED SIX

Gibbs forgot where he was. He forgot about Naomi Downes. About Ronan Carver. About the helicopter and the fact that he was now a fugitive. All he knew was that someone was shooting at him with a very big gun that fired very big bullets.

He needed to get away. He ran as fast as he could. Away from it all. He saw the road off to his left. The empty darkness ahead of him. Long strands of grass tangled around his ankles. But he powered on, ripping through the foliage.

Then he heard something horrible. A bullet flying past his head.

He had nothing to compare the sound to. Maybe it was like a nest of angry hornets, or the screech of a thousand lost souls. It pushed him past his breaking point, beyond fear, and into the realm of cold logic.

Suddenly, everything became clear. He dropped down onto his face, flattening himself in the grass. Without thinking, he started to crawl forward. Slowly. Trying not to disturb the grass too much.

The sniper had seen where he dropped down. He wanted to get away from that spot. But he didn't want to telegraph his movements.

He moved about ten feet. Then he poked his head up. Looking around. He needed to get to safety. Shelter.

But there wasn't any. To his left was the road, with a cornfield beyond it. To his right and front was a vast field of grass. There were trees and shrubs dotted around. He thought he even saw a toolshed. But it would take forever to crawl to one of those.

If he stood up to try and run, the next bullet might take his head off.

Gibbs glanced back toward the chopper. He no longer saw Carver. But the big man had to be somewhere close by, lying low.

The chopper was the closest sanctuary. But with a sniper suppressing them, they wouldn't be able to take off.

Gibbs suddenly felt a choking sensation. He grabbed at his throat. Realized it was the shoulder strap from the assault rifle Carver had given him. He untwisted it from his neck, looked down at the gun.

This was something he knew. He could use guns. He could shoot—if he could get close enough to the sniper, which was probably impossible.

But what else could he do? There was nowhere to run. The only option was to try and eliminate the threat.

Gibbs turned toward the road and started crawling.

ONE-HUNDRED SEVEN

Harvey Carrol was getting sick of waiting.

The hours kept passing. Einer and his two goons kept loitering around. There was always at least one of them in the room with Harvey at any given moment. No privacy. No chance at enacting any sort of plan.

He had one in mind, something drastic. If it went wrong, he was dead meat. But since he was probably dead meat anyway, what did it matter?

They were still in the living room. Harvey had finished his sudoku book a while ago. Now he was just twiddling his thumbs. Getting up every so often to use the bathroom. With an escort, of course.

"Get any sports channels out here?" Einer asked. "I've missed a couple of games. Maybe I can catch a rerun."

Harvey tossed him the remote. Einer caught it, spilling his glass of bourbon in the process.

"Whoa!" He grabbed the glass with his other hand. "Alcohol abuse! Someone cut me off."

"Nah, go ahead and keep drinking," Harvey replied with a grin.

"Yeah, you'd like that, wouldn't you?" Einer sneered. "You'd like it if I drank the whole liquor cabinet and passed out. But you'd still have my two friends to contend with, huh?"

"Sure," Harvey said. "But they don't look like much."

One of the meatheads was currently scrounging for food in the kitchen. The other stood a few feet from Einer. He gave Harvey a mean bulldog stare.

"Sheesh, calm down, Pierre," Einer barked. "He's just messing around. We both know you could break him in half with one hand."

"I don't fight old men," Pierre responded. "No honor in that."

"But this is pretty honorable, huh?" Harvey chuckled. "Holding an old fella hostage for a whole day without even telling him the score."

"I did tell you the score," said Einer. "The score is you shut up and do what I say."

Harvey just nodded and laughed some more. He didn't feel so scared anymore. He figured the sun was setting on this whole thing. He could sense it, the end approaching.

It was just about time to try out his plan.

It all relied on what he found when he reached his hand between the couch cushions. He couldn't remember where he'd stashed all his guns. He liked to keep one in every room of the house, just in case. But "just in case" never seemed to arrive. So, he forgot.

He hadn't checked yet.

Slowly, he dropped his right hand off his lap. Sneaked it across the cushion and into the gap. Straight away, he felt it. Cold metal. The butt of a compact pistol. He pretended to adjust his position. Scooting a bit further to the right. Covering up what his hand was doing.

Einer's phone rang again. He grabbed it off an end table, looked at the screen, and frowned. He answered it right there in the living room, rather than walking away like he usually did.

"Yes, sir?" he said. A moment passed. "Yes, Colonel. I had a feeling this call was coming soon. I'll get it done."

He hung up and got to his feet. Despite his three glasses of whiskey, he looked very sober. He picked up his mammoth handgun, pointed it at Harvey.

"Sorry, old man," Einer said. "Looks like you're no longer useful."

ONE-HUNDRED EIGHT

Carver leaped out of the helicopter. He dashed around to the back, hiding from the sniper. No more shots came. He assumed the guy was still focused on Gibbs, trying to confirm the kill. Or maybe he was reloading.

There was no point in waiting. The passage of time was only going to make the situation worse. Carver peered out of his hiding spot, toward the road. He saw that the land sloped downward on the other side of it, forming a ditch that separated the road from the cornfield.

He made a run for it, cutting toward the road at a dead sprint. At least at first. Once he'd covered fifteen feet, he dropped low and zig-zagged. Crouch-running back and forth in a serpentine pattern.

Another shot came. A second later, another. They thudded into the ground. The first bullet missed him by several feet. The second was a little closer.

By the third shot, the sniper would be dialed in. He would compensate for Carver's movement pattern, adjust his aim and his timing.

The third shot would hit.

It was time to mix things up again.

Carver dove forward. Somersaulting through the grass. He came up on his feet and ran as fast as he possibly could, pumping his arms and legs.

He reached the road. His feet slamming down on the compacted dirt.

He felt the third shot coming. Anticipated it. He dropped onto his right knee. Rolled to the side. Then he pushed himself up and went serpentine again. Weaving his way across the road.

The third shot missed him as well. But by an even smaller margin than the second. The sniper was cool and calm. He was not getting frustrated by Carver's erratic movements.

Carver dropped into a prone position at the far side of the road. He pulled himself quickly into the ditch, making himself flat.

It wasn't a much better position than before, but at least he was closer. He could regroup. Take a breath. Plan his next move.

But not for long. The ditch was shallow. He couldn't be sure he was completely hidden.

From here, he could see back up into the grass he'd just come from.

There was movement to the left, not far from where Gibbs had gone down. The grass was shaking around. Rustling as if someone had crawled through it.

Gibbs hadn't been shot after all. He was coming toward the road. Apparently, he thought he was being stealthy. But there was no way the sniper didn't see the grass moving.

In just a few seconds, Gibbs would reach the road. He'd be out of grass. And out of time.

ONE-HUNDRED NINE

"Pierre?" Einer said. "You said you don't fight old men. How do you feel about watching them die?"

Pierre shrugged his massive shoulders. "Sometimes messy things have to be done."

"You're right about that." Einer nodded slowly. "Sometimes you gotta follow orders. I *always* follow orders."

For a moment, Harvey thought the guy was stalling. Then he looked into Einer's eyes and saw the truth.

Einer was savoring the moment. Tasting it. Enjoying it. The job was about to be finished. He could get out of this boring old house. Away from the boring old man who lived in it.

"No hard feelings, huh?" Einer said.

"Nope," Harvey agreed. "It's all right, son. I've lived a full life."

Einer smiled. "Thanks for understanding. I heard your daughter's dead, right? She was Carver's girlfriend?"

"His fiancée," Harvey said. "Her name was Annie."

"Cool. Maybe we'll send Carver to see the two of you in the afterlife. Pretty soon."

"You think you'll be able to take that boy on?" Harvey laughed. "Good luck."

"Oh, shut up," Einer snapped.

His thumb moved, hitting the safety latch on his handgun. It was now ready to fire. Einer was already squeezing the trigger. No hesitation now.

Harvey didn't hesitate either.

He had grown up with guns. Living out in the countryside, it helped if you could shoot. But he'd never been all that good with firearms. Never had much of an occasion to use them.

That was until Ronan Carver came along. The kid trained Harvey and Annie up. Taught them to feel comfortable with a gun in their hand. How to use them. How to get over the fear. The reluctance.

How to kill someone if you really had to.

Harvey ripped the pistol out from between the couch cushions. He didn't have time to aim. To think about what he was doing. That was what the training was for, how to make it all feel natural. So, when the time came, you didn't *have* to think. Or even aim.

The bullet went a little lower than Harvey would have liked, punching a penny-sized hole in Einer's throat.

The young guy with the goofy hair immediately dropped his gun, using both hands to try and plug the hole. It didn't work. Blood welled between his fingers. He choked and gasped, falling to his knees.

Not a pretty sight. But Harvey wasn't looking. He had already turned his sights on Pierre.

The meathead was slow to react, just as Harvey predicted he would be. Pierre was only standing because he would have fallen asleep otherwise. He was tired. Bored. He had lost focus.

He got his focus back just in time for a bullet to fire through his skull. He was dead before he hit the floor, much quicker and more merciful than Einer. But Harvey didn't have time to put the man out of his misery.

There was still a third guy in the house. Somewhere.

He listened.

Footsteps came thundering from the direction of the kitchen.

The big man came swinging into the room, already firing. Harvey fell off the couch, grunting as he felt his bad knee pop out of place. He was showered with bits of stuffing as his sofa was shredded by bullets.

Lunging forward, he dove out from behind the coffee table. Shooting several blind shots. One of them hit their mark, and the third guy went down.

Grunting with effort and pain, Harvey got up on one knee. He dragged himself over to Einer.

"Sorry, son," Harvey said. "I waited until the last moment. Figured there was still a chance we could all walk away from this."

He put another bullet in Einer's head, ending his pain.

Then he fell back against the couch. Felt warmth and wetness running across his chest. A cold feeling gave way to burning pain.

He'd been shot.

ONE-HUNDRED TEN

Carver didn't know what to do. He was about to watch the death of Trooper Gibbs.

On one hand, the distraction would be helpful. While the sniper was focused on Gibbs, Carver could seize the moment. Close some more distance.

On the other hand, Gibbs didn't deserve any of this. And Carver still felt bad for the traffic stop that had kicked all this off.

A few crucial seconds passed. Time was running out. But Carver made up his mind.

Getting onto his knees, he stuck his head and shoulders up out of the ditch. He aimed in the general direction of the muzzle flash he'd seen earlier, and squeezed his trigger, sending a short spray of bullets toward the trees.

He hoped Gibbs would realize what was going on, and get a move on.

His hope was fulfilled a second later when Gibbs dove into the ditch, sending up a puff of dust as he landed hard.

"Holy cow!" Gibbs cried out.

Carver stopped shooting. He dropped back down out of sight.

"I almost died," Gibbs added. "I didn't know I was so close to the road. Thanks for saving me."

Carver frowned. "What was your plan?"

"To get to that sniper nest and take the son-of-a-gun down," Gibbs scoffed. "Wasn't that your plan, too?"

"It's still my plan," Carver said. "But I might not have time."

"Whaddya mean?" Gibbs demanded.

"I mean, I know who the sniper is. Not his name, but his reason for being here. He's Naomi's contact. He figures we're here to try and stop her."

"Which we are," Gibbs added.

"And he's trying to stop *us*," Carver added.

"So, what do we do?"

Carver took a breath. Checked the magazine on his rifle. "Nothing. For now. That semi-truck should be here soon."

"With Naomi in it," said Gibbs. "As far as we know."

"She's in it," Carver said with conviction. "And when she gets here, the sniper's going to have to start making moves. We'll see what happens."

"Sure. Sounds fair." Gibbs coughed, sending up another puff of dust. "I guess, this is better."

"What is?" asked Carver.

"Us working together, instead of trying to kill each other."

"I never tried to kill you," Carver replied.

Gibbs shrugged. "Yeah, I guess not. I never tried to kill you, either. Are we even? You're not going to beat me up again, right?"

Carver smiled. "Gibbs, you're not even on my radar."

"But you just saved my life!"

"And I'm almost starting to regret it. Now be quiet and let me listen."

ONE-HUNDRED ELEVEN

A few seconds passed. A soft wind blew. Gibbs fidgeted around, antsy and nervous.

"What are we listening for?" he asked.

Carver silenced him with a hand wave. In the quiet, they heard a growing rumble. A diesel engine coming up the road. It was the semi-truck, finally approaching the border.

But it was still a half mile out or more. The sound was faint. There was another noise, much closer. Footsteps over desiccated cornhusks, crunching toward them.

Gibbs gave Carver a wide-eyed stare. Clenching his mouth shut so hard his lips went white. Carver signaled the trooper to stay down. Then he readied his weapon, putting his finger on the trigger.

The footsteps stopped a few meters away. Carver couldn't see anything over the lip of the ditch. Just the sky, twinkling with stars.

"Carver, you can come out," a man's voice said. "I'm not going to shoot."

Gibbs's expression turned from fear to confusion. But Carver didn't have any answers. The voice sounded familiar, but he couldn't place it.

Who was this guy? And how did he know Carver's name?

"Come on," the man's impatient voice continued. "We don't need to fight. Just come out. Hear this?"

There was a heavy thud. Something hitting the ground.

"That was my rifle. I dropped it. Come on out. I know you're there."

"How do I know you don't have another weapon?" Carver called.

"You don't," came the reply. "Which is why you should probably hold onto that AR of yours for now. Point it at me as you climb out of that ditch. Just don't shoot. Please."

"That sounds reasonable," said Carver.

"Then let's go," the man answered.

Carver stood up slowly. Aiming his weapon at a man standing eight feet away. But he quickly realized there was no reason to shoot. In the moonlight, he recognized the face straight away.

He lowered the rifle. "Good to see you, Warren. Strange circumstances, though."

Warren smiled. "Strange indeed. But I guess we never exactly meet for coffee, do we?"

"Who is it?" Gibbs asked.

"He's an intelligence officer for the US Navy," Carver replied. "I worked with him several times when he was in the SEALs. He's a good man."

"Then why was he shooting at us?" Gibbs added.

Carver looked Warren in the eyes. "That's a good question. I'd like to know the answer."

ONE-HUNDRED TWELVE

A few seconds went by. Warren and Carver stared at one another. Then their faces were slashed by approaching headlights. Glancing over, they saw the semi approaching. It was a quarter mile out. Moving slow.

"Looks like our time's almost up," Warren said. "But I'll tell you what I can. First of all, I want to apologize. I should have recognized you sooner."

Carver shrugged. "It's dark. Things happened fast. We survived."

"Barely!" Gibbs protested. He got to his knees, coughing and dusting himself off.

"Who's this guy?" asked Warren.

Carver smiled. "State cop. I'd tell you the full story, but it would take longer than we have. We're looking for Naomi Downes."

Warren gestured toward the truck. "She's about to arrive. But you don't have to worry about her. I've got it covered."

"You're her contact," Carver said. "The one she's been communicating with."

"That's right," Warren confirmed. "I've got things lined up. A way to get her out of the country until it's safe for her to come back. She'll be fine."

"That's the problem," Carver grunted.

"What do you mean?" Warren asked.

"We're here to bring her to justice," Carver added. "She's trying to sell us out. She has names. Identities of undercover operatives around the world. Americans. People we know. People we've worked with."

Warren shook his head. "Who told you that? It isn't true. She has evidence of political corruption. Murder."

"That's what I thought too, Warren. She lied to both of us. Did you ever see her supposed evidence?"

"Not yet, but... Come on, Carver. Maybe you don't believe her, but I do. And I made a promise to her. Please don't make me fight you."

Gibbs stood up straight. "You don't want to fight this guy, Warren. You'll lose. You might want to think about switching sides."

Warren shook his head again and said nothing.

Nearby, the sound of squealing brakes rang out. The truck was pulling to a stop less than fifty feet away, right in the middle of the road.

"Let's see what Naomi has to say for herself," Carver said.

ONE-HUNDRED THIRTEEN

Harvey wanted to stay right where he was. Sitting on the living room floor with his back against the couch. It was surprisingly comfy, despite the corpses of three men littering the place.

But the blood was pumping out of his bullet wound, and it was hurting something fierce. The pain reminded him he was still alive.

If he wanted to stay that way, he'd best get his butt in gear.

With a prolonged grunt, Harvey pushed himself to his feet. He stepped around Einer's corpse, then Pierre's, and then the unnamed third gunman's. He entered the hallway, stumbling against the wall. Leaving a smear of blood.

He still had no idea where he was hit. It looked like it might be his chest. If that was the case…

It would be bad news. A death sentence, considering how far the nearest hospital was. And the lack of anyone to help him.

He reached the bathroom before collapsing, landing hard on his knees. He threw out a hand, catching himself on the edge of the bathtub. His vision darkened. His stomach heaved. It could be shock doing it to him. Or it could be blood loss.

Harvey reached into the tub, turned the cold water on, full blast. He cupped some of it in his hands, threw it into his face. The icy water shocked him back to reality.

"Let's go, old man," he grunted.

There was a first aid kit under the sink. A proper one. Carver had bought it from some military surplus place. It had everything you could need in it.

Harvey used a pair of scissors to cut through his shirt. He peeled the garment away, getting his first clear look at the wound.

He was relieved to see it was a single bullet hole. In his shoulder. Not a great place to be hit, but not the worst either. He was looking at a lengthy recovery time, but it was survivable. As long as he stopped the bleeding.

He dug through the med kit. Found some iodine. A sachet of clotting powder. A needle and thread. And a pair of forceps.

He sterilized the forceps, used them to dig the bullet out. It hurt like nothing he'd ever experienced. He nearly passed out. Sweat dripped down his face. He shivered with cold and agony.

But he got it done.

Next up, he used the clotting powder. Following it up with some rudimentary sutures, the best he could do. Deep inside the first aid kit, he found a bottle of pain meds. The strong stuff. He popped two into his mouth. Swallowed them with more tub water. Then he turned the water off.

Using the remains of his shirt, he tied himself a quick sling to support his injured arm. With a deep breath, he got back to his feet and moved into the kitchen.

He used the landline to try and dial Carver. No use. The line was dead. The thugs must have cut it.

Harvey made his way back to the living room. Found Einer's phone. He used the dead man's finger to unlock it. Rather than call 911, he took a quick detour. Peering through the files Einer had stored.

What he saw made his jaw drop.

"Well, I'll be," he whispered.

His wound was tended to. He'd live for now. But Carver was still out there, embroiled in God only knew what kind of mess.

It was time for Harvey to step in.

ONE-HUNDRED FOURTEEN

All eyes were on the semi-truck.

The passenger door popped open. The interior light came on, illuminating the face of the driver. A middle-aged guy with a beard. He was staring to his left, at the helicopter parked in the nearby field.

Naomi got out of the truck. She stood beside the open door. Unzipped Carver's duffel bag and pulled out the M4 carbine. The driver looked around and saw the gun. His eyes went wide.

Stepping away from the truck, Naomi slammed the door shut. That was the driver's cue to get out of Dodge. He stepped on the gas, all eighteen wheels tearing up the dirt as he hightailed it north.

In a moment, he was just a set of tail lights, fading into the distance.

Naomi approached slowly. Keeping her gun aimed vaguely in the direction of Carver and Gibbs.

Suddenly, Warren had a pistol in his hand. Pulled from some secret holster on his person. He pointed it at Carver's face.

"Hey!" Gibbs yelled, aiming at Warren in turn.

Carver also held his gun on Warren. A moment later, he thought better of it, and aimed at Naomi instead.

She stopped on the side of the road. Just above them on the lip of the shallow ditch.

"I guess, this answers the question of who flew that chopper here," she said. "I'm glad you made it out of that RV, Carver. But I wish you weren't here."

"Too bad," Carver said. "You made a mistake, letting me live."

"No, I didn't," she shot back. "I never wanted anything bad to happen to you."

"Then why did you do it?" Carver demanded. "Why did you turn on me?"

"I got scared!" she snapped. "We were moving too slow, Carver. I needed to give myself a head start. I needed a decoy. I'm sorry it had to be you. But I didn't see any other way."

"We could have gotten out together," Carver growled. "You just had to trust me. But I'm glad you did it, Naomi, because I know who you are now."

She shook her head slowly. "I… I'm sorry for what I did. I really am. It was just survival. Maybe it was the wrong move. But maybe not. I made it here, after all."

"So did I," Carver reminded her. "And you aren't getting away."

She ignored him. "Warren, is everything ready?"

"It is," Warren said. "The plane's stashed in the next field over. Past those trees. Fueled up and ready."

His words were confident, but his tone of voice was not. Warren was starting to feel doubt, casting a questioning eye on Naomi.

ONE-HUNDRED FIFTEEN

"Was any of it true?" Warren asked.

Naomi didn't answer right away, because she had no idea he was talking to her. When she realized it, she looked surprised.

"Was any of *what* true?" she asked.

"About Senator Unger," Warren went on. "Is it true? Or are you just out to make a quick buck? Tell me the truth."

"I've been telling you the truth all along!" Naomi protested. "I didn't lie about anything. I have the proof right here in my pocket. I'm ready to share it with the world, as soon as we get somewhere safe."

"Nowhere is safe from me," Carver said darkly. "Stop lying, Naomi. I've seen the truth with my own eyes."

She scoffed. "What did you see, exactly? And who showed it to you? Don't tell me it was Unger. Is that where you got the chopper from?"

Warren suddenly lowered his gun.

"Put that back up!" Naomi yelled. "I'm telling the truth, Warren."

He aimed his pistol at Carver again reluctantly. His finger was off the trigger. But it moved back as soon as they heard more helicopters approaching.

Carver glanced to the south. Saw the fleet of choppers bearing down on them.

"It was only a matter of time," Carver said with a grin. "Your truck driver must have called the cops. And the information got back to Colonel Bell."

"Hey, maybe they followed us from that other roadblock," Gibbs pointed out. "Tracked us on radar. How about them apples, Naomi? You're going down."

Naomi's arms shook. But she kept her aim true. The standoff continued.

But Carver wasn't worried. They only had to hold Naomi here until the cavalry arrived. She was all alone. Even Warren was barely on her side anymore.

The whole nightmare was just about over.

ONE-HUNDRED SIXTEEN

"You've still got a chance," Gibbs said. "Just put the gun down. We can end this peacefully. What do you say, Naomi?"

She barked out a laugh. "Still acting like a cop, huh? Come on, Gibbs. I'm screwed if I stay here. Just like you are. But there's room for another passenger on Warren's plane. An express ticket to a non-extradition country."

"Which one?" Gibbs asked.

"Nice try," Warren added. "But I guess the offer stands. You can come with us if you like. It doesn't matter to me."

Gibbs didn't say anything. He licked his lips. He was considering it, thinking hard.

"How about you, Carver?" Warren asked. "If Naomi's telling the truth, the people in those choppers are pure evil. You don't want to be here when they land."

Carver glanced at the helicopters again. They were hovering above the border crossing now. Churning the air loudly. Slowly descending toward the ground.

"Please, Carver," Naomi gasped. "Senator Unger… he'll kill me. Just like his wife. He'll bury me so deep the worms won't even find me. Is that what you want?"

Carver shook his head. "You manipulated Gibbs. And now you're trying to manipulate me. Not going to happen."

He sighted her head down the barrel of his rifle. She was less than six feet away. The easiest shot in the world. Except she had that look in her eyes. Lost. Terrified.

The same look Annie must have had just before she died.

Carver winced. Expelling his pain and sorrow in an angry roar. It made Naomi flinch. But he didn't pull the trigger.

Suddenly, he had no earthly idea what to do.

But it didn't matter. Not unless Naomi was stupid enough to start shooting. Carver was about to be absolved of any responsibility.

The choppers were landing.

ONE-HUNDRED SEVENTEEN

As the helicopters touched down nearby, the noise was overwhelming. Wind blasted across the road. Fuel fumes choked the air.

Then the engines were shut down. The rotors spun to a stop. And dozens of men and women flooded out into the grass, hurrying across the road.

Amidst their numbers, Carver spotted three official-looking men. Colonel Bell. Senator Unger. Vice President Lamay.

"Last chance to surrender peacefully," Carver said to Naomi.

The barrel of her gun wavered around. Her body trembled uncontrollably. She refused to look at the mercenaries. She didn't want to watch her approaching doom.

The mercs stopped on the other side of the road. They were waved back by Lamay. They kept their weapons trained on Naomi and the others, ready to fire.

Unger kept coming, trailed by Lamay and Bell. The senator raised his hands high above his head, smiling triumphantly. Then he brought his hands down, clapping a few times.

"Ronan Carver, why am I not surprised to see *you* here?" he called out. "I knew putting you in that helicopter was asking for trouble. But my friend Colonel Bell seemed to think you'd play by the rules. I guess, I won that bet. And it all paid off. Thanks for stopping her."

He looked at Naomi. His smile turned sour.

"You're not even going to look at me?" he asked. "After everything you put us all through?"

"Screw you," Naomi spat.

Unger laughed. He turned toward the mercenaries. "All right, people! Let's take her into custody, along with her little helper."

Naomi kept shaking. Holding her gun. But Warren was smarter. He immediately set his pistol on the ground and raised his hands.

Unger's private army started across the road, ready to get the job done.

"Wait!" Lamay suddenly boomed. "Everyone stop!"

ONE-HUNDRED EIGHTEEN

The mercenaries froze in their tracks. Faces implacable. Unger stared at them in disbelief, then at Lamay.

"What are we waiting for, people?" Unger demanded. "We have her right here. It's over. We can destroy whatever evidence she's holding and lock her up where she belongs. What's the hold up?"

Desperation poured off him in waves. Lamay didn't even acknowledge the man. He was too busy staring at his phone. The screen lit his face with a pale glow.

"Mr. Vice President, sir," Unger went on. "Is this really the time to check your email, or whatever you're doing?"

"Shut up," Lamay said.

Unger took a quick step back, as if the VP's words were a physical punch. There was fear on his usually confident face.

Something was wrong. Carver slowly lowered his weapon. But Naomi didn't notice. She was finally looking at Unger. Something like hope glittered in her eyes.

Finally, Lamay held up his phone. "A strange thing just happened, ladies and gentlemen. Some interesting news has reached me via the Boise, Idaho FBI office. Senator Unger… Colonel Bell…"

As he said the names, the respective men perked up expectantly.

"I can't believe I trusted you," the vice president finished.

"Sir!" Unger yelled. "I don't know what kind of news you just got, but it must be wrong. Naomi managed to get this guy… whoever he is… to help her out." He pointed at Warren. "And she managed to trick Ronan Carver, too. Which I bet isn't easy, right? She's good at manipulating people. She—"

"I said shut up!" Lamay shouted. He looked at the mercenaries. "My friends, I urge you to take these two men into custody. Quickly. Before my disgust with them grows further."

The job was carried out in short order. Colonel Bell went silently, grinning the whole time, like it was all a joke. But Unger complained loudly as he was dragged to the choppers.

"This is outrageous! I am an elected senator! I will not be treated this way. That woman is a liar! You hear me? *A liar!* She's fooling all of you!"

Then a door was slammed shut in his face, and his whining was cut off.

ONE-HUNDRED NINETEEN

Nothing happened for another few seconds. No one knew what to do. Naomi was too weak to hold up her carbine, and she let it fall.

Gibbs was the last man standing. He was still aiming at Warren, seemingly frozen in time.

Suddenly, Lamay was there. Gliding regally between them all. He put a hand on Gibbs's shoulder.

"You can put that down now, Trooper," Lamay said. "It's over."

"Huh?" Gibbs looked at the man, and dropped the gun fast. "Sir! Sorry, sir."

Lamay chuckled warmly. Patted Gibbs on the arm. "That's perfectly all right. Thank you for doing your job so diligently, son. If you would step over beside this man… What's your name?"

"Warren, sir," Warren replied.

Lamay nodded. "Trooper, go ahead and stand beside Warren. You'll both be gathered for debriefing momentarily."

Gibbs did as he was told. He was shocked. At a loss for words.

Lamay left the trooper behind. Stepping over between Carver and Naomi. He spoke without looking at either of them.

"I'd like both of you to take a ride with me," he said. "We have some things to talk about."

He walked away.

Carver gestured for Naomi to go first. She shook her head and gestured at him. He stayed where he was. She grunted in frustration and started walking.

Lamay led them to a helicopter. They got in. It took off, heading south.

***

A little while later, they were back in the town of Bassett. Being herded into the police station, and placed inside a cramped interrogation room.

Just Carver and Naomi. Alone. Neither of them knew how to break the silence.

Thankfully, they weren't forced to wait long. It was only a couple of minutes before the door opened. Lamay stepped in carrying a tray of coffee and donuts.

He sat down, setting the treats on the table.

"I need to return to Washington soon," he said. "But since the men I was working with are now in jail cells, I decided I should be the one to fill you two in. Care for a bite?"

Naomi grabbed a glazed donut and tore into it, dunking it in coffee and shoving it in her mouth. After a moment, Carver grabbed a cup for himself.

"What I'm about to say should not leave this room," Lamay went on. "Not that I have to tell either of you that. Some of it will come out in upcoming trials. Some of it will be kept hidden away forever. I suppose I'll begin."

ONE-HUNDRED TWENTY

"I'll start by acknowledging what should already be obvious," said Lamay. "Naomi has been telling you the truth, Carver. But not all of it."

Carver looked at Naomi. She gave him a sheepish look over the rim of her coffee cup.

"She has been carrying information that incriminates Senator Unger," Lamay went on. "Carver, I believe you know about the accusation regarding his wife?"

"Naomi said he had her killed," Carver replied. "He had a large life insurance policy on her. And she didn't want him to get into politics. It wasn't the life she was after."

Lamay nodded. "All true. But it goes beyond that. Naomi also possesses evidence of further corruption. During his first run for office, Unger was up against a younger man. A formidable opponent who stood a good chance of winning. He happened to perish in a plane crash during the race."

"I assume that wasn't a coincidence," Carver said.

"Your assumption would be correct. It seems Unger hired someone to tamper with the plane. To make sure it failed. And there's also the list of names, the list Unger tried showing you back in that barn. It's a real list. But it wasn't Naomi who wanted to sell it."

"It was *him*," Naomi added. "He needed campaign funds. Cash to pay off his lackeys. I found that out, right before I ran off with the flash drive. I guess, it was the catalyst. When I only knew about his wife, it felt smaller. As soon as I realized so many other people were in danger… I had to do it. I had no choice."

Carver stared at her. "Why didn't you tell me any of this?"

She shrugged. "It's a burden of information, Carver. You were already dealing with enough, trying to keep us both alive. That kind of knowledge is dangerous. It was better if I was the only one who had it."

"You weren't the only one," Lamay said. "But I'll get to that in a moment. Unger's plan was as solid as it could be. He knew Naomi had the list on her flash drive, so he figured he could frame her for his own plan. As long as he found a way to quickly destroy the other evidence, the proof of his assassinations."

Carver frowned. "It would have been a difficult trick to pull off. But he had no other options. And it almost worked."

"Fortunately, someone had a change of heart," Lamay added. "Unger apparently has an ex-con by the name of Einer under his employ. This Einer possessed copies of the same evidence, perhaps as a way to blackmail more payment out of Unger. Whatever the case may be…"

"He forwarded his evidence to the FBI," Carver finished for him. "And they wasted no time in getting it into your hands."

Lamay smiled. "That's exactly right."

ONE-HUNDRED TWENTY-ONE

"Where does Colonel Bell play into this?" Carver asked.

"We're unclear on that," Lamay answered. "But we do know that the two of them go far back. Bell and Unger were best friends in elementary school. They grew up together, and Bell has been with Unger through every step of his political career. It's safe to assume Bell is every bit as guilty as Unger."

Carver took a sip of coffee. It warmed him. "He's the head of the state police. A good tool for Unger to keep in his arsenal. A tool he's probably used many times before. I have two more questions."

"Go ahead," said Lamay. "I'm here to answer."

"You learned all this from your phone?"

Lamay nodded. "It was laid out very plainly in the communique I received from Boise. Before I came into this room, I contacted the field office to get some more details. And that's the first time I've heard any of it. Until now, I assumed that Unger was a good man."

"As good as any politician can be, anyway," Naomi scoffed.

Lamay took the jab in stride. "You've both had an exhausting few days. And I think you probably have your own issues to talk over. So, let's hear your last question, Mr. Carver."

"Gibbs and Warren," said Carver. "What's going to happen to them?"

Lamay shrugged. "Nothing. With Colonel Bell out of the picture, there's no one to accuse Gibbs of insubordination. He'll be allowed to return to his work. As for Warren… if anyone questions his actions, I'll say he was operating under my orders. Who's going to argue with that?"

Carver smiled. "You're not so bad, sir."

"Oh, don't tell me that. I want to keep my ego in check." Lamay stood up. He grabbed a donut. "You're both free to go whenever you please. No one will stop you."

He stepped out. Shutting the door behind him. Carver almost got up to make sure it was unlocked, but he didn't see the need.

He turned to the woman beside him. "Naomi… I'm sorry. I should have believed you."

She shrugged. "I can't blame you. I kind of killed any reason you might have had to trust me. I acted like an idiot."

Carver reached out a hand. She hesitated, but decided to go for it. He grabbed her hand and held it gently. "Like you said, you were just surviving. I hope nothing like this happens to you again. But if it does, you'll do better the second time."

She reached up with her free hand. Wiped a tear from her eye. "I'm so sorry."

He squeezed her hand. "We both made bad calls, but we've both been through a lot together. I'd say we're even. Friends?"

She nodded. "Of course, we're friends. I'm glad I ended up in your trunk, Carver. Which is a really weird thing to say."

He pulled her into his chest, giving her a long hug.

A knock on the door interrupted them. A cop stuck his head into the room. "Mr. Carver? You have a phone call."

ONE-HUNDRED TWENTY-TWO

"Excuse me," Carver said to Naomi. He got up and hurried into the hall. He was led to a phone on the wall. He grabbed the handset, mashing it against his ear.

"Harvey?" he said.

"Hey, kid!" the old man's voice replied. "Glad I could finally get you on the horn. Things must be pretty crazy out there in corn-land, huh?"

"They're calming down now," said Carver. "That was you, wasn't it?"

"What was me?" Harvey asked with mock innocence. "Just give me a second here. I'm hurting."

Carver's heart skipped a beat. "What happened?"

"Oh, just a little gunshot wound. Nothing to lose your dinner over. We can talk about it some other time, when I'm a little more lucid. Point is, I'll be fine."

"Where were you hit?" Carver asked.

"Left shoulder. Better than the right, eh? I was going to drive myself to the hospital like a proud fool, but then I remembered something that got invented a while back. A little old thing called an ambulance. One phone call, and they were on their way. Dragged my old carcass straight to the ER."

"I'm glad to hear you're okay," said Carver. "Who's Einer?"

"Einer? Hm… I don't know any Einers. Oh, wait. Maybe it's that guy who's lying dead in my living room right now. The guy whose phone I used to send a bunch of stuff to the FBI."

Carver let out a breath. "Harvey… you don't even know what you did."

"Why? Is it bad?" Harvey muttered.

"No. The opposite. You saved the day," Carver replied. "I'll tell you everything soon. As much as I can, at least."

"Sounds good, son. Speaking of this Einer business, I think the cops are here to ask me some questions. But before I go… How are you, Ronan? Did you find a purpose out there?"

Carver looked down the hall. Naomi was there, just outside the interrogation room. Nibbling her donut. Safe and comfortable for the first time in what probably felt like an eternity.

"I did," Carver answered. "But it's over now. I'm not sure what's next. I'll try and get back to Idaho as soon as I can."

"Hey, whatever you need to do," said Harvey. "I'll be just fine on my own. I hope you will be, too."

***

Sanders took one last look at the teal minivan as Gibbs drove them out of the rental place in his squad car. "Well, we brought it back in one piece," she said.

Gibbs laughed. "No extra charges for us. We did drive into an action movie, though."

"And you got to ride in a helicopter piloted by the lead hero," she joked.

"Yeah, but I was just the sidekick," he quipped back.

They were silent for a moment. Finally, Sanders said, "Whoever could have thought Colonel Bell was a dirty cop?"

"A dirty lackey to Senator Unger, more like," Gibbs said. "Well, it's all over but the shouting now."

"The vice president sure turned out to be all right, though," Sanders observed. "He was one of the good guys."

"Yeah, he was the good-guy-in-chief on this one. Say, partner, how about we find some breakfast in Burwell?"

"Sure," Sanders replied. "Just as long as we don't hear about a stolen car before we go in."

Gibbs chuckled. "Yeah, we've had enough excitement for a lifetime." Then he turned serious, glancing at Sanders. "Thanks for watching my back."

She looked at him and then smiled. "What are partners for?"

EPILOGUE

With a private jet, you could get anywhere in the world in no time at all.

Four hours earlier, William Lamay had been in northern Nebraska. Talking to Ronan Carver and Naomi Downes in a tiny police station. Now he was back home, showered and dressed, in his private residence just outside Washington, D.C.

It was early morning. Any chance of getting sleep was out the window. The sun had risen. The day had begun.

Lamay was in his office. Sipping coffee with a splash of cream and bourbon. He stared at his computer, knowing there was work to do. Knowing even more was about to arrive.

He was refilling his mug when a knock sounded at his door.

"Come in!" he said.

The door opened slightly. His secretary, Yvonne, put one foot over the threshold, leaning into the room.

"Line one, sir," she said.

Lamay looked at his desk phone. At the little red light, blinking slowly.

"Is it him?" Lamay asked.

"The Director of the CIA," Yvonne confirmed.

Lamay nodded and thanked her. Yvonne retreated, shutting the door tight. Lamay picked up the phone and hit the button for line one.

"I assume you received my emails?" he asked.

"I did," said the Director.

"I wasn't sure how good the WiFi signal was on the jet. What do you think?"

"I think he's exactly what we've been looking for, sir. As long as you vouch for him."

Lamay almost laughed at that. He took a drink of coffee. "His record is something to behold. And he conducted himself in an impressive manner throughout this Senator Unger business. I think Ronan Carver could be very useful to us in the future."

"Hm." The Director clicked his tongue a few times. Mulling things over. "People like Carver are hard to find. I think he can be trusted with things that would crush an ordinary man. Do you think he will allow himself to be recruited?"

This time, Lamay couldn't contain a chuckle. "Carver is a man who values his independence. His self-reliance. So, I can't say for sure what he would agree to. However…"

He leaned forward, setting his cup down.

"We'll keep an eye on him," Lamay went on. "Track his movements, so we have the option to call on him when need be. When things get bad, it's good to have a wild card up your sleeve."

Visit the author's website:
www.finchambooks.com

Contact:
contact@finchambooks.com

THOMAS FINCHAM holds a graduate degree in Economics. His travels throughout the world have given him an appreciation for other cultures and beliefs. He has lived in Africa, Asia, and North America. An avid reader of mysteries and thrillers, he decided to give writing a try. Several novels later, he can honestly say he has found his calling. He is married and lives in a hundred-year-old house. He is the author of the Lee Callaway Series, the Echo Rose Series, the Martin Rhodes Series, and the Hyder Ali Series.

Printed in Great Britain
by Amazon